Rough I

Graham Ison

© Graham Ison 1995

Graham Ison has asserted his rights under the Copyright, Design and Patents Act, 1988, to be identified as the author of this work.

First published in 1995 by Little, Brown and Company.

This edition published in 2017 by Endeavour Press Ltd.

Table of Contents

One

The sergeant of the police armed response vehicle acknowledged the call.

"Did I hear that right, skip?" asked the driver. "Shooting at Hyde Park Corner?"

"That's what the lady said." The sergeant looked out of his window at the traffic in Edgware Road and wondered what was happening at Hyde Park Corner that merited their special attention.

"Where at Hyde Park Corner?"

"Didn't say. Just said Hyde Park Corner."

The driver sighed and thumbed down the siren switch. "The sooner we get there, the sooner we get back." He adjusted his driving position slightly and cursed at a bus that seèmed hellbent on running him off the road, siren or no siren. "Bloody ten to three," continued the driver. "Isn't it bloody marvelous? Ten minutes to booking-off time and we get a call to what'll probably turn out to be a poxy car backfiring."

"Don't you ever stop whingeing?" asked the sergeant, trying to complete the entry in his log book and not being helped by the way his colleague was throwing the car around. Deep down, they both knew that the constant cross-talk that went on between them was pure bravado. Minutes from now either one of them could be dead. But they would never admit to thinking about it. Even to themselves.

A small car stopped in the center of the junction and its driver, a pensioner in a cloth cap, held up his hands in a gesture of surrender.

"Well, don't sit there looking bloody helpless," muttered the police driver as he braked hard and switched the siren from wail to yelp. "Where did you get your licence from, bloody Woolworths?"

"The lights were in his favor," said the sergeant mildly.

"Whose side are you on, skip?" The police driver grinned and swung the car round the back of the obstruction, accelerating.

Everything was at a standstill around Hyde Park Corner when the ARV arrived and three Traffic Division motorcyclists were attempting to maneuver some of it around a stationary cab near the Machine Gun Corps Memorial.

"Never realized they were detachable," said the ARV driver caustically, nodding at the three empty motor cycles as he and the sergeant got out of the car and made their way towards one of the policemen.

"Where's this shooting then, mate?" asked the sergeant of one of the motor-cyclists.

"Over there, sarge," said the traffic man. He waved at the stationary cab. "But you won't need those." He nodded at the pistols in the men's hands. "It's all over." He grinned and turned to berate a van driver who had offended him.

Still holding their firearms at the ready, the crew of the ARV strode purposefully towards the cab. A young, uniformed constable was standing by it talking to the driver. At the approach of the ARV crew, he turned a white face towards them.

"What you got, son?" The sergeant lowered his Smith and Wesson so that it pointed at the ground.

"A dead'un, sarge," said the PC.

The sergeant walked over and peered into the taxi. "Bloody hell!" he said.

Sprawled on the back seat of the cab was a man of about forty-five. On his lap was an open executive brief-case. And there was a bullet hole between his eyes.

*

At New Scotland Yard, Detective Chief Superintendent Tommy Fox, operational head of the Flying Squad, had just started to stir his afternoon cup of Earl Grey tea when the telephone rang. For a moment or two, he glared malevolently at it before snatching at the handset. "Fox," he said tersely.

"Tommy, it's Alec Myers. Spare me a minute, will you."

Fox sighed. "Yes, sir."

"And bring your tea with you, Tommy," Myers added. He was familiar with Fox's routine.

Commander Alex Myers, Fox's immediate boss, was standing at the window of his office peering down into Broadway. He turned as Fox entered and waved towards a chair. "Have a seat, Tommy, and help yourself to a cigarette." He pointed at the packet on his desk and then poured two measures of Scotch from the bottle on the flap of his open drinks cabinet. "Prefer that to tea, wouldn't you?" he asked unnecessarily, putting the tumbler of whisky on the desk.

Fox plucked carefully at his trousers before sitting down and then flicked a speck of dust from his sleeve. "I gather you want something, guv?" The offer of a cigarette was rare; a glass of Scotch even rarer.

"New suit, Tommy?" Myers appraised Fox's latest button-one-show-two acquisition from Hackett and placed the water carafe beside Fox's whisky.

"Not that new," said Fox guardedly. "It's just that I take care of them."

Fox's reputation as an elegant dresser was widely known at Scotland Yard, but anyone who believed that he was a dandy was in for a nasty surprise. Many policemen had found that Fox was a very hard-nosed copper, and even more villains had made the same discovery, particularly one audacious robber whose near-fatal mistake of threatening Fox with a loaded pistol had landed him with a broken jaw. Too late, he had been made aware that it needed more than a firearm to stop the head of the Flying Squad from making an arrest; seconds later, Fox had felled him with a right-handed upper cut.

"This shooting at Hyde Park Corner this afternoon, Tommy..."

"Yes, sir?"

"You know about it, of course."

"Of course, sir," said Fox in a tone of voice that implied that he knew exactly what was going on among the villainry and resented any suggestion that he didn't.

"The detective superintendent at Charing Cross, name of Semple—"

"Oh God!" muttered Fox.

Myers ignored the jibe. "He's identified the victim—"

"I should bloody well hope so," said Fox.

"Tommy, just shut up and listen for a moment, will you," said Myers, beginning to tire of Fox's interjections. "The victim is a villain called Wally Proctor. He's got a string of previous for jewelery heists going way back, but nothing in the past five or six years."

Fox assumed a sour expression. "Why are you telling me all this, sir?" he asked. But he knew.

"I want you to investigate it," said Myers. "You see, Tommy, there are complications."

Fox groaned. "Aren't there always," he said.

*

Detective Superintendent Jim Semple of Number Eight Area Major Investigation Pool sat down at his desk in Charing Cross police station and glumly considered his immediate future. His first reaction to the news that a detective chief superintendent from the Commissioner's Office, as policemen called New Scotland Yard, was to take charge, was one of relief that such a complicated case was about to be taken off his hands. But when he heard that the DCS concerned was Tommy Fox, he was overcome with a sense of foreboding based on previous experience and information received. Semple knew instinctively that he would continue to investigate the extraordinary death of Wally Proctor, but that Tommy Fox would be breathing down his neck the whole time.

"I think he's here, guv." A DC poked his head round the superintendent's door. "Anyhow, a Ford Scorpio has just come into the yard."

"Haven't you got any work to do?" asked Semple nastily.

Seconds later, the tall immaculate figure of Tommy Fox appeared in the doorway of Semple's office. "I'm reliably informed that you've got a sudden death that's puzzling you, Mr Semple," he said. "I take it you know Denzil Evans?" He indicated the Flying Squad detective inspector who was with him with a casual wave of the hand.

"Evening, sir." Semple stood up. "Yes, I know Denzil." He nodded a greeting at Fox's "bag carrier".

"Wally Proctor, yes?" Fox gazed enquiringly at the superintendent.

"Yes, sir." Semple fingered a slim folder on his desk.

"Tell me about it." Fox wandered across to Semple's notice-board and started to read one of numerous pieces of paper on it, most of which were held in place by a single drawing pin. Fox was a great believer in reading other people's notice boards; he always claimed that it gave him a greater insight into the efficiency of a CID office than any formal inspection would.

"The cab driver picked Proctor up at the Agincourt Hotel in Park Lane," said Semple. "Asked to be taken to Victoria Station. When they got to Hyde Park Corner, the driver heard a loud report from the back of

8

the cab and when he looked round, he found that Proctor had been shot. Quite unnerved him, it did."

"Who? The cab driver... or Proctor?" Fox switched his attention to a memorandum about the slovenly preparation of Forms 151F for the Crown Prosecution Service, and hummed tunelessly.

"No, the cab driver, sir." Semple had heard about Tommy Fox's obscure sense of humor, but decided to play it straight for the time being.

Tiring of the notice board, Fox turned and sat down in a chair opposite the superintendent's desk. "Do go on, Mr Semple," he said. "I'm fascinated."

"We recovered the brief-case that Proctor was carrying—"

"Oh!" said Fox. "He had a briefcase, did he?"

"Yes, sir." Semple was already beginning to feel oppressed and Fox had been in his office less than ten minutes. It did not bode well for the future. "It contained an ingenious device that shot Proctor the moment the case was opened."

"Good gracious," said Fox.

"Er, d'you fancy a Scotch, sir?" Semple posed the question hesitantly. He had heard that Fox was one of the few hard-drinking CID officers still left in the force.

"Thought you'd never ask." Fox turned to DI Evans. "I'd heard that they were very generous here at Charing Cross, Denzil, hadn't you?" he asked.

"Yes, sir, very," said Evans and lapsed into silence once more. He had worked for Fox for some years now and had become wary of his sarcasm.

"Are you going to show me this diabolical briefcase then, Mr Semple?" Fox lifted the glass of whisky and gazed at it reflectively, as if assessing its quality.

"Oh, er, it's gone for forensic, sir."

"By which, I take it, you mean it's been submitted for scientific examination?" Fox believed in fighting his war against the misuse of the word "forensic" whenever the opportunity arose. As the Flying Squad had discovered over the years, Fox, despite his cockney accent, was a stickler for correct English. When it suited him.

"Er, yes, sir. I didn't realize that you—"

"Good," said Fox. "For one awful minute, I thought you were going to say that it was still languishing within the precincts of this police station." He waved a hand airily around the office and took a sip of whisky. "What have your enquiries at the Agincourt Hotel revealed?"

Nervously, Semple shuffled the papers in the folder on his desk. "I don't seem to have had a result on that yet, sir."

"Oh dear!" Fox smiled. "But someone is out doing it, at this very moment, I imagine."

"Yes, sir, definitely." Semple hoped that the detective sergeant who had been deputed to interview the hotel staff had already left the office.

"Splendid. Now, this man Proctor. Got a bit of form, I believe."

Myers had told Fox that in recent years, Proctor had not come to the notice of police. That is to say, he had not been convicted of any crime, but Fox knew villains, and he knew that Proctor had undoubtedly been "at it". The fact that he had met an untimely end in a cab at Hyde Park Corner merely confirmed the theory. And the ingenious device which had killed him, only served to heighten the belief of Fox, well versed in the practices of the villainry as he was, that other villains had been involved in the murder.

"Well known to police, sir," said Semple, and pushed Proctor's criminal record across the desk, pleased that he was able, at last, to come up with something positive. "That's the printout from the microfiche," he added. "It was in the dead section."

"How very appropriate," said Fox and skimmed through Proctor's criminal biography. "But what's he been up to since his last conviction? According to this—" Fox slung the file on the desk. "—he came out in 1988 following a two-stretch. Then nothing."

"It all went quiet after that, sir, so it seemed."

"I gathered that," said Fox. "What do your snouts have to say?"

Semple looked unhappy. His informants, such as they were, were deployed to assist in solving the vast catalogue of outstanding crimes, with which, the Area Pool was dealing. There was little time for enquiring into the activities of those criminals who appeared to have gone straight. "There's been no word on the ground, sir," he said.

Fox glanced at his watch. "Well, I can see that there's little for me to do here, and I have an appointment." He stood up. "I'll leave you to do the groundwork then, Mr Semple," he said. "Lay the foundations. See you in the morning." He paused at the door. "I shall be interested to see the outcome of the enquiries at the hotel. There should be a sheaf of statements by, shall we say, half-past eight?"

"Yes, of course, sir."

Fox beamed at the superintendent and then turned to DI Evans. "You take the car back to the Yard, Denzil," he said. "I'll take a cab. I suppose it's safe enough," he added drily.

Once Fox was clear of the building, Semple strode into the main CID office. "Which of you bastards is supposed to be doing the enquiries at the hotel?" he asked.

*

Fox's taxi set him down at a block of mansion flats behind Harrods of Knightsbridge. As usual, he opted for the stairs rather than the lift and made his way to the first floor.

The woman who answered the door was in her mid-thirties, and was tall and slim with long brown hair. "Tommy," she said excitedly. "I thought you weren't going to get here."

"You should know me better than that, Jane," said Fox, pecking her on the cheek and walking through into the large sitting room. "Got stuck with a murder enquiry."

"Oh!" Jane looked grave. Fox had investigated the murder of her sister, Lady Dawn Sims, the previous year, and the mere mention of murder evoked unhappy memories. But it had meant that Fox and Lady Jane Sims had become acquainted, a relationship which she was hoping would advance beyond mere friendship. "What sort is it?" She poured two measures of Scotch and handed one to Fox. "Another of your domestic murders?" she asked as she sat down opposite him.

Fox sipped his whisky and stretched out his legs. "No, not this time. The Finger who got topped had got form as long as your arm. Looks as though another hood decided to take him out."

Jane Sims threw back her head and laughed. "What on earth does that mean?" she asked. "I'm sure you make up this language of yours just to tease me."

"It means," said Fox slowly, "That one villain appears to have murdered another villain. Probably some vendetta, or he was doublé-crossed."

"Was this the shooting at Hyde Park Corner that was on the news?" Jane glanced at the Regency cabinet that had been expertly converted to house her television set. The first time he had called on her, Fox had displayed a mild disapproval of the starkly functional decor of her flat, since when she had begun to replace some of the more austere items of furniture.

"That's the one."

"But they said he'd shot himself."

Fox took out his cigarette case and offered it to Jane. "That's because I chose to let the media think that," he said. "Don't want the villains to know how much we know. Time enough when we nick them."

Jane shook her head at the proffered cigarette case. "But shouldn't you be working on the case, Tommy?" she asked.

"Good Lord no," said Fox. "I have a vast team of accomplished detectives who are, at this very moment, combing the capital for information. I'm more like the conductor of a huge orchestra. I tell the musicians what to do and they do it." But both he and Detective Superintendent Semple of Charing Cross knew that that was not the way it happened. Fox could not resist interfering at every turn.

Jane laughed at his overt indifference to a job that she knew he took very seriously. "You're a real enigma, Tommy, d'you know that?" She glanced at his immaculately suited figure, his McAfee shoes, his beautifully laundered Thomas Pink shirt – she noted, with pleasure, that he was wearing the silk tie she had bought for him from Liberty – and the gold Tissot watch on his wrist, and smiled. "You just don't look the sort who spends all his working life mixing it with villains."

Fox chuckled at her use of the criminal vernacular. "That's the mistake the villains make," he said, "And usually too late."

Jane refilled Fox's whisky glass. "Are we eating out tonight, Tommy?"

Fox grinned. "No," he said firmly. "I'm not taking you out in jeans and a sweater."

"Good," said Jane. "Be a dear and open some wine."

*

At Charing Cross police station, Detective Superintendent Semple glanced at the clock and sighed. Then he stood up and stretched before walking to the door of his office. "Got those statements ready yet, Ken?" he asked. "I need them by half-past eight tomorrow morning."

"Just about, guv. Is there a panic for them then?"

"You could say that," said Semple drily.

Two

The enquiries that Detective Superintendent Semple's officers had made at the Agincourt Hotel in Park Lane had elicited only one statement that was of any value. And that amounted to very little. The hall porter remembered Proctor, although he did not know his name, entering the hotel at a little before half-past two in the afternoon and reclaiming a brief-case for which he had produced a ticket. The hall porter could not recall who had left the case there or how long it had been in the hotel's care.

"Did your Detective Sergeant..." Fox glanced at the name of the officer who had conducted the interview. "Horton. Did this DS Horton rattle this bloke's bars for him?" He dropped the form casually on Semple's desk.

"He's a very good officer is DS Horton," said Semple defensively.

"Really?" Fox tutted and lit a cigarete. "Well, it looks as though we'll have to talk to this hall porter chappie again, doesn't it?" He shrugged at the apparent unfairness of being surrounded by incompetents. "And what news on this device that saw off the bold Proctor?"

"Heard nothing from the lab yet, sir," said Semple, secure in the knowledge that he could hardly be blamed for the forensic science laboratory's seeming delay. He was wrong.

"Well, I really think you ought to have chased them up, Mr Semple." Fox turned to DI Evans. "Looks as though we'll have to talk seriously to these people, Denzil," he said. He switched his gaze back to the detective superintendent. "Post-mortem?"

"Being conducted this morning, sir."

"Who's doing it?"

Semple moved a few pieces of paper around on his desk and then gave up. "That'll be in the incident room, sir."

"Good," said Fox. "Time we had a look at the incident room."

Semple sighed, convinced that he had just made another mistake, and led the way down the corridor.

Fox stood in the doorway of the incident room and surveyed the activity. "Who is doing the post-mortem?" he asked of no one in particular.

"Pamela Hatcher, sir," said a DC from the corner.

"Splendid," said Fox. "Inquest?" he asked, turning to Semple once more.

"Er ..." Semple looked at the DI in charge of the incident room. He was beginning to feel like a trainee tennis player facing a machine that delivered balls non-stop and at a fast speed.

"Provisionally for tomorrow, guv," said the DI. "Horseferry Road. Straight adjournment, of course."

"Of course," murmured Fox and turned on his heel. "Come, Denzil, we shall visit the laboratory."

*

Hugh Donovan was the senior ballistics officer at the Metropolitan Police Forensic Science Laboratory at Lambeth, and he and Fox had done business on many previous occasions. "Fascinating device this, Tommy," he said.

Fox examined the open briefcase on Donovan's bench. "How did it work, Hugh?"

Donovan picked up a pencil and, using it as a pointer, indicated a .22 pistol that was held in a clamp with its barrel slighdy elevated towards the lock side of the case.

"That, you'll see," he said, "is held at an angle of about thirty degrees so that the muzzle just clears the front side of the lower part of the case. It's operated by this spring and wire apparatus, so that when the case is opened the tension here—" he touched the spring with the pencil. "— activates the trigger and discharges a round." He put down the pencil and grinned at Fox. "Bloody ingenious, that," he said.

"Bit hit-and-miss, isn't it?"

"Oh yes. But on this occasion it hit. Right between the eyes, they tell me. Whoever made it relied on the fact that most people will open a briefcase on their lap or on a table. You usually lay your briefcase flat before you open it, don't you?"

"I used to," said Fox drily. "But how did he load the bloody thing without shooting himself? Surely the tension is on the trigger all the while the lid is up."

"Yes, it would have been, but this is one cunning little bastard." Donovan closed the case and turned it over. "He went to a great deal of trouble. Here, here, here and here—" he pointed to the four edges on the underside of the case. "—You'll see marks where the base has been removed and then put back into place after the pistol was loaded. This guy obviously spent a lot of time working out how to see off your victim."

"An engineer of some sort?" Fox raised an eyebrow.

"Probably. And no stranger to guns, either."

"What about the weapon itself, Hugh? Known, is it?"

"I'm waiting until I get the round from the pathologist before I do a test firing, but there'll be no doubt that the round that killed Proctor came from this weapon. The number's been filed off, naturally—"

"Naturally," murmured Fox.

"But we should be able to bring it up, with a bit of luck. I'll be able to give you more once that's all done."

"When?"

Donovan paused in thought. "Day after tomorrow?" he suggested tentatively.

"Make it tomorrow," said Fox and grinned.

*

"Why is it, Denzil," asked Fox as he led the way through the revolving doors of the Agincourt Hotel, "That I always have to go around doing things that detective sergeants have cocked up?"

"Don't know, sir," said Evans. He did know, of course. Fox could never let other people get on with it. But this was neither the time nor the place to say so.

"You are Mr Brian Buck, I take it?" Fox addressed himself to the tail-coated hall porter who was seated importantly behind a curved desk in the foyer.

"Indeed, sir. How can I help you?"

"I am Detective Chief Superintendent Fox… of the Flying Squad."

"How d'you do, sir."

"Is there somewhere quiet where we can discuss a certain matter that is of consuming interest to me?" Fox gazed around the foyer as if seeking some oasis of peace and tranquility.

The hall porter gazed around too. "I am rather busy at the moment, sir," he said.

"So am I," said Fox tersely. "I am investigating a murder. What are you doing?"

"If you'll just bear with me for one moment, sir, I'll get my assistant to take over." Recognizing defeat when it was staring him in the face, Buck disappeared into the small office behind his desk. Moments later, he returned with a younger man who was in the act of donning his jacket. "If you care to come round the counter, sir, we can use my office."

Fox examined the hall porter's office with a sour expression. "Now then, in this statement..." He held out his hand and waited for Denzil Evans to pass him the sheet of paper. "In this statement, which you made last evening to Detective Sergeant Horton, you say that you recall a man coming into the hotel at about twenty-five past two yesterday afternoon and claiming a brief-case which had been left for safekeeping here in the hotel." He glanced up. "Yes?"

"Yes, sir. Absolutely." Buck leaned forward, a helpful expression on his face.

"When was the briefcase left here, Mr Buck?"

The hall porter spread his hands. "I really don't know, sir," he said.

"I see." Fox studied the ceiling before realigning his gaze on Buck. "I understand that you attach tickets to those items that are left."

"Indeed, sir."

"Indeed," repeated Fox. "And these tickets have numbers on them, do they not?"

"Of course, sir. Otherwise we wouldn't know which item belonged to which person, if you take my meaning." Buck grinned and put his head on one side, silently deciding that the detective opposite him clearly did not have the potential to be a hall porter.

"And they run in some sort of numerical order."

"Yes."

"So a ticket bearing, for example, the number one would be issued some considerable time before the ticket numbered, say, twenty?"

"Yes, sir. We go up to a hundred before starting a new book, you see."

"Oh I do, I do," said Fox warmly. "Now do you, by any chance, remember the number of the ticket presented by the gentleman who reclaimed the briefcase that we're talking about?"

"Oh yes, it was number fifty-five," said Buck without hesitation.

Fox sighed. "Why, as a matter of interest, do you recall that so readily?"

"The bloke bunged me a fiver," said Buck and then paused, obviously persuaded by Fox's sartorial elegance that, despite his accent and occupation, he was a gentleman after all. "That is to say, he very graciously gave me a tip of five pounds... sir. And I thought to myself, that's a coincidence, I thought. Two fives on the ticket and one in my hand."

"Good gracious me," said Fox. "So far, so good." He leaned forward, as if taking Buck into his confidence. "I can see that you're a very experienced hall porter," he continued.

"Twenty-seven years I've been in the business, sir," said Buck, preening himself. "Began as a lift-starter at the Hilton when it opened."

"What in hell's name is a lift-starter?" asked Fox.

Buck grinned. "He waits by the lifts in the foyer and when he sees a guest approaching, he presses the button to call the lift."

"Good God!" said Fox and shook his head. "However, as I was saying, you obviously know the hotel business inside out. I'll wager there's not much that gets past you."

"I think I can say, in all modesty, sir, that I know my way around, yes."

"Good. In that case, you should be able to tell, from the run of the numbers, approximately when that case was lodged."

The hall porter leaned back in his chair and toyed briefly with one of the brass buttons on his waistcoat before leaning forward again. "If you can give me a moment, sir, I might be able to come up with an approximation."

"Excellent," said Fox.

The hall porter went next door to the left-luggage office and examined some of the items in there. Then he went to the counter and riffled through the book of deposit tickets. "As far as I can tell, sir," he said, returning to his own office, "The briefcase you're interested in would probably have been left here on Monday."

"Any idea of time?" asked Fox, pushing his luck.

Buck shook his head. "Sorry, sir, but I can't be more positive than that. And," he added cautiously, "saying it was Monday is only a guess."

Fox nodded. "The day before yesterday then."

"I reckon so, sir," said Buck.

*

Detective Sergeant Percy Fletcher had been lumbered again. It seemed that whenever Fox needed someone to delve into masses of paper, he always selected Fletcher.

"Well, Perce, what can you tell me about the late Wally Proctor?"

"Forty-three years old, sir. Came out of the 'Ville six years ago after doing a two-stretch. Got full remission. That was for a jewelery heist in the West End." Fletcher looked up expectantly. He knew what Fox was going to ask next, but always kept some of his information back to counter the quick-fire questions that inevitably arose in an interview with his governor.

"Method?"

"Old as the hills, sir. Proctor went into a high-class jewelers and asked to see some expensive rings. To cut a long story short, he palmed one – valued at five grand – and stuck it under the front edge of the counter with chewing gum. But as he left, he was challenged by a brave member of staff. Proctor got all arsey, turned out his pockets, threatened an action for slander and left the shop. But the manager wasn't happy. He'd come across this scam before, apparently, and had a look round. When he found the ring under the ledge of the counter, he rang the Old Bill and they had a young DC sit in the office..." Fletcher looked up. "That was in the days when we had enough blokes to do that sort of thing, guv. Anyhow, about an hour later, Proctor's accomplice turned up and promptly got his collar felt. The two of them had worked the trick before, so it was dead easy to pick up Proctor. And because of his form, Proctor went down for two."

"Nice one," said Fox. "A bit flash, this Proctor, was he? I mean, the average toe-rag can't just wander into the sort of West End jewelers that holds that sort of stock."

"Fourth-rate public school," said Fletcher. "Held a commission in the army for a while, but got the bum's rush. Helped himself to some mess funds somewhere along the line. There's only a brief reference to it on his antecedents. But he was always turned out well, according to the description on the docket. Savile Row suits, all that."

Fox nodded approvingly. "A villain of taste, you might say, Perce."

Fletcher grinned. "Yeah, he was that all right, guv."

19

"But nothing since he came out?"

"No convictions, sir. There is a docket…" Fletcher reached down and took a file from the pile he had put on the floor when he had first entered Fox's office. "He tried the black pearl scam about a year back."

"Elucidate, Perce, for the benefit of Mr Evans here."

"Black pearls are very rare, guv, but Proctor got hold of one. Probably nicked it, but nothing was ever proved. Anyway, he waltzes into a jeweler's and plonks it on the counter, saying nothing. The geezer in the shop whips out his glass and peers at it. ''Fraid I can only offer you a grand for that, sir', he says. Proctor tells him that he doesn't want to sell it, but is willing to pay over the odds to match it – £1750 was the sum mentioned – so he could have a set of earrings made up for his bird, some such tosh like that. Anyway, he leaves a bogus name and address and goes merrily on his way. So the jeweler puts out the word that he's prepared to pay £1500 for a black pearl. A couple of days later, Proctor goes into another jeweler's, haggles a bit, and walks out with twelve hundred and fifty notes in his sky rocket—"

"Sky rocket: pocket, Denzil," Fox said in an aside. He always assumed that because Evans was Welsh, he didn't understand rhyming slang, despite the fact that the DI had been a London policeman for years.

"Thank you, sir," said Evans in a tone barely short of sarcastic.

"Of course," continued Fletcher, "when the first jeweler takes the black pearl off the second jeweler for fifteen hundred sovs, he finds that the name and address Proctor gave him was duff."

"So what happened?" asked Evans.

"Nothing," said Fletcher. "No offence."

"How did it come to notice then?" Evans leaned forward and rested his elbows on his knees.

"The DI at West End Central…" Fletcher glanced at Fox. "Name of Dickie Lord, guv."

"Yes, I know him," said Fox.

"Well, Dickie Lord, who always took an interest in the jewelery game, spotted the MO straightaway. And he went round and gave Proctor a talking to. In short, told him to keep off his ground." Fletcher sighed. "That was in the days when we could do that, of course," he added. Fletcher was very fond of reminiscing about the old days.

Fox teased a paper clip on to the end of his letter opener and toyed with it for some moments. "Where's Dickie Lord now, Perce?"

"Doing very nicely, guv, as a matter of fact. Set himself up as an independent insurance investigator. Deals mainly with expensive jewelery blaggings."

"Does he now," said Fox thoughtfully. "I think we shall pay Dickie Lord a visit. Where does he have his offices, Perce?"

"Hatton Garden, guvnor."

"Of course," said Fox. "Where else?"

*

"The test firing proved that the round that killed Proctor came from the weapon in the briefcase, Tommy," said Hugh Donovan.

"Which comes as no surprise to any of us," said Fox. "But what about the weapon?"

"Now that's interesting," said Donovan, warming to his subject. "It was used in a case about five years ago. The weapon itself was never recovered."

"What sort of job was it?" asked Fox.

Donovan flicked over a page in the file before him. "A domestic murder so far as I can tell. I've only got the brief details here, of course, but I can give you the docket number."

*

Detective Superintendent Semple had something to tell Fox at last. "We've turned over Proctor's drum, sir," he said.

"How did you find it?"

"He had five credit cards in his possession when he was topped. I got one of the lads to check with each of the companies that issued them. Four of the addresses were duff, but the fifth, a modern flat in the Bayswater Road, was where he lived."

"Very good," said Fox. "Anything interesting?"

Semple paused, relishing the moment. "Only about two hundred grand's worth of tomfoolery, sir."

"Checked in Property Index, Mr Semple?" Fox spoke casually despite his sudden interest that the late Wally Proctor should have some two hundred thousand pounds worth of jewelery in his flat.

Semple was disappointed at Fox's flat response. "There's no record of it having been stolen, sir."

"Well now, isn't that a funny thing? Are you sure it's genuine?"

"Yes, pretty certain, but there were some paste replicas of some of it as well."

"Were there indeed?" Fox looked thoughtful as he considered the implications. "Well, Mr Semple…" He paused. "James, isn't it?"

"Jim, actually, sir."

But Semple's belief that he was at last being accepted by Fox was canceled out by the detective chief superintendent's next statement.

"Well, Jim, it looks as though we're going to have to do some hard work from now on."

Semple looked at his own DI. "And what the hell does he think we've been doing so far?" he asked. But he waited until Fox was well clear of the building before he said it.

Three

"Mr Lord's expecting you, Mr Fox." The busty redhead spoke huskily as she rose from her seat at the computer station, smoothed her dress and moved towards the door leading to Lord's office.

"How kind," murmured Fox. Knowing him as well as he did, he suspected that ex-Detective Inspector Dickie Lord's personal assistant had been engaged more for her looks than her secretarial skills.

"Mr Fox!" Lord walked across the office and held out his hand. "How are you?"

Fox shook hands with the former policeman and indicated DI Evans. "D'you know Denzil Evans?" he asked. He gazed around the sumptuous office and nodded approvingly. It was richly carpeted, and Lord's desk, in front of an expensively curtained window, was curved and large. On a side table were a battery of telephones and a fax machine. Along an adjacent wall was a built-in bookcase containing an impressive array of books, legal and actuarial. "Seem to be doing all right for yourself, Dickie."

"Bit hand to mouth," said Lord with no hint of amusement on his face. "But I'm scratching a living, if you know what I mean?" He shook hands with Evans. "Must have bumped into you at the Yard sometime," he said. It was the standard greeting from one detective to another whom he had never set eyes on before.

"Probably," said Evans.

"Vicky, love, see if you can find three cups of tea, there's a good girl." Lord paused and glanced at Fox. "Unless you'd prefer..." he began.

Fox nodded. "I would."

"Forget the tea, love," said Lord. He crossed to the bookcase, opened a section of "books" and poured three large Scotches. "Now then, what can I do for you, Mr Fox?" he asked when all three of them were settled in his comfortable suite of armchairs.

"Wally Proctor," said Fox without preamble.

"Thought it might be," said Lord and crossed to a filing cabinet. He dropped a bulky folder on the small table between them. "You're welcome to have a go through that," he said, "but most of it's probably rubbish. Titbits of information I've picked up over the years."

"Thought you'd have had all that on your computer," said Fox, making no move to read the file.

"Not likely," said Lord. "I never put the 'iffy' stuff where someone else can read it."

"Tell me the bones of it, then," said Fox. He took a sip of whisky. "This is a decent malt."

"Knockando. Gift from a grateful client." Lord grinned. "Proctor..." He leaned back in his chair and gazed briefly at the ceiling. "Good iceman in his day." The beauty of dealing with one's own was that the conversation could be conducted in the verbal shorthand that was a feature of the profession.

"How good?" Fox knew that the late Wally Proctor had been an iceman, a jewel thief with a preference for diamonds. He had stolen either by confidence trick or, when the opportunity had presented itself, by a straight blagging.

"Well, he came out of the 'Ville about six years ago following a two-stretch—"

"Yes, I know," said Fox. "Percy Fletcher's been doing some ferreting for me. Who was his accomplice on that job, Dickie?"

Lord looked thoughtful. Eventually he said, "Skelton, first name Robin."

"How appropriate," murmured Fox. "Can't say I've heard of him."

"I suppose Percy Fletcher told you about the black pearl scam, as well."

Fox nodded. "Yes."

"But I'm in no doubt that he's been at it since." Lord leaned forward to top up Fox's glass and then held the bottle towards Evans. Evans shook his head. "I've investigated one or two claims recently that seem to have his name on them."

"In what way?"

"The method's got to be Proctor's." Lord flicked open the file. "There have been two or three jobs recently where women, usually in their sixties, but some older, some younger, have reported the theft of jewelery. In most cases, the Old Bill have found no signs of forced entry, but the victims have been adamant that they've admitted no one they didn't know, and that they made the discovery on returning from a day out, or a weekend with their families. That sort of thing."

"And what d'you think?" Fox offered Lord a cigarette.

"I'm bloody sure that they were conned. In one case I got an admission that the woman had been befriended by a smooth-talking operator, almost certainly Proctor, and that he'd done a runner with the gear. About fifty grand's worth, that one was. Did a bit of digging and it turned out that she'd given him permission to try and sell it on her behalf. She never saw the bastard again."

"Anything come of it?"

"No," said Lord. "The company I was doing the job for refused to pay out and the woman said she wouldn't go to court even if the bloke was found. She seemed to think he might turn up one day, even though it was six months since she last saw him. By rights, she should have been done for making a false claim." He grinned. "And who says insurance companies haven't got hearts?"

"Is that the only one?" asked Fox.

"The only one I've proved, but I'm bloody sure there've been others."

Fox leaned forward to tap ash into the ashtray. "What's the latest one you dealt with, Dickie? One that might fit Proctor's MO, I mean."

"There's about three, all within months of each other, that might fit." Lord crossed to the filing cabinet once more and plucked out a handful of files. "Six weeks ago a Mrs Linda Ward, aged fifty with an address in Earls Court, reported a theft from her flat—"

"A theft? Not a break-in?"

"Well, she reported to police that she'd been burgled, but the local law couldn't find any signs of a break-in. She confessed herself mystified. She'd been on holiday for a fortnight and claimed that she'd left about seventy K's worth of jewelery in the flat, daft bitch, and when she came back it had gone. The company withheld payment of the claim pending a full investigation."

"And how are you getting on with it?"

"Zilch!" said Lord. "She won't budge from her story. She says she never met a dark, handsome stranger and that no one, apart from her married daughter, had a key to her flat."

"Is there a porter at these flats, Dickie?"

"Yeah, but he's been there years. Apparently he's trusted by everyone."

"Got any form, this porter?" asked Fox.

Lord grinned. "Well," he said, "Now that I'm no longer in the job, I don't have access to the PNC, but I'm reliably informed that he's clean. The DC I at Kensington accidentally let it slip."

"Careless of him," said Fox. "He shouldn't be telling civilians what's on the Police National Computer."

"That's what I told him," said Lord.

"What about Mrs Ward's daughter? Suddenly looking more prosperous, is she?"

"Not that you'd notice. She's married to some filthy rich architect nearly twice her age – she's only twenty-three – and lives in Chalfont St Giles. Doesn't look as though she'd need an extra seventy thousand."

"Your clients going to pay, are they?" asked Fox.

Lord shrugged. "Probably have to in the long run," he said. "Unless I can come up with something. Why? D'you want to have a go at her?"

"Might have a chat with her," said Fox. "What about the others?"

"There's one in Surbiton, a Mrs Joyce Bourne, and another in Chiswick…" Lord turned up the file. "Mrs Audrey Harker. They're both widows. Mrs Bourne's sixty and Mrs Harker's sixty-three." He flung the files on to the table. "Same story in each case. Both claim to have been broken into, but neither premises showed any signs of a forced entry."

"And presumably they deny that they knew any smooth-talking bastards like Proctor."

"That's about the size of it," said Lord.

"All right with you if Denzil takes a few details, Dickie?" asked Fox.

"Be my guest," said Lord and pushed the files towards Evans.

"Well, one thing's certain," said Fox as he stood up. "You can close your file on Proctor now."

Lord sighed. "He might be dead," he said, "but I'm sure that he'll trouble me for a while yet. But d'you think any of this could be connected with Proctor's topping?"

Fox grinned. "Got to start somewhere, Dickie," he said. "As a matter of interest, when Jim Semple turned over Proctor's drum, he found about two hundred grand's worth of jewelery. According to Property Index, it's not listed as stolen, but you know as well as I do that the descriptions

26

given by losers are often too vague to be certain. You might like to take a look at it."

"Thanks," said Lord as he shook hands.

"One other thing," said Fox. "Who, in your opinion, is the best iceman now that Proctor's no longer with us?"

Lord looked thoughtful, but only for a moment or two. "Robin Skelton, aforementioned," he said.

*

"This weapon," said Fox, placing a .22 pistol on Detective Superintendent Semple's desk, "was the one which killed Proctor, but a ballistic comparison shows that it was last used in a murder in Shepperton. Get one of your lads to find out what it was all about, will you."

"Think it might be relevant, sir?" asked Semple.

"If it was a domestic murder, it might be," said Fox. "On the other hand, it might have been doing the rounds before Proctor's killer laid his hands on it."

"I suppose…" began Semple and then stopped.

"What?"

"I suppose it is a murder we're dealing with here, sir."

"Oh! Don't tell me you think it may have been a suicide." Fox looked at Semple with an expression of despair on his face. "Because if it is, he went to a great deal of trouble when he could simply have shot himself."

"No, sir. I was thinking more that he might have set the thing up himself, intending to plant the briefcase on someone else."

"I see," said Fox. "And just couldn't resist the temptation to test it." He gave the detective superintendent a withering glance.

*

Among Tommy Fox's coterie of informants was a man called Arnold Bertram Pogson who, because of his initials, was invariably known as "Sailor" Pogson. Pogson had begun his criminal career while at university, where he had specialized in accountancy – and stealing other people's credit cards. Because of his criminal conviction – and the sentence of three years that went with it – Pogson had been unable to secure membership of the more discerning professional bodies and made his money by creative book-keeping, advising dubious clients on the best way to invest their felonious profits and occasionally by "taking in laundry" as the cleansing of ill-gotten gains was known. At a percentage, of course, rather than for a straight fee.

Pogson's role as a sporadic informant was not derived from an overwhelming desire to ingratiate himself with the police – he was usually too cautious to require the sort of protection that many informants mistakenly thought that aiding the police provided – but found that it was a useful way of dealing with those of his clients who welshed on him. In short, Pogson and Fox each found the other useful, when it suited them. Unfortunately for Pogson, it was Fox who always held the upper hand in these transactions.

Fox entered the suite of seedy offices that Pogson rented just off City Road, ascended the rickety staircase and, ignoring the receptionist-cum-secretary and sleeping partner, strode into Pogson's office.

"Hallo, Sailor," said Fox, and grinned as he slammed the door behind him.

Pogson looked alarmed at the sudden arrival of the head of the Flying Squad. Normally, they met in more discreet surroundings or even conducted their business by telephone. But Pogson recognized Fox's presence as the detective's customary way of bringing pressure to bear. "You want something, Mr Fox?" he said.

"Very perspicacious of you, Sailor," said Fox and, after carefully appraising the poor-quality furniture, sat down in the armchair opposite Pogson's desk.

"It's not a good idea, you coming here, Mr Fox," said Pogson. "People might talk."

"That's the whole object of my visit, Sailor." Fox glanced around the office and wrinkled his nose before lighting a cigarette. "Wally Proctor."

Pogson sucked through his teeth and rocked slowly back and forth in his chair. "A tragedy, Mr Fox, a tragedy," he said.

"Think so?" Fox grinned at the accountant. "Why? Owe you some money, did he?"

Pogson removed his rimless spectacles and began polishing them with a handkerchief. "I don't do business with people of that sort, Mr Fox."

"Oh, do leave off, Sailor."

Ignoring the jibe, Pogson held the spectacles up to the window and peered through them. Satisfied that they were clean, he replaced them on his nose and stared at Fox. "Is there something I can do for you?" He suddenly felt an overwhelming desire to get Fox out of his office.

"I understand that you gave some investment advice to the late Mr Proctor from time to time."

Pogson silently washed his hands and smiled benignly. "It's possible that I may have done," he said. "A long time ago though."

"Yes, I'm sure you did, Sailor." Fox paused and gazed at Pogson. The accountant found it disconcerting. "And Robin Skelton, no doubt."

Pogson contrived to look perplexed. "Skelton, Skelton..." He repeated the name several times. "I don't think I've—"

"Let's stop buggering about, Sailor, shall we?" Fox leaned forward, an earnest expression on his face. "First and foremost, I have found about two hundred K's worth of tomfoolery in Proctor's abode, together with a wealth of paper about how he fenced previous acquisitions, and what he did with the money when he, how shall we say, realized his assets. I've no doubt that when we come to do the financial analysis of all this, your name will feature quite prominently." He leaned back and waited. It was all fiction. Proctor had been a careful villain and there had been nothing in his flat to show how he had disposed of any of the jewelery that he had stolen over the years.

Pogson was fairly certain that there would have been no such documents, but despite being a shrewd operator on the financial markets, he was still naive enough to think that Fox would overlook any evidence that involved him in anything illegal. But that just proved that, after all these years, he still did not know Fox as well as he thought he did. "Name doesn't ring any bells," he said.

"Oh dear!" Fox looked genuinely distressed. "It looks as though we're going to have to do this the hard way," he said, and glanced pointedly at Pogson's filing cabinet.

"Skelton. Yes, of course. Handles jewelery from time to time." Pogson was suddenly overtaken by a restoration of memory.

"Nicks jewelery is the expression, Sailor, but yes, you're thinking along the right lines. Where can I find him?" Fox had already told Detective Sergeant Percy Fletcher to go out and "beat on the ground, just to see what came up", but he believed in setting more than one trap. And if it upset the villainy in the process, so much the better.

"Ah, now there you have me, Mr Fox." Pogson appeared to ponder the problem. He had always been paid what he called the laundry bill, for converting Skelton's profit into something legitimate, and he had no reason to shop the jewel thief. But, when it came to it, it was every man for himself. "I could make a few enquiries, I suppose, and perhaps give you a bell." He looked hopefully at Fox.

"Yes, why don't you do that, Sailor?"

"It might take some time."

"I've no doubt, Sailor. Shall we say tomorrow? At the latest."

Pogson waited until he had seen Fox's car pulling away from the kerb in the direction of Finsbury Circus, and promptly telephoned Skelton. "Robin? The Old Bill's looking for you." There was a pause and then he added the gladdening information that it was Tommy Fox of the Flying Squad who was doing the looking.

But Fox had known that Pogson would make that call, and he would not have visited the bent accountant unless DS Percy Fletcher had already located Skelton. It was all part of another of Fox's little plans designed to upset the villainry and flush out the unrighteous. As he later said to DI Evans, "They never learn, Denzil. They never learn."

Four

It had not taken Detective Sergeant Percy Fletcher long to discover where Robin Skelton was living. Deploying his stable of snouts, as informants are known to the police, he had learned that the jewel thief's center of operations was now concentrated on an elegant flat in a modern block just off Queensway in the heart of Bays water. Ironically, it was less than half a mile from the flat that Proctor had occupied until his untimely demise.

Having passed the information to Fox, Fletcher had been surprised when told to do nothing. But now, Fletcher and the rest of DI Jack Gilroy's team were secreted in and around the street where Skelton lived. Why it was necessary to complicate the operation by mounting a surveillance was a mystery to Fletcher, but then much of what Fox did was a mystery to him. To say nothing of the rest of the Flying Squad.

Within minutes of receiving the radio message from Fox that Skelton was likely to make a hurried departure – a message which had been transmitted the moment Fox had left Sailor Pogson's premises – the one detective who had been left loitering saw the jewel thief emerging from his block of flats. He immediately alerted DI Gilroy who was parked around the corner, and maintained a running commentary on Skelton's movements.

Carrying a brown nylon holdall, Skelton crossed the road and unlocked a Rover 400 parked in one of the side streets. Putting the holdall in the boot, he drove off only to find himself hemmed in by three Flying Squad cars before he had traveled fifty yards.

"Afternoon." Gilroy approached Skelton's car and produced his warrant card.

"What's the problem, Constable?" Skelton addressed the detective inspector with all the dignity of a helpful citizen.

"We have had several reports of burglaries from the block of flats you've just left, sir," said Gilroy, ignoring the slight to his rank, "and we've been asked by the residents to keep a look out. We just happened to be passing when we saw you come out carrying a holdall."

"I'm going away for a few days." Skelton smiled. "But I must commend you for your vigilance, Constable, and I'm very pleased to hear that you're safeguarding our interests."

"All part of the service," said Gilroy. "So perhaps you'd be good enough to show me what you have in the holdall."

"But I live there," said Skelton.

Gilroy immediately adopted the role of the dim detective. "I'm sorry?"

"I live there, in that block of flats. The flats you were just talking about."

Gilroy reached out for the pocket book that Fletcher was proffering. "According to the police national computer, sir, you are Mr Robin Skelton. Yes?"

"That's right."

"And this is your car?"

"Yes, of course it is."

"But the computer gives your address as somewhere in Notting Hill." Gilroy smiled sympathetically.

"Oh, I, er, I must have forgotten to change it when I moved," Skelton said lamely.

"Mmm!" Gilroy nodded slowly. "Shall we look in the holdall now?" he said.

Slowly, Skelton got out of the car. He was a tall, slender man, in his mid-forties, and dressed in a gray suit with a white shirt and a discreet tie. In his buttonhole, he wore a red carnation. But as he turned to face Gilroy, he suddenly lunged forward and ran down the street.

Gilroy sighed and leaned against the car, watching as four members of his team set off in pursuit. Skelton had reached the traffic lights at the junction and was in the act of hailing a cab when DS Ernie Crabtree laid hands on him and hustled him, still struggling, back to his car.

"Ah, nice of you to come back," said Gilroy. "Shall we open the holdall now?"

Glowering at the police officers now surrounding him, Skelton watched as DS Fletcher opened the boot of his car and took out the holdall. After rummaging among underclothes and dirty shirts, he produced a chamois leather bag. Inside the bag was a quantity of jewelery.

*

An hour or two later, Fox strode into the interview room at Notting Hill police station and beamed at the hunched figure of Robin Skelton. "I'm Thomas Fox... of the Flying Squad," he said. "I don't think we've had the pleasure."

Skelton remained silent, glaring at Fox with an expression that implied that pleasure was not a term he would have used to describe this latest encounter with the police.

"And what have you to tell me, Jack?" asked Fox, turning to DI Gilroy.

"We found Mr Skelton to be in possession of a quantity of jewelery for which, so far, he has failed to account, sir." Gilroy looked sorrowful. "And I understand from DS Fletcher, who is currently searching Mr Skelton's flat, that more jewelery has been found there. DS Buckley is searching the address in Notting Hill but, so far, I've not heard from him."

"Good gracious me," said Fox and looked at the prisoner with renewed interest.

"I'm in the trade," said Skelton sullenly.

"Oh, that's all right, then." Fox appeared to consider this statement for a while. "And where d'you have your commercial premises, Mr Skelton?"

"I don't. I trade from home."

Fox nodded understandingly. "Don't blame you, really," he said, "What with uniform business rate, and heating and lighting, and all that. But how do your clients like the idea of trotting into your flat to view the merchandise?"

"I've got nothing to say," said Skelton, realizing that he had probably said too much already. The last time he had been arrested, his solicitor had reproved him for making a verbal statement and had cautioned him that, in the event of a future unhappy event of that nature, he should remain shtoom. "I want a solicitor."

"Why? Is there some problem with unpaid VAT?" Fox nodded slowly. "Well, if that's the case, I have to tell you not to bother. That's all dealt with by Her Majesty's Customs and Excise. Not the sort of thing we worry about." Not unless there's nothing else, Fox thought to himself.

"Why have I been brought here?" Skelton decided to go on the attack.

"Oh, didn't the officers tell you?" Fox glanced at Gilroy. "Surely, Jack, you explained to this gentleman why you wanted him to assist us in our enquiries."

"Not exactly, sir," said Gilroy. "I told him I was arresting him for possession of a quantity of jewelery suspected of having been stolen."

"Ah! Now we're getting to the nub of it. What d'you have to say about that, Mr Skelton?"

"Nothing," said Skelton churlishly.

Thoughtfully, Fox took out his case and selected a cigarette. After a moment's hesitation, he offered one to Skelton. "These things have a way of sorting themselves out," he said, applying a flame to Skelton's cigarette. "But there are much more important things to talk about."

"There are?" Skelton looked unhappy.

"Yes," said Fox. "The unfortunate demise of Mr Wally Proctor. It was reported in *The Times*, although he was not accorded an entry on the obituary page."

"What about it?"

"I understand from my informants, who are many and various, that you and he had a falling out. Something to do with the attempted theft of a diamond ring from a high-class firm of West End jewelers, as a result of which the pair of you went down for a couple of years."

"So what?" Skelton's pseudo-public school accent, and the phraseology that went with it, had started to slip since the start of the interview.

"Have you ever studied engineering?" asked Fox suddenly.

"Eh?" The change in tack obviously disconcerted Skelton. "No, never."

Fox nodded amiably. "You see, Robin, old sport, someone of felonious intent rigged up a briefcase with a firearm in it, and when poor old Wally opened it up, it went bang, thereby sending a lethal projectile into his brain, such as it was. Cab driver's none too pleased either. Quite unnerved him, apparently."

"That was nothing to do with me." Skelton's reserve now began to crumble quite dramatically and an expression of mild panic crossed his face. Although he had never encountered Fox before, he, in common with many other villains, had heard of him. And his methods. And what he had heard did not imbue him with any sense of well-being.

"Well, I'm pleased to have your assurance on that point, Robin. But you'll forgive me if I don't take your word for it, won't you?" Fox turned to Gilroy. "I presume that you have enough upon which to frame a charge, Jack?"

"More than enough, sir," said Gilroy. "Might even be enough to convince the Crown Prosecution Service."

"From which, Robin," said Fox turning back to Skelton, "You will deduce that my detective inspector is brimming with confidence." He stood up. "I'll leave you to deal with the paperwork then, Jack."

*

"The murder you enquired about, sir," said Detective Superintendent Semple, "The one in which the firearm was used." "Ah yes," said Fox. "You have intelligence regarding that outrage, I take it?"

"Yes, sir." Semple turned up a file. "Took place on a houseboat between Dumsey Eyot and Dockett Eddy."

"Is that in the Metropolitan Police District, Jim?"

"Just, sir. At Shepperton, on the River Thames. A man was shot dead and his body dumped in the river. It was a dispute over a woman—"

Fox groaned. "Isn't it always," he said.

"Apparently the victim had recently been seeing the girl, and her first boyfriend – the alleged murderer – didn't like it. Happens all the time."

"Really?" Fox affected surprise. "What, people shooting each other on houseboats? Well, who'd've thought it?"

"No, sir," said Semple, who was still struggling to come to terms with Fox's bizarre sense of humor. "The eternal triangle."

"Any names, Jim?"

Semple thumbed open a file. "The girl was called Julie Strange. The deceased was Jason Bright, and the alleged murderer is Kevin Povey."

"You keep saying the *alleged* murderer, Jim. Am I to take it there was no conviction?"

"There wasn't even a knock-off, guv'nor," said Semple gloomily.

"Why?"

"Did a runner apparently. When Povey's drum in Battersea was turned over, there were signs of a hurried departure. No one has the faintest idea where he went or where he is now. Might even be dead, I suppose. One thing that might be useful though – they found a picture of him in a photograph album when they searched the flat in Battersea. Here."

Semple passed Fox the photo. "I did a check with Hugh Donovan at the lab, sir, and he has no record of the weapon having been used between then and now."

Fox glanced at the photo then handed it back to Semple. "Have you made up-to-date enquiries about this fellow? What was his name again?"

"Kevin Povey, sir. The only trace of him is that he's still on the PNC as wanted for questioning in connection with the Shepperton job."

"I should bloody well hope so," said Fox. "But what do we know about him? Or the woman for that matter."

"The docket's got quite a lot about him," said Semple. "He was twenty-four at the time of the offence, and apparently a bit of a waster. He came from a good family, went to a decent school, but never settled to anything. His old man was quite well off and indulged him. Got the impression that he would rather have given him fifty quid than fifty minutes, if you know what I mean."

"Yes, I get the idea," said Fox. "Were the parents interviewed?"

"Only by the French police, sir."

"How original," said Fox. "Is there a reason?"

Semple grinned. "Yes, they were living in Cannes at the time. Apparently hadn't seen their son for some time. The officer in the case saw no profit in interviewing them."

"Strange fellow," said Fox. "Must be one of those dedicated bastards that we seem to be recruiting these days." He shook his head. "Fancy turning down the chance of a trip to the Riviera. And the woman, Julie Strange?"

"There's a statement on file, sir, in which she puts the killing firmly down to Povey. Witnessed it, apparently, but took no part in either that or the disposal of the body. She claims that Povey threatened her and that's why she didn't inform police immediately. The murder was only discovered when Bright's body was found in the river some two or three days later."

"What's known about her?"

"Aged twenty-one at the time, sir, and a model apparendy. Whatever that means."

Fox reached across the desk and took the file. He read through Julie Strange's statement and glanced up. "She doesn't say what happened to the firearm," he said. "She doesn't say, for example, whether it was thrown overboard, or whether Povey took it with him."

"I suspect that he took it with him, sir," said Semple. "She claimed he threatened her, and if he'd just slung the weapon over the side, she might not have been so intimidated. Apart from which, if it was thrown overboard, it's unlikely to have been recovered to commit another murder. It would still have been in the mud, I imagine."

"Good thinking," said Fox. "But where's this woman now?"

"No idea, sir. There's a note on the docket that says the houseboat was sold shortly afterwards."

Fox nodded slowly. "Perhaps it might be a good idea to find out, Jim," he said. "See if she can remember exactly what happened to the firearm that, five years later, took poor old Wally Proctor out."

*

Mrs Joyce Bourne was a sixty-year-old widow who lived in a house at the better end of Surbiton. Although she was well preserved and still boasted a good figure, she had begun to behave, since the death of her husband, as though she was just waiting to die.

When Fox arrived at her door, she was delighted that the police should be so concerned at her loss that they had now sent a detective chief superintendent from Scotland Yard to talk to her about it. No sooner had she ushered Fox and Detective Inspector Denzil Evans into her sitting room than she disappeared into her kitchen, intent on making tea.

Fox leaned back in the chintz-covered armchair and took a sip of tea from a bone china cup. "Mrs Bourne," he began, "I am sorry to trouble you again about the loss of your jewelery."

"Not at all," said Mrs Bourne. "I'm most grateful that you're taking such an interest."

"Perhaps you could just run through what happened."

"It's funny you should ask that, but I'd been to see my married daughter. She lives in Cardiff, you see. She's got a lovely house there, but then property's cheaper out of London. At least, that's what her husband said. He's a surveyor, you know, and surveyors know about these things. They've been married for ten years now. Well, it's her second marriage, you see. Her first husband was an absolute—"

Fox held up his hand. "Yes, madam, I'm sure that she's very happy now, but could we get back to the jewelery you lost."

"The what?" Mrs Bourne leaned forward as though she were deaf.

"The jewelery you had stolen, Mrs Bourne."

"Oh yes, the jewelery. Er, would you like some more tea?"

"No, thank you. That was very nice." Fox placed his cup and saucer on the occasional table.

"Inspector?" Mrs Bourne looked expectantly at Evans.

"No, thank you, madam. One's quite sufficient for me."

"Oh," said Mrs Bourne, "You're Welsh, Inspector. Where d'you come from?"

"Wales," said Evans.

"Yes, yes, but I mean where in Wales?"

"Just outside Cardiff, madam," said Evans with a sigh. "A little place called Pen-y-groes."

"Well," said Mrs Bourne, "Isn't that a coincidence?"

"The jewelery, Mrs Bourne?" said Fox.

"Oh yes, of course, the jewelery. Well, I'd been with my married daughter for a week and when I got back, it had gone. I called the police straightaway, naturally…"

"Naturally," murmured Fox. He knew all this. Evans had got details from the investigating officer at Kingston police station. "But your house hadn't been broken into, I understand."

"No, at least that's what the young policewoman said. She went all over and said there was no way anyone could have got in without a key. Apparently they can tell, you know."

"So I gather," said Fox drily. "And you can't explain how your jewelery was stolen. What was its value, incidentally?" Mrs Bourne paused, and for the first time she hesitated. "About forty-five thousand pounds, I suppose."

"You suppose? You mean that's the amount you claimed from the insurance?"

"Well, yes." Mrs Bourne gave a guilty little smile and poured herself another cup of tea. "Are you sure you won't have another cup?" she asked.

"No, thank you," said Fox and nodded to Evans. Fortunately, Wally Proctor had been a vain man and the police had found a good portrait of him, in a frame, in his flat. And it was a copy of this that Evans now handed to Fox.

"Have you ever seen this man before, Mrs Bourne?" Fox laid the quarter-plate print of Proctor on the table.

Mrs Bourne gave a little gasp and put her hand to her mouth. "Oh my!" she said.

"When did you first meet him?"

"I, er, well, I suppose it must have been about six months ago…"

Five

Mrs Audrey Harker of Chiswick, one of the other losers whose names Dickie Lord had provided Fox with, was also widowed and was three years older than Mrs Joyce Bourne. But her story was similar. She had spent the weekend with her sister in Basingstoke and when she returned, she said, she found that all her jewelery, which she valued at about thirty thousand pounds, had vanished. She was unable to explain how the thief had managed to enter her premises, but pointedly suggested that the police ought to be telling her, not asking.

Fox placed the photograph of Wally Proctor in front of Mrs Harker. "Have you seen this man before, Mrs Harker?" he asked.

Audrey Harker afforded the print the merest of glances. "No," she said. "Why? Should I have done?"

Fox replaced Proctor's photograph with one of Robin Skelton that had been taken just after his arrest. "This man, then?"

"Oh, God, it's Charles. You know then." Mrs Harker looked accusingly at Fox. "Why have you been wasting everyone's time if you knew all along?" she demanded.

"We didn't know all along, Mrs Harker. In fact, we've only just arrested this man. His name is Robin Skelton and he was in possession of a quantity of stolen jewelery." Fox picked up the photograph and handed it back to Evans.

"What name did you know him by?"

"Charles Beveridge. He was absolutely charming. So helpful, too."

"So it would seem," said Fox. "Tell me, Mrs Harker, how did you come to meet him?"

No one likes to appear foolish and Audrey Harker was no exception. "I'm afraid I took him on face value," she said. "He called here one day and said that he worked for my late husband's firm. He said that he was in the area and that part of his job was to look in on pensioners' widows, just to make sure that they were all right." She shook her head, as if unable to comprehend her own stupidity.

"And you accepted that? Didn't do any checking?"

"No, I'm afraid not. He seemed so, well, so caring and he didn't seem to want anything. I mean, he just sat, there where you're sitting, and he had a cup of tea and he talked about how difficult things were for people living on a fixed income."

"At what point did you part with your jewelery, Mrs Harker?"

"It must have been the third time he called, I suppose. The first time, when he was talking about fixed incomes, he said that if he could help in any way, he'd be more than happy to do so."

"I'll bet," murmured Fox.

"Anyhow, I happened to mention that I'd got some jewelery, quite a lot in fact, and that I'd thought about selling it. I never have occasion to wear it these days, you see. Never go out very much, not the sort of going out that involves getting dressed up, anyway."

"Are you sure you mentioned the jewelery first? Or did he?"

"Oh, he might have done. I can't really remember. Anyway, he kindly offered to make some enquiries. I asked him if he wanted to take it with him, but he said no, he'd find out first, but he did have a look at it."

Fox shook his head in amazement. "You offered to allow a complete stranger to take your jewelery, the first time you'd met him?"

"Well, he did say he was from Peter's old company. Anyway, as I say, he refused, but the third or fourth time he came, he said that he'd got a buyer and quoted a very good price."

"So you handed it over and never saw him again."

"Yes. He'd given me a phone number and after about six weeks had passed, when I'd started to get a bit worried, I telephoned him, but the operator told me that the line had been discontinued, or something like that."

"What was the number, Mrs Harker?"

"I'm not sure if I've still got it. He told me it was the new number for my late husband's old firm." Mrs Harker rose from her chair and walked across to a Regency table and opened one of the drawers. She moved the contents about and then turned. "No, I'm sorry, I must have thrown it away."

"Not to worry," said Fox. "It wouldn't have meant very much. I daresay a young lady would have answered, claiming to be your husband's old company, and then she'd have put you through to a man who would have vouched for this Charles Beveridge. So why did you tell the police that you'd been broken into?"

"I didn't. I just told them that I'd come back from Basingstoke and the jewelery had gone. Well, that was the truth. But the police seemed to think I'd been burgled, but then they said that they couldn't see how anyone had got in. The detective, a nice young man, helped me fill in the forms for the insurance company."

"Did he indeed," said Fox. "Don't happen to remember his name, I suppose?"

"No, I'm sorry."

"Never mind," said Fox. "I'll find him."

Did he but know it, a CID officer at the local police station was about to be subjected to a very uncomfortable interview with the head of the Flying Squad.

*

"Get on to Kingston and Chiswick nicks, Denzil," said Fox, "And arrange for Mesdames Bourne and Harker to have a gander at the gear Jack Gilroy's team found in Skelton's possession. Never know, they might get lucky. Not that they deserve to. If they score, let Dickie Lord know. I reckon we owe him one." He shook his head. "Isn't it bloody marvelous. Some bastard turns up and because he's well dressed and speaks with a posh accent, these old birds will give him anything he asks for." He stood up and stared out of the window. "I ask you, Denzil, what chance do we stand?"

"But we're no nearer knowing who topped Wally Proctor, guv'nor," said Evans.

Fox turned and glared at Evans. "I am aware of that, Denzil," he said.

*

"We've tracked down Julie Strange, sir," said Semple. "The girl who witnessed the murder on the houseboat."

"Good," said Fox. "How did you do that?"

"Got one of the lads to do a trawl through the marriage register at St Catherine's House, on the off chance that she may have got married."

"I thought that was a bit of rare occurrence these days, Jim."

"What's that, sir?"

"Getting married."

"Oh, I see," said Semple. He did not see at all, but then he had not known Fox all that long. "She's now Mrs Lockhart. Her spouse was shown on the certificate as a dental surgeon so we looked in the Dental Register, found out where he practised and hey-presto!"

*

"I'm afraid Skelton got bail, sir," said DI Jack Gilroy.

"What?" Fox looked up, stark disbelief evident on his face. "How the hell did that happen?"

"The Crown Prosecution Service bloke didn't put up a very good fight."

"That, Jack, is what happens when you send a boy to do a man's job," said Fox. "Conditions?"

"That he surrenders his passport and reports to police daily, sir. At Notting Hill nick."

"It's no wonder that crime is rife, Jack." Fox stared moodily at the file on his desk. "There we have a bloody villain bang to rights and he gets bail. I sometimes wonder why the hell we bother."

*

Lady Jane Sims was wearing a long baggy sweater and black leggings when she answered the door. "Tommy, I was just thinking about you. Come on in." She led the way into her sitting room and pushed her drawing board into a corner.

"Working?" asked Fox. He had been mildly surprised, when they had first met, to discover that Jane Sims was a highly qualified architect.

"Just roughing out a few designs." Jane pushed the hair out of her eyes and poured drinks for them both.

"What is it?" asked Fox, peering at the drawing.

"A new sports center. It's only in the early stages. We don't even know if we're going to get the contract, but I've never done a sports center before. It could be rather fun."

Fox nodded gravely. "Looks like an aircraft hangar to me," he said.

"Oh, you!" Jane gave him a playful punch and handed him a glass. "Well," she said, "It's nice to see you, but is there a special reason for your dropping in?"

"Does there have to be?" asked Fox. "I thought you found my company irresistible, whatever the reason."

"I do." Jane smiled at him and sat down on the settee, crossing her legs.

"As a matter of fact, there is a reason," said Fox hesitantly. "At least there was, but I've thought better of it."

"Out with it, Tommy Fox," said Jane. "What is it? A dirty weekend somewhere?"

"Worse," said Fox and smiled at her.

"Oh, come on. Don't keep me in suspense."

"Every three months the Flying Squad has a dinner at the Yard. It's usually for the senior officers only, but some fool suggested that we included wives this time."

Jane laughed. "Tommy, this is so sudden."

"Or girlfriends," said Fox hurriedly. "I wasn't quick enough to put the kibosh on it. I must admit that the file slipped through without my noticing what the secretary had proposed. I was going to ask you if you'd like to come, but then I thought better of it. It's not quite your scene."

"Oh rubbish. I'd love to come. When is it?"

"Thursday. The day after tomorrow. But look, I know it's short notice and if you can't make it, I shall quite—"

"Oh nonsense. Of course I'll come. What shall I wear? How exciting. I've never seen the inside of Scotland Yard before."

"Wish I hadn't," said Fox gloomily, regretting his impulse in mentioning the Squad senior officers' dining club.

"Well, what do I wear?" Jane was clearly excited at the prospect of so unusual an outing.

"The men wear dinner jackets," said Fox, "If that's any help. Incidentally, it's nothing like regimental dinners in the Guards, you know."

"I never went to one," said Jane. Her former husband had been an officer in the Guards, but they had divorced some nine years ago. "The Guards are a chauvinistic lot. Anyway, I'd prefer to forget that period of my life."

"Sorry," said Fox, realizing that it was a tactless thing to have said.

"Will I meet all your friends, Tommy?"

"I don't have any friends in the Flying Squad," said Fox. "They're all slaves."

*

44

Linda Ward was the third name on Dickie Lord's list. According to the ex-DI, she was fifty years of age, but she looked at least ten years younger. She had ash blonde hair, cut stylishly so that it curled under and was just clear of her collar, and her dress – obviously from one of the better fashion houses of London – was patently expensive. The brooch she wore was a silver and diamond depiction of a rose. Apparently she had not lost all her jewelery to the iceman, if in fact, Proctor – or even Skelton – had been the thief.

She sat down opposite Fox and Evans and arranged the skirt of her dress carefully. "I must say that I'm impressed by the attention I'm getting," she said, giving each of the detectives a frosty smile.

"The police at Kensington have told me about the theft of your jewelery, Mrs Ward," said Fox. He deliberately avoided mentioning burglary.

"So sad," said Linda Ward. "I'd had some of it since I was a girl, you know."

Fox nodded sympathetically. "I wonder if you'd just go over what happened."

"Of course." Linda Ward brushed absently at the arm of her chair. "I'd been on holiday in the South of France. My married daughter and her husband own a rather large villa there, in a charming little place just outside Cannes, and they very kindly invite me down every year. They really spoil me. Even pick me up from the airport in the Rolls. However, it was ruined by what happened when I got home."

"And what happened?" asked Fox. He was unimpressed by people who felt obliged to tell him, albeit obliquely, how rich they and their family were.

"All my jewelery had gone." Linda Ward raised her hands in a brief attitude of desperation, before allowing them to fall, once more, into her lap. "Apart from what I had with me, of course. Thank God, I'd had the sense to take my best pieces with me."

"When you say it was gone, Mrs Ward, was there any sign that your flat had been broken into?"

"Now that's the strange thing, Inspector—"

"Chief superintendent, madam. *Detective* chief superintendent," said Fox.

"But there was absolutely no sign of anyone having been in." Linda Ward ignored Fox's correction to his rank. To her, all policemen were the same, regardless of what they chose to call themselves. And policemen, in her view, were best lumped in with tradesmen.

"Yes," said Fox. "That's the conclusion drawn by the officers who first investigated the matter."

"Well, it's obvious that someone had broken in."

"The entire flat was examined scientifically," said Fox, "And there was no evidence to support the theory that you'd been the victim of a burglary. No sign whatever of a forced entry."

"Well, I can't explain it, Chief Inspector. Perhaps you can." Mrs Ward stared haughtily at the two policemen.

"Perhaps I can," said Fox quietly as he took the photograph of Proctor from Denzil Evans. "When did you first meet this man, Mrs Ward?" he asked as he handed the print to her.

Linda Ward froze. Her face paled several shades, but the expression on her face did not change. After a few seconds, during which she studied the portrait closely, she looked up. "Where did you get that?" she asked.

"We took it from the flat of a jewelery thief with the uninspiring name of Wally Proctor, Mrs Ward, shortly after someone had murdered him."

Linda Ward stared at Fox. "But what was this Proctor man doing with a photograph of James?" she asked.

"James who?"

"James Dangerfield. I don't understand it."

Fox picked up the photograph and returned it to Evans. "The man you knew as James Dangerfield was, in fact, Wally Proctor," he said. "Small world, isn't it?"

Linda Ward rose from her chair and, walking across the room to a side table, poured herself a brandy which she drank down at a gulp. Then she turned. "I'm sorry, would either of you gentlemen like a drink?" she asked.

"No thanks," said Fox. "I never drink on duty." Evans shot his chief a sharp sideways glance.

"No, of course not," said Linda Ward, and sat down again.

"Now, Mrs Ward, would you like to tell me what really happened?"

"I first met James last year, when I was in the South of France," began Linda Ward, and then went on to relate how he had struck up an acquaintanceship with her, wined and dined her, and arranged to meet her in London. "He was an absolute gentleman, so courteous, and obviously of good family."

"Did he have a key to your flat, Mrs Ward?" asked Fox, rather brutally.

At first, Linda Ward looked as though she would take exception to the question, but then she just nodded. "Yes," she said softly.

"He was living with you then?"

Again, the woman nodded. "He talked of marriage," she said. "It gets very lonely when you're a widow," she added defensively.

"Why didn't he go with you to the South of France this year then?"

"He said that he wanted to, but that he had business in London. He promised to keep an eye on the flat while I was away, but I never saw him again."

"Why then did you not tell the police this, instead of pretending that your flat had been broken into, Mrs Ward?"

"I really thought it had. I couldn't believe that James would do such a thing." Linda Ward had been staring at the empty fireplace, but now she looked up. "He's dead, you say?"

"Yes. He was shot in a cab at Hyde Park Corner."

"Oh my God! I saw that in the papers. I didn't realize it was him." Mrs Ward clutched hopefully at a sudden thought. "Then perhaps he didn't take my jewelery. Perhaps he was going to come back, but—"

"No chance," said Fox. "He was well known to the police as a jewel thief. He had convictions stretching back a long way. His method, unfortunately, was to prey on rich and lonely widows. Like you, Mrs Ward."

*

The lugubrious figure of Swann, Fox's driver, appeared in the doorway of the detective chief superintendent's office. "You wanted me, guv?"

"Yes, Swann. You know where Ladyjane Sims lives, don't you?"

"Yes, sir."

"Good. Pick her up at seven o'clock and bring her back here."

"Right, guv." Swann grinned.

"And give me a call when you're ten minutes away from the Yard," said Fox. "That's ten minutes from arriving here, not ten minutes after you've left," he added pointedly.

Swann looked crestfallen. "Of course, sir," he said.

47

Six

Although Swann had duly sent the message to say that he was ten minutes from Scotland Yard, Lady Jane Sims was already in Back Hall, as the front entrance is perversely called, when Fox stepped out of the lift. Clearly impressed by Fox's guest, the Back Hall Inspector, usually the most taciturn of officers, was enthusiastically explaining the Roll of Honor which was in a glass case by the door.

"Well, I must say you look rather stunning," said Fox, once he had escorted Jane into the lift. She was wearing a calf length soft velvet black dress with a matching serape. Her hair, styled to a fringe at the front, was curled under at the ends so that it just reached her shoulders. "And you've had your hair cut."

"Don't look so bad yourself, officer," said Jane with a smile as she admired Fox's well-cut dinner jacket.

"This is going to be a bore, Jane," said Fox as the lift reached the fifth floor.

"Don't be such a spoilsport. I've made up my mind that I'm going to enjoy myself." Jane stopped as Fox was leading her through the thickly carpeted foyer outside the dining room, and glanced around at the sporting trophies in a glass cabinet and at the portraits of bygone commissioners. "Is your picture here somewhere?" she asked teasingly.

"No," said Fox, "And never likely to be either. Let me take your wrap." As Jane revealed bare shoulders, he smiled and said, "I can see I shall have to keep a close eye on you this evening."

The long dining room was crowded with Flying Squad officers, their wives and guests, but they parted with barely concealed admiration as Jane made her entrance, followed by Fox.

"Let me get you a drink," said Fox, "And then I'll introduce you to some of the more acceptable of my colleagues."

The next twenty minutes were taken up in small talk and introductions as, one after another, Squad officers vied with each other to be presented to the earl's good-looking daughter about whom there had been so many rumors. It was not the first time that Fox had been seen in the company of a woman – he had brought a partner to each of the previous Squad dinner-dances – but this one was the most attractive so far.

"You know Jack Gilroy, of course," said Fox. Gilroy had been Fox's principal assistant into the investigation of Jane's sister's murder the previous year. "And this is another reprobate, Denzil Evans."

"Evening, m'lady," said Evans.

"Jane, please," said Jane with a smile as she held out her hand.

Fox winced and made a mental note to refer Evans to *Debrett's Correct Form* and explain to him that he was not a butler. "And this is the Commissioner, Sir James Gilmore," he said.

"My dear Lady Jane, how good to meet you," said Gilmore, holding Jane's hand for a fraction longer than was necessary. "May I present my wife," he added, steering a mousey little woman in a blue dress towards Fox's guest.

Fox, as chairman, sat in the center of the long table with his back to the pictures of the Queen and Prince Philip. Jane was on one side of him and the Commissioner, as guest of honor, was on the other. Commander Alec Myers sat at Jane's left hand. Opposite her was Detective Superintendent Gavin Brace, whom Fox had, at last, managed to bring to the Flying Squad as his deputy.

Jane clearly enjoyed herself during the meal, making animated converstion with all around her, and leaving Fox to talk to the Commissioner. Gilmore, as always, insisted on discussing the Metropolitan Police and all its problems.

But as coffee was about to be served, Detective Sergeant Percy Fletcher appeared at the door of the dining room and hovered, waiting to catch Fox's eye. Reluctantly, Fox excused himself and walked across. "What is it, Perce?" he asked.

"Sorry to butt in, guv," said Fletcher, "but I've just had a call from Notting Hill nick."

"What about?"

"Robin Skelton should have reported to the nick at four o'clock, guv, but he didn't show."

"Is that all?" Fox was irritated at being interrupted for so paltry a matter as a prisoner on bail not complying with the conditions of that bail.

"No, sir. They sent a PC round to his drum, but he couldn't get an answer. To cut a long story short, guv, they eventually broke in. Skelton's been topped, sir."

"Bugger it!" said Fox. "Who's dealing?"

"Well at the moment, sir, the DCI from Notting Hill."

Fox groaned. "I suppose I'd better take a look," he said. "Get hold of Swann and tell him to be on the front in five minutes, Perce." And, after apologizing to Jane for having to leave – and cautioning Gilroy to make sure she got home safely – Fox left for Skelton's Bayswater flat.

*

Pamela Hatcher, the Home Office pathologist, was hard at work when Fox arrived at Skelton's flat. The photographic team had taken shots from every conceivable angle and the scientific officers were meticulously examining the entire flat in their search for fingermarks or other evidence likely to lead to the killer.

"What have we got, Pamela?" asked Fox.

"Gunshot wounds to the body, Tommy," said Pamela Hatcher as she stood up. "Four points of entry as far as I can see, but—"

"Yes, I know," said Fox with a grin, "but I'll have to wait for the postmortem."

"Is this one of the Commissioner's new policies, Tommy, dressing for a murder?" Pamela Hatcher cast an amused glance at Fox's dinner-jacketed figure.

"Very funny," said Fox. "How long's he been dead? Any idea?"

"Between four and six hours is the best I can offer you, Tommy." Pamela Hatcher spoke over her shoulder as she began to pack away her instruments and thermometers. "I might be able to narrow it down once I've done the postmortem," she added. "I'll let you know."

"Thanks a lot," said Fox and turned to the detective chief inspector from Notting Hill police station. "What do we know?" he asked.

"Nothing appears to have been stolen, sir, not at first glance, and there's no sign of forced entry. Looks as though Skelton admitted his killer. Whether he knew him or not, well..." The DCI shrugged.

*

Hugh Donovan, the senior ballistics officer at the laboratory at Lambeth, grinned as Fox entered his workshop. "You're doing well, Tommy," he said. "One a week, isn't it?"

"Never mind the small talk, Hugh, what's the verdict?"

"Those are the rounds recovered from the body and the scene..." Donovan gestured at a kidney-shaped bowl on his bench. "They were .22 caliber and obviously not from the weapon that killed Proctor, because you've got that. Unless..." He grinned.

"This is no time for jokes, Hugh," said Fox. "Even though I might have felt like topping the bastard, I think I might have preferred to do for the Crown Prosecution Service solicitor who couldn't be bothered to object to bail." He smiled spitefully. "I shall have great pleasure in telling him about the demise of Robin Skelton."

"I've done tests on the rounds and they don't match any ballistic records we've got, Tommy," said Donovan, becoming serious again. "I'm afraid you're out on a limb."

"Aren't I always," muttered Fox.

*

Detective Sergeant Rosie Webster was a very attractive six-foot-tall blonde. She weighed fourteen stone and was beautifully proportioned. Although unmarried, she was never without a boyfriend, but she had yet to go out with a policeman, preferring, as she put it, men who could keep her in the style, to which, she could easily become accustomed. But there was nothing soft about Rosie Webster, and many a female prisoner, and not a few men, had found that it was unwise either to cross her, or attempt to deceive her. Consequently, when Fox had to interview a woman suspect, he invariably took Rosie with him. And in Fox's view, Julie Lockhart, formerly Strange, who had witnessed the murder of Jason Bright on the houseboat at Shepperton, fell into that category.

The telephone directory contained two addresses for Julie's husband, Peter Lockhart. One was obviously where he practiced dentistry and the other was his home address. Both were in Barnes, in south-west London, and Fox decided that it would be better to interview Lockhart's wife when he was not there.

Julie Lockhart answered the door wearing jeans and a sweater. Her hair, a rich auburn, was tied at the nape of her neck with a black ribbon and she wore no make-up. She did not look much like the model that the police docket said she had been. The room into which she led them, on the front of the house, was tastefully furnished but untidy. There was an overflowing ashtray on the occasional table next to a pile of newspapers, and a dirty cup and saucer stood on the floor, near the settee. In the corner of the room, the television was switched on, but the sound had been muted. It was not an ideal setting for an interview about a murder that had taken place some five years previously.

"You'll have to excuse the mess, I'm afraid, but I haven't got around to doing any housework yet." Julie Lockhart sat down on the sofa and glanced distractedly at the two detectives. "What's this all about?" she asked.

"It's about the murder of Jason Bright," said Fox.

"Oh that." Julie Lockhart did not seem at all perturbed that the subject was being raised again. "I told the police all I know at the time."

"Perhaps, Mrs Lockhart, but I'd like to go over it again, if you don't mind."

A sudden expression of fear crossed the girl's face. "Have you caught him?" she asked.

"No. Not yet. Tell me, Mrs Lockhart, what exactly happened?"

"I'd been going out with Kevin—"

"That's Kevin Povey," said Fox.

Julie Lockhart nodded. "I'd been going out with him for about eight months, I suppose. He lived in Battersea and I had this houseboat on the Thames at Shepperton."

"Was it yours?"

"Good heavens, no. I rented it. I was modeling at the time and making quite a good income, and I decided to leave home."

"Where was home?"

"Newcastle," said Julie, but there was no trace of a north-eastern accent. "There's not much work for models in Newcastle," she added with a smile. "Anyway, I'd got fed up with Kevin. He was so possessive. D'you know what I mean?" She glanced at Rosie. "And I began to feel stifled. Well, a couple of months before it all happened, I'd met Jason. He was a designer – a dress designer – and we kept bumping into each other at shows and so on. After a while he dated me and we started going out fairly regularly."

"And you were still seeing Kevin at this time?" Rosie raised an eyebrow.

"Yes. Why not?"

"Go on," said Fox.

"But it all ended on that terrible Saturday night. I'd told Kevin that I wasn't going to see him that evening. Said I was busy, or wanted to catch up on my letter-writing. Something like that." Julie looked into the middle distance as though conjuring up the scene in her mind's eye. "But I'd actually arranged to get dinner for Jason on the boat."

"And Kevin Povey turned up, I suppose?" said Rosie.

"Yes. Frightful scene. I'd never seen him so angry."

"Were you still having dinner when he arrived?" asked Fox.

"Oh gosh no. We were in bed together."

"And that upset him, I imagine?" asked Fox with masterful understatement.

"I've never seen him so angry, or so violent. He dragged the covers off us and pulled Jason out of bed. He started calling him names and hitting him. Well, Jason wasn't a big man, and he just tried to defend himself. I tried to pull Kevin away, but I wasn't strong enough, and anyway I was naked, which is not the best way to start fighting. Not real fighting," she added with a mischievous smile.

"And then Kevin produced a gun, I take it?" asked Fox.

"Mmm! Yes, he did. I was terrified. I'd never seen a real gun before, but Kevin started to wave it about, threatening Jason and telling him that if he didn't leave me alone, he'd kill him. Well, I'm not sure what happened next, because I ran across the cabin trying to get back to the berth where Jason and I had been making love. But then I heard this loud bang and I stopped and turned round. And then I screamed. Kevin was standing there with this stunned look on his face and Jason was lying on the floor with blood oozing out of this hole in his head."

"What happened next?" asked Rosie.

"Kevin bent over him and then stood up. And he said that Jason was dead. He said that it was an accident and—"

"And was it? An accident?"

"I don't know. As I said, I had my back to them both when it happened."

"Go on, Mrs Lockhart."

"I said that we ought to call the police – I had a phone on the boat – but Kevin wouldn't let me. He dragged Jason's body up on deck and dropped it over the side into the river. I think he was drunk, and he started waving the pistol about again. There was a wild look in his eyes.

He said that he was going away, but if I told the police, he would find me and kill me. Then he left."

"And you've not seen him since?" Rosie looked as though she disbelieved the whole story, mainly because of the matter-of-fact way in which Julie had related it. But she realized that the girl must have told it many times before.

"No. Never."

"What was his job at the time you were going out with him, Mrs Lockhart?" asked Fox.

"I, er, I don't think he had one. His father had a lot of money and I think that Kevin just lived on his allowance."

"What sort of car did he have?"

"A Mercedes. At least that's what he was driving that night."

"How d'you know that?" asked Fox.

"I stood on deck and watched him drive away."

"What, naked?" asked Rosie acidly.

Julie Lockhart raised her chin slightly. "Well, there's nothing wrong with that, is there?"

*

"What did you think, Rosie?" asked Fox.

Rosie Webster looked at Fox with a cynical smile on her face. "I didn't believe her, sir," she said. "She was much too offhand about the whole thing. I think she was lying through her teeth."

*

Having been assured by Jack Gilroy that Jane Sims had been taken home and seen safely into her Knightsbridge flat, Fox left it until the next evening before he called on her.

Jane threw the door wide and smiled. "Hallo, guv," she said.

Fox groaned. "I knew I should never have taken you there," he said.

"Why do they all call you guv?" asked Jane as they sat down.

"Simple," said Fox. "It's because I'm the governor. Anyway, you got home all right, I see."

"Yes, and I've got a frightful hangover, Tommy."

"Oh?" Fox looked sharply at the girl. "How did that happen?"

"After you'd left, the Commissioner made a speech." Jane smiled. "I must say, he's a bit of a bore, isn't he, and so intense. Anyway, after the bigwigs had left, the party began."

"What party?" Fox was beginning to have grave misgivings about having introduced Jane into the doubtful company of the Flying Squad at play.

"Well, the brandy and the port began to circulate..." Jane paused. "They drink a lot, your chaps, don't they?"

"Sometimes." Fox nodded gloomily.

"And the curator of the Black Museum was there—"

"I know."

"And he opened it up and took a party of us down there. It was awfully interesting, Tommy."

"Matter of opinion," muttered Fox.

"Then we went back upstairs and had a look at the Flying Squad office with all those gorgeous hunky detectives of yours, and we had a few more drinks. And then Alec—"

"Alec who?"

Jane looked thoughtful for a moment or two. "Alec Myers. He is one of your chaps, isn't he?"

"In a manner of speaking," said Fox, wondering how his commander had got involved in all this.

"Well, he made me an honorary guv. And they all started calling me Lady Guv from then on. It was great fun, Tommy. Will there be another one soon?"

"No," said Fox firmly.

"And then they put me in a police car and your Jack Gilroy brought me home. But he wouldn't come in for a drink."

"More than his life's worth," said Fox darkly. "Lady Guv indeed."

Jane laid a hand on his arm. "Promise me you won't be cross with them, Tommy. They're a lovely crowd and I haven't had so much fun in years."

Seven

Fox had told Lady Jane Sims that his job as the officer in charge of a murder investigation accorded with that of the conductor of a huge orchestra. Today, in the incident room at Charing Cross police station, he had all his players assembled. Beside him, Detective Superintendent Jim Semple of Eight Area major investigation pool was beginning to wonder why he was there; the Flying Squad appeared to have taken over.

"The story so far, gentlemen," Fox began, "Is that Wally Proctor was murdered in a cab at Hyde Park Corner which, apart from being an arrestable offence, probably contravenes one of the multifarious regulations regarding the use of motor hackney carriages." The audience laughed dutifully. "But to add to our grief, his erstwhile henchman, Robin Skelton, was murdered in his flat at Bayswater by person or persons unknown. However," he went on, "I do not intend that the person or persons in question should remain unknown for much longer. Between them, these two undesirable icemen had hit on a profitable scam of befriending widowed ladies and relieving them of their tomfoolery with the aid of the guile and charm that is the stock-in-trade of the confidence trickster. Jack, what news from Bayswater?"

Gilroy passed a folder of scene-of-crime photographs to Fox and referred him to page five. "That is a fingermark found on the inside of the sitting-room door at Skelton's flat, sir."

"Splendid," said Fox. "All we have to do now is find the finger that matches the mark and we've cracked it. Maybe. I presume that this finger's not on record, Jack?" Fox was accustomed to the misfortunes that normally attended his investigations.

"It is, as a matter of fact, sir," said Gilroy. "At least we think it is. I spoke to Sam Marland, the senior fingerprint officer, just before I came in here, and he's matched it to marks found on a houseboat at Shepperton."

Fox eased down the cuffs of his shirt. "I hope you're not going to tell me that they tally with the victim, Jason Bright, Jack."

Gilroy grinned. "No, sir. But they probably belong to Kevin Povey, who's still wanted for questioning in connection with Bright's murder."

Fox perched on the edge of a table. "Why only probably?"

"Povey had no previous convictions and his dabs aren't on record. But when the houseboat was done, after Bright's murder, they found five different sets of marks. Four were identified almost immediately. One set belonged to Bright, another to Julie Strange, a third to a former boyfriend, and the fourth to the bloke who owned the houseboat, a chap called—"

"Never mind what he was called, Jack. So that leaves the one, which probably belongs to Kevin Povey. Yes?"

"That's about the strength of it, guv," said Gilroy.

"Why the hell should a bloke who killed someone he found screwing his girlfriend suddenly decide to top an iceman? If they are his dabs, of course."

"There's obviously a connection, sir," said Gilroy and immediately he wished he had remained silent.

"Now that is the sort of earth-shattering observation, Jack," said Fox, "That could result in your being invited to lecture on it at Bramshill." A ripple of laughter greeted this remark; Fox's views on the Police College were well known to his audience. He lit a cigarette and pondered the problem. But only briefly. "Seems to me, Jack, that we'll have to find this Povey. What do we know about him?" He glanced around the room. "Anybody?"

"There's a description on the docket," said Semple, "And, of course, the photograph that was found in his flat, but they're both at least five years old now and he could have changed his appearance quite substantially."

"I know. It's the usual sort of description that could apply to half the male population." Fox looked around the room until he saw Rosie Webster. "Rosie, go and see Julie Lockhart again and see if you can build on that description. And take Kate what's-her-name with you. See if you can rattle Mrs Lockhart's bars for her." Fox was the first to recognize that when it came to interviewing women under about fifty, Rosie Webster was more skilled at it than he was. "Denzil..." Fox switched his gaze to DI Evans. "Yes, sir?"

"How are the enquiries into Proctor going?"

"We've got no further with the hotel, sir," said Evans. "It looks as though whoever deposited the brief-case at the Agincourt Hotel, the case containing the pistol that—"

"Yes, yes, I know all that," said Fox impatiently. "What about it?"

"It's gone cold, sir," continued Evans. "I don't think we'll ever track him down now."

Fox nodded. Even he realized that some things were impossible. Not that he ever admitted it. "Associates, friends, family? Anything on that?"

"Enquiries are continuing, sir," said Evans with a grin. "You mean you've got nowhere." Fox turned to Gilroy. "And Skelton, Jack? Anyone confess to knowing him?"

"One possible lead, sir," said Gilroy. "I spoke to the neighbors and one old dear claimed to have seen a young woman leaving Skelton's flat a couple of times first thing in the morning. Quite accidental, of course. The informant reckoned she was putting out the milk bottles at the time."

"Of course," said Fox. "You know, Jack, the investigation of crime in this country will undoubtedly suffer a severe setback if doorstep deliveries of milk ever stop. Keep me posted."

*

The young woman to whom Fox had referred as Kate what's-her-name was Detective Constable Kate Ebdon. A twenty-five-year-old Australian, she had only recently been posted to the Flying Squad from Leman Street police station in the East End of London where she had built a reputation as a determined and hard-working detective. Her colorful language had frightened quite a few villains and even more senior officers, but she had impressed Fox on the few occasions he had come into contact with her.

"Got a job for you, Kate," said Rosie Webster.

"Right, skip. What is it?" Kate looked keen.

Rosie outlined the background to the houseboat murder enquiry and gave Kate the docket to read before the pair of them set off for Barnes.

Julie Lockhart looked distinctly nervous when she opened her front door to the two women officers. "Oh, er, hallo," she said. "Er, look, it's not really convenient at the moment."

But Rosie Webster was not that easily dissuaded. She had deliberately not telephoned to make an appointment and, like Fox, she and DC Ebdon had called mid-afternoon in the hope that Julie Lockhart's husband would be hard at work in his surgery.

"Are we interrupting something?" asked Kate.

"No, it's not that, but my husband's at home."

"Oh, I see," said Kate with a shrug. "Well, are we going to come in or what? We can have a chat here on the doorstep if you like."

"No, you'd better come in." Julie led the way into the sitting room and invited the two detectives to take a seat before perching nervously on the edge of the settee. Of Julie's husband, there was no sign and Rosie wondered if the woman had pretended that he was there as a lame excuse for not wanting to talk to the police again.

"When I came down the other day with Detective Chief Superintendent Fox, Mrs Lockhart," Rosie began, "you went over what had happened the night of Jason Bright's death."

"Yes." Julie had been quite ebullient on the previous occasion Rosie had seen her, but she seemed oddly restrained this afternoon.

"Seems odd," said Kate, who had made herself as conversant with the case as was possible from reading the docket, "that you didn't see what happened."

"Well, I didn't," said Julie defensively.

"Let me get this straight, Mrs Lockhart," said Kate. "You were prancing about in the nude while Povey was waving a gun about and threatening Jason Bright. Right?"

"Yes."

"But you said that you had your back to him when the shot was fired."

"Yes."

"Did you hear anything? Like Povey tripping over something? Or did he say anything?"

"No. I told the police, and I told you the other day…" Julie nodded at Rosie Webster. "I was scared and I was trying to get away, into the berth where Jason and I had—"

"Where you'd been screwing," said Kate. Her Australian accent came out quite strongly.

Julie Lockhart wrinkled her nose in distaste at DC Ebdon's coarse expression, although it was one she had used herself quite often in the past. "I didn't see what happened," she said, emphasizing each word.

"Are you shielding Povey, Mrs Lockhart?" Kate was not going to let Julie escape too easily. "Surely to God he doesn't still frighten you, does he?"

"No, of course not, but that's the truth."

"When did you last see Kevin Povey, Mrs Lockhart?" Rosie Webster's question came quietly and caught Julie off guard.

"I, er, well, the night of the murder."

"And you haven't seen him since?"

"No, of course not."

"Did he leave the country after Jason Bright was killed?" Kate returned to the questioning.

"I don't know." Julie's hands were intertwined and she was clenching them with nervousness. "I told you. I keep telling all of you. I never saw him again."

"Supposing you were to see him again, Mrs Lockhart. What would you do?"

"I'd tell the police, of course."

"I sincerely hope you would, Mrs Lockhart. Otherwise it might be regarded as an obstruction of justice." Kate Ebdon was determined to worry the woman.

"We omitted to ask you for a description of Kevin Povey when we were here last." Rosie flipped open her pocket book.

"I gave the police a description of him at the time and I think they took a photograph album from his flat in Battersea—"

"How did you know that?" Kate interrupted with her customary bluntness.

Julie looked up sharply. DC Ebdon's Australian accent grated on the ex-model's ear and disconcerted her. "I think the police who were dealing with it must have told me," she said.

Kate nodded. "Maybe," she said. "Bit unusual though."

"Anyway, if you'd care to tell me what you can remember, Mrs Lockhart, it would be a great help," said Rosie Webster.

"Yes, of course," said Julie and went on to describe as much as she could recall of Kevin Povey's appearance.

"Thanks. I'm sure that'll be a great help," said Rosie as she closed her pocket book. She was about to stand up when the door to the sitting room opened.

A man stood in the doorway. He was about thirty years of age, was tall and quite good-looking in a rugged sort of way. But his hair was slightly disarranged and he appeared to be wearing nothing more than a short dressing gown. "Oh!" he said, looking at Julie. "Sorry, honey, I didn't realize you had company." He glanced admiringly at Rosie's legs.

"You're Mr Lockhart, I presume," said Rosie.

There was a moment's hesitation before the man replied. "Yes, I am," he said. "Who are you?"

"We're police officers, Mr Lockhart."

"Oh! Sorry I interrupted," said the man and promptly left the room, closing the door firmly behind him.

*

"You don't think this bloke was her husband then, Rosie," said Fox.

"No I don't, sir. She was on edge the whole time we were there. At first I thought it was because she had something to hide, about Bright's murder, I mean, but then this chap came in wearing a shortie dressing gown. It was obvious that he didn't know we were in the house, and he disappeared again as soon as I told him who we were."

"And this was three o'clock in the afternoon. Presumably her husband should still have been at his surgery at that time."

"That's what I thought," said Rosie.

"Or filling cavities somewhere else," said Kate Ebdon with a cheeky smile.

Fox grinned. "I suppose it wasn't Povey?"

Rosie Webster looked at her chief with a pained expression on her face. "No, guv'nor it wasn't," she said.

*

Fox did not like leaving loose ends and although the suggestion that Julie Lockhart may have been entertaining a man friend in her husband's absence had no direct bearing on the murders, the Flying Squad chief decided to make further enquiries. Himself.

The moment that they were ushered into the dentist's presence, Rosie knew that the man she had seen at the house was not, in fact, Julie Lockhart's husband. The dentist was much shorter than Julie's visitor, had an almost bald head, a small toothbrush moustache and wore wire-framed spectacles. Fox thought he looked like Dr Crippen.

"Sorry to trouble you, Mr Lockhart," said Fox, who was not sorry at all, "but I wonder if you'd have a look at this." He produced the photograph of Povey that had been removed from Povey's flat in Battersea.

Lockhart took the print and gazed at it. "Am I supposed to know this man, officer?"

For once, Fox had not introduced himself as a detective chief superintendent; that would have alerted the dentist to the fact that this was more than a routine enquiry. "We're just making enquiries to see whether this man had visited anyone in the neighborhood." Fox gazed around the surgery with all the apparent disinterest of a detective tired of making footling enquiries.

"No, officer, I'm sure I've never seen him before."

Fox shrugged. "Sorry to have troubled you, sir," he said. "I'm afraid that boring legwork forms quite a large part of our business." He smiled disarmingly.

"What's he done, officer?"

"He murdered someone, Mr Lockhart," said Fox. "Good day to you."

*

It was two days later that Detective Chief Inspector Leslie Balls of the Complaints Investigation Bureau appeared in Fox's office and introduced himself.

Fox looked up. "And what can I do for you, Mr Balls?" he asked.

"I'm dealing with a complaint from a Mrs Julie Lockhart, sir," said Balls.

"Oh?" Fox put his pen down on the desk and leaned back in his chair. "Sit down."

"She stated in her telephone call, sir, that she has been harassed by police investigating a five-year-old murder. She names Detective Sergeant Webster and Detective Constable Ebdon, both of the Flying Squad."

"Does she really?" Fox smiled. "Tell me, Mr Balls, when did you receive this telephone call?"

"This morning, sir."

"My word, you chaps are quick off the mark, aren't you?"

"Serious things, complaints, sir," said Balls.

"Indeed they are. And you've been appointed to investigate this serious complaint, have you?"

"Yes, sir."

"Tricky," said Fox.

"It seems fairly straightforward to me, sir."

"Ah, but that's because you don't know the full facts, Mr Balls. You see, I also interviewed Mrs Lockhart. Then I sent the two officers to whom you refer to see her a second time. So they were acting under my specific orders, you see."

"Oh!"

"Yes," said Fox. "Creates problems, doesn't it?"

"It means that I can't investigate it, sir."

"I imagine so," said Fox.

"I'll have to refer back to Mr Thomas, sir."

"Yes, I suppose you will. Well, I'm sure that Commander Thomas will be happy to appoint a commander to investigate this. Rather lets you off the hook, doesn't it?"

"I suppose it does, sir." Balls closed the file that had been open on his knee and stuffed it into his briefcase.

"I'd be careful about opening your briefcase like that, Mr Balls," said Fox. Balls looked up in surprise. "I'm currently investigating the murder of a man who opened his briefcase as you have just done. Blew his head off."

"Really?" Balls smiled a sickly smile.

"Tell me," said Fox. "What criminal offences have been alleged against my two officers?"

"No criminal offences, sir." Balls stood up.

"Then why, might I ask, is an officer from your department investigating it?"

"I'm afraid I don't know the answer to that, sir. You'll have to ask the commander."

"I'll do better than that," said Fox. "I'll ask the Assistant Commissioner."

Eight

Fox made a number of snap decisions. Following the appearance of Detective Chief Inspector Balls with a complaint against two of his officers, Fox immediately made for Commander Alec Myers's office. "I've just had some prat from Complaints come to see me, sir, belly-aching about a Mrs Julie Lockhart."

Myers smiled and held up a hand. "Calm down, Tommy, and take a seat. Now, what's it all about?"

Fox explained and then went on, "This is a deliberate attempt to obstruct an investigation into a case of murder, sir. In fact, into three cases of murder."

"By whom?" asked Myers mildly.

"It's bloody obvious, guv'nor," said Fox. "This woman knows something. I'm convinced of that. She waited two days before making a complaint, and that tells me that she's taken advice. Someone doesn't want us poking about. We rattled her bars a bit and she doesn't like it. Or more to the point, someone else doesn't like it."

"Like who?"

"Like Kevin Povey, I should think. Or the bloke who was giving her a seeing to when Rosie and DC Ebdon called on her."

Myers smiled. "Are you sure you're not jumping to conclusions, Tommy?" he asked.

"Look guv'nor, she's very touchy about answering questions. She's tried to row herself out of this thing altogether. She says that she didn't see what happened the night that Bright was murdered—"

"Perhaps she didn't."

"Pah!" Fox snorted. "I don't believe it. I think she knows more than she's telling. And furthermore, I wouldn't be surprised to find that she knows exactly where Povey is. Probably still seeing him."

"I still think you might be jumping to conclusions, Tommy, but what d'you want me to do?" Myers refused to be excited by Fox's outburst.

"I want this complaint held over until we've sorted this thing out, sir. If Balls, or worse, some uniformed commander, goes tramping about, taking statements from the Lockhart woman and God knows who else, it could completely bugger up my enquiries."

Myers looked doubtful. "I don't know, Tommy. It would mean getting the Deputy Commissioner's approval."

"Yes," said Fox, and waited.

"All right," said Myers. "I'll see DACSO for a start."

As good as his word, Myers spoke to Dick Campbell, the Deputy Assistant Commissioner Specialist Operations, better known by the acronym DACSO, who in turn saw the Assistant Commissioner, Peter Frobisher. Frobisher listened carefully to the argument and reluctantly referred the matter to the Deputy Commissioner, who as disciplinary head of the Metropolitan Police was the only man who could withhold a complaint. After careful consideration, he agreed that Mrs Lockhart's complaint that she was being harassed should be suspended. But, he ruled, it would be reviewed after two weeks. It was a partial victory.

*

The second decision that Fox made was to circulate details of Kevin Povey. In a welter of directions, he ordered that Povey's description and his photograph should be circulated to the *Police Gazette*, to Interpol, and to every port and airport in the United Kingdom. Details were also forwarded to the National Criminal Intelligence Service and to the newly formed Europol.

That done, Fox sent for Detective Inspector Henry Findlater, the quiet, Calvinistic Scot who headed the Flying Squad's unofficial surveillance team, and instructed him to mount a round-the-clock observation on Julie Lockhart. But not because Fox was much interested in Julie Lockhart. He was playing a hunch. The man seen by Rosie Webster when she and Kate Ebdon called on Julie Lockhart was, at the moment, a mystery to Fox. And he wanted to know more about him.

*

Mrs Linda Ward, the attractive widow who lived at Earls Court, had as good as confessed to having had an affair with Wally Proctor and that he had made off with her jewelry. And that interested Fox. Interested him because Proctor, masquerading as James Dangerfield, had first made Mrs Ward's acquaintance in the South of France. It was possible, therefore, that Proctor may have had some criminal associates there. And knowing also that honor among thieves was a fable, it was also possible that one of them may have murdered him. For a start, Fox decided to interview Mrs Ward's married daughter, Michelle, who, according to Dickie Lord, was married to a "filthy rich" architect nearly twice her age with whom she lived at Chalfont St Giles.

But it transpired that Michelle White's husband was a property developer, not an architect. Fox assumed that Mrs Ward thought that architect sounded better.

Their house at Chalfont St Giles was sumptuous by any standards. The circular graveled drive would have accommodated about seven or eight cars, but when Fox and Gilroy arrived, there were just two. A Rolls-Royce, and a BMW that proved to be Michelle White's runabout.

"Nice Roller, sir," said Gilroy, admiring the Rolls-Royce.

"Bottom of the range," said Fox dismissively.

"You must be from the fuzz." The man who answered the door wore a pale blue polo shirt, light trousers and a pair of moccasins. He was about forty-two, bronzed, overweight and had curly hair flecked with gray. "I'm Paul White," he said. "Come in. My wife's by the pool."

White led the two detectives through the house and along a corridor into a room at the rear that contained a large oval-shaped swimming pool. The pool itself was tiled in blue as were the surrounds, and the floor-to-ceiling windows were hung with expensive curtains drawn back to reveal a huge, landscaped garden. Michelle White, wearing a scarlet one-piece swimsuit, was lying on one of the seven or eight recliners that were dotted around the pool.

"Mrs White, I'm Detective Chief Superintendent Thomas Fox... of the Flying Squad, and this is Detective Inspector Gilroy."

"Hallo." Michelle White sat up and adjusted the backrest of her recliner to the halfway position but made no attempt to shake hands. She raised one knee and flicked her long brown hair over her shoulders so that it hung down her back. She certainly looked no older than the twenty-three that Dickie Lord had said she was. "I guessed you might be coming." She smiled and looked at her husband. "Paulie, why don't you get the gentlemen a drink?"

"No thank you," said Fox, answering for both himself and Gilroy.

"Do sit down then." Michelle waved nonchalantly towards the other recliners. "Mummy said that you'd been to see her. It's quite awful about her jewelery, isn't it?"

"Yes," said Fox. "Quite awful. Did she tell you about James Dangerfield?"

"Oh, we've known about him for some time, haven't we, Paulie?" Michelle glanced at her husband. "But Mummy was always secretive about him, once she got back to England that is. God knows why. Why shouldn't she have it off with a fellah she fancies? After all, she's still a young woman, and not bad looking either." She looked at her husband again. "Is she, Paulie?"

"No, not bad," said White.

"Did she tell you that it was almost certainly Dangerfield who stole her jewelery, Mrs White?"

"No!" Michelle sat up and stared at Fox. "Surely not."

"His real name was Wally Proctor and he was murdered, in a taxi at Hyde Park Corner."

"Oh no!" Michelle put a hand to her mouth. It was a theatrical and somewhat artificial gesture.

"You probably read about it," said Fox.

"Yes, we certainly did, didn't we, Paulie?" Once again, Michelle glanced at Paul White.

"Your mother told me that she first met Dangerfield, or Proctor as we prefer to call him, last year when she was staying at your villa in the South of France."

"Never did like the guy," said White, swinging his legs off the recliner so that he was sitting sideways-on and facing Fox.

"What particularly didn't you like about him, Mr White?" Fox suspected that White had just come to that conclusion in the light of what Fox had told him. Either that or he had seen in Proctor a like image and may have been afraid that he was muscling in, perhaps on his own wife, Michelle. Fox had already concluded that Paul White was a bit of a con man himself.

"I don't know. There was something about him. Something that didn't ring true."

"Did you express those fears to your mother-in-law, Mr White?" Fox knew damned well that he had not.

"Well, no. None of my business really, was it? Wouldn't have been any point, anyway. When Linda gets it into her head to do something, no one on God's earth will stop her. It would have been a waste of breath, quite frankly."

"I see. Tell me, how did Mrs Ward meet this man?" Fox's gaze encompassed both Paul White and his wife.

Paul White answered the question. "Our villa's about eight or nine kilometers from Cannes," he said. "Halfway between there and Miramar. The minute Linda gets there, she's away to the casino in Cannes. She loves playing the tables. Apparently she met this Dangerfield chap..." He paused. "What did you say his real name was?"

"Proctor," said Gilroy.

"Yes, well, she met him at the roulette tables one night. Then she met him again the next night. Need I go on?"

"No, I think I understand," said Fox. "I imagine there are quite a few Proctors hanging about the casinos in the South of France."

"Oh, believe me, there are," said White.

"Did Mrs Ward remain friendly with him the whole time she was there?"

"Yes, she did." Michelle White smiled. "I wasn't as doubtful about him as Paulie," she said. "He seemed a very nice man. Very personable, and he had beautiful manners." Her husband snorted. "He was a bit younger than Mummy, but that doesn't matter, does it?"

"You met him then."

"Oh yes. Mummy asked if she could bring him to the villa. Naturally, we said yes. He was awfully nice. Brought me a beautiful bouquet of flowers and a huge box of chocolates. We spent all day round the pool, just swimming and lazing and talking."

"Around the pool?"

"Yes. We've got one at the villa as well. Paulie indulges me, you see." Michelle smiled across to where her husband was sitting, a sullen expression on his face.

"I'd have spotted him as a con man a million miles away," said White. "Written all over him. Know what I mean?"

"Did he mention jewelery at all, while he was at the villa, Mr White? Or perhaps suggest that he was hard up? Money tied up in shares? Anything like that?"

"No. Well he wouldn't, would he? Too clever by half, these guys. It's all softly-softly with them. Well, he proved it, right? Waited damned nearly a year to relieve Linda of her sparklers."

"Did you meet him at all, once you were all back in England?" Fox was still trying to get a picture of Wally Proctor. And more particularly, any associates he may have had. So far, he had not had much luck.

"No," said Michelle. "When Mummy telephoned, she said that she'd met him once or twice in London. Then suddenly, she wasn't mentioning him any more. But I dropped in on her one day when I went into town to do some shopping at Harrods. I must admit that I had a bit of a nose around. There was an electric razor in the bathroom and a man's dressing gown hanging up in Mummy's bedroom." She shrugged. "I just put two and two together."

"Did you tackle your mother about it?"

"Sort of," said Michelle. "I asked if James had moved in. Frankly, I thought, well, good luck to you, Mummy."

"James?" Fox knew who she meant, but wanted to confirm it.

"Yes, James Dangerfield. Who turned out to be this Proctor man you mentioned."

"What did your mother say?"

"She told me to mind my own business." Michelle giggled. "Well, a nod's as good as a wink, isn't it?"

"So they say," said Fox. "So they say."

*

Fox went to see Linda Ward again.

"Mrs Ward, how long did Proctor, or James Dangerfield, as you knew him, live with you?"

"How dare you." Linda Ward was clearly outraged at Fox's question. But he knew that she would be, however he framed it. And that was why he had brought Rosie Webster with him. "What business is it of yours, may I ask?"

"I'm not interested in your private life, Mrs Ward. But I am very interested in Proctor's private life, and as the two of you appear to have had a close association, I must ask these questions." Fox smiled at the woman opposite him. "I'm investigating three murders, Mrs Ward, and that means that I have to ask a lot of questions, some of which may well be embarrassing. But you have my assurance that anything you tell me will not go beyond this room." He glanced at Rosie and nodded. Rosie ostentatiously closed her pocket book and dropped it into her handbag. Fox had told her not to take notes, but to have the book out so that she could make this gesture of confidentiality.

Mrs Ward appeared somewhat mollified by Fox's words and Rosie's actions. "Well, I suppose you are just doing your job," she said. "But it's still a shock to think that James turned out to be some cheap criminal."

"He wasn't all that cheap," said Fox. "My officers have been making enquiries all over the place and I now know that at least five other women were relieved of their jewelery in the same way that you were."

Linda Ward looked up, the expression on her face implying that she did not believe the detective. Then she shrugged her shoulders and sighed. "And I suppose they were all silly old women like me." She stared at the empty fireplace.

"I wouldn't call you silly, Mrs Ward," said Fox and, with a smile, added, "And certainly not old. In fact, you're a very attractive woman."

Rosie Webster thought what a smarmy bastard her chief was and made a mental note to regale the other sergeants with this latest piece of Tommy Fox lore.

For the first time since their arrival, Linda Ward smiled. "I don't suppose you'd like a cup of tea, would you?" she asked. "Or perhaps something stronger?"

"A cup of tea would be fine, Mrs Ward."

Once Linda Ward had made the tea and the three of them were settled again, Fox resumed his questioning. "Did you ever meet any of Proctor's friends, Mrs Ward?"

"No, I didn't. We went out from time to time, but only for dinner, usually at some exclusive restaurant. I think he was as much a stranger there as I was. You can always tell, you know. Head waiters tend to know you if you're a regular. You know what I mean, don't you?"

"Oh I do, Mrs Ward," said Fox warmly. "Indeed I do. So you never met anyone who seemed to know Proctor."

"No, no one. But there was a rather strange phone call for him one day."

"Oh? Who from?"

"I don't know, but oddly enough, the voice sounded familiar." Linda Ward put her head to one side as though it would aid her memory.

"He didn't say who he was then?"

"No. And he sounded quite aggressive. Well, not so much aggressive but rather that he was trying to disguise his voice."

"What did this caller say, Mrs Ward?"

"I told him that James wasn't here, and this man on the telephone said something like, Well, tell him I'm coming for him."

"D'you mean that he meant he was going to collect him? Pick him up in a car, or something like that?"

"Oh no. He sounded much too angry. I thought he meant he was going to get him. You know, like these thugs you see on television."

"And not only on television," Fox muttered. "And what did Proctor say when you relayed this message to him?"

"I didn't. You see, James had already left me by then."

"As a matter of interest, Mrs Ward, why didn't you tell me all this the last time I came to see you?"

"I'm sorry, but I've only just remembered it."

*

"Well, Rosie, what did you think of that?" asked Fox as they reached the car.

"Looks like a case of a lonely sex-hungry widow being had over by a sharp con man who eventually got his come-uppance, sir," said Rosie with a grin.

"You do have a way of summarizing things rather neatly, Rosie." Fox paused and glanced across the road. "I suppose you'd rather have had a gin and tonic than that cup of Lapsang Souchong."

"Yes, sir."

"So would I," said Fox and, leaving Swann to fester behind the wheel of the car, steered Rosie Webster across the road to the nearest pub.

Nine

"You know when we nicked Skelton, sir…"

"Yes, Jack." Fox stirred absently at his tea.

"I got the fingerprint lads to go over his Notting Hill flat, just for the hell of it," said Gilroy.

"Of course," said Fox.

"They've come up with a partial."

Fox placed his teaspoon carefully in the saucer. "Has it been identified, Jack?"

"Well, as I said, it's only a partial and they couldn't get enough points off it for proof, but they're as sure as hell that it tallies with the unidentified marks found in Skelton's Bayswater flat after his murder, and on the houseboat following the Jason Bright killing." Gilroy grinned at his chief.

"Povey?"

"Looks like it, sir."

"In that case, Jack, we shall have to find this Povey. He's rapidly becoming a pain in the arse. What's more, he's getting in the way of an honest bit of thief-taking. D'you realize, Jack, that there are villains marauding all over London while we're wasting our time on this tosser? Get hold of Percy Fletcher for me, will you?"

Detective Sergeant Percy Fletcher was renowned for his string of informants, most of whom had been cultivated during Fletcher's period at West End Central police station. "You wanted me, guv?" he asked when he ambled into Fox's office mintues later.

"Yes, Perce. We need to find Kevin Povey. Get out and beat on the ground. See what comes up."

"Right, sir." Fletcher nodded gloomily.

"And give Mr Evans a shout on your way out."

Detective Inspector Denzil Evans was clutching a file when he entered Fox's office. "Identified the jewelery, sir. Well, at least, some of it. Most of it belongs to Mrs Ward. The police report reckoned that Proctor had

had about seventy grand's worth off her. The rest is an equal split between Mrs Bourne and Mrs Harker."

"Splendid, Denzil. Any not accounted for?"

"Each-way bet, sir."

Fox raised his eyebrows at Evans's unusual lapse into race-course jargon. "Would you care to elucidate, Denzil?"

"Yes, sir. Not all Mrs Bourne's and Mrs Harker's losses have been recovered, and some of the gear that was found hasn't been tied up with a loser yet."

"Ah, I see," said Fox. "Well, keep at it, there's a good chap. And when you've got a minute, send someone round to the Agincourt Hotel. Tell them to see that hall porter fellow. What was his name?"

"Buck, sir. Brian Buck."

"That's the chap. Show him the photographs of Skelton and Povey. Show them to the staff as well. See if anyone recognizes either of them as the finger who deposited the despatch case."

"Briefcase, sir," corrected Evans.

"Matter of opinion, Denzil. It despatched Wally Proctor, didn't it?"

*

Detective Inspectors Gilroy and Evans were both known to have informants and they too were instructed to put out feelers in the search for Kevin Povey. And Fox went after his own favorite snout.

Spider Walsh's idea of discretion was about as subtle as a charging rhinoceros, and Fox, sitting in the downstairs bar of the Cat and Fiddle public house in Belgravia, watched with amusement as the old informant entered.

Walsh oiled his way round the door and stopped. He peered first at the bar, giving his lips a cursory lick, and then stared around the room until he sighted Tommy Fox sitting in a corner with his back to the wall. "Hallo, Mr Fox."

"I do wish you'd give up these arcane approaches, Spider."

Walsh looked hurt. "I've never done drugs, Mr Fox," he said. "You know that."

"Sit down," said Fox. "I've got you a stout."

"Oh, ta, Mr Fox." Walsh seized the pint of Guinness and thirstily took the top off it. He wiped the froth from his upper lip with the back of his hand and sighed. "Dunno if I can help you this time, Mr Fox," he said.

"You haven't heard the question yet, Spider." Fox took a sip of his Scotch. "I'm anxious to interview a man called Kevin Povey, and I'm equally anxious that he does not learn that I wish to interview him. Got the drift?"

Walsh nodded thoughtfully. "Ain't never heard of him," he said. "What's his MO?" In common with most people on the fringe of the criminal fraternity, Walsh knew the Latin phrase *modus operandi*. In fact, it was probably the only Latin phrase that he knew, with the possible exception of *sine die*, a term bandied about in the courts to indicate that a case was being remanded to a date yet to be fixed.

"His MO, as you so succinctly put it, Spider, is that he goes about murdering people."

Unfortunately, Spider was taking his second draught of Guinness at that point and promptly coughed and spluttered and spilt a liberal quantity of stout down the front of his raincoat. "Oh, my Gawd," he said, when eventually he had recovered his composure.

"That's very expensive stuff that Guinness, Spider," said Fox mildly. "Shouldn't waste it."

"I don't know nothing about no toppings, Mr Fox." Walsh peered around the bar as if lining up an escape route. "Who's he done, this Povey?"

"I reckon there's three down to him, Spider. But you'll remember two of them." Briefly, he told Walsh about the deaths of Proctor and Skelton.

"I heard about that geezer in the flounder, Mr Fox. Very nasty."

"Murders always are, Spider, but particularly ones in taxis. Tends to upset the hackney-carriage trade, that sort of thing."

Walsh drained his glass and looked hopeful. "I'll see what I can do, Mr Fox, but I ain't making no promises."

"Get yourself another stout, Spider, seeing that you wasted half the first one." And with an uncharacteristic display of generosity, Fox placed a ten-pound note on the table before leaving.

*

"Mr Gilroy's looking for you, sir," said a detective constable as Fox put his head round the door of the Flying Squad office. "Something about a pawn shop in Staines apparently."

"Where is he?"

"In his office, I think, sir."

"Right," said Fox. "Tell him I'm back." He walked down the corridor to his office and started, reluctantly, to sift through the files that had appeared on his desk during his absence.

"Got a call from the local Old Bill at Staines, guv'nor," said Gilroy as he entered Fox's office. "Don't know whether there's anything in it, but they thought there might be."

"Go on then."

"Seems a bloke tried to hock some gems in a pawn shop in Staines. The assistant didn't like the look of the sparklers or the bloke who was trying to pledge them. And he told this finger that they were paste and he wasn't interested."

"What happened?"

"The bloke left and the chap in the pawn shop rang the law, but by the time they got down there, our hero had taken it on the toes. No trace of him in the vicinity."

"Was it paste, Jack?"

"No, it was the real thing apparently."

"What did he reckon this tomfoolery was worth then, Jack? Did he say?"

"The local law reckoned he put a value on it of about ten grand, sir."

"Why the bloody hell didn't he hang on to him then?" asked Fox.

"They won't take the risk these days, sir," said Gilroy. "They're frightened of getting stabbed. And I don't blame them. Half these blokes are on drugs. Anyway, the bloke would probably get a pound out of the poor box if we'd nicked him and the pawnbroker'd finish up getting done for assault."

Fox shook his head. "Things have come to a pretty pass, Jack. Description?"

"The usual, sir," said Gilroy, which meant that the description would have fitted half the male population of London, "but there was one point about him…"

"Which was?"

"He had a tattoo on the back of his left hand. The pawnbroker's assistant is pretty sure that it was a heart with an arrow through it."

"How distasteful," said Fox. "Anyone ever heard of this chap?"

"Enquiries are in hand, sir."

"Good. Give Dickie Lord a bell. He might know this finger."

Gilroy paused, his hand resting lightly on the handle of Fox's office door. "Why are we interested in this bloke, sir?"

"According to Dickie Lord, the late Mr Proctor, and to a lesser degree Skelton, weren't above doing a bit of fencing, as well as thieving. Given that both are now permanently out of circulation, this poor sod's likely roaming the streets trying to find a buyer for his ill-gotten gains. It's worth a try, Jack, but don't waste too much time on it."

*

One of the Flying Squad's strengths is that it manages to acquire some very good detectives, and one of the attributes of a very good detective is that he, or she, has a very good memory. In this case, it was Detective Constable Kate Ebdon, the recently recruited Australian who had cut her teeth on the villains of Leman Street, who came up with the answer to Fox's query.

DI Gilroy had broadcast the brief description of the man who had attempted to pawn ten thousand pounds' worth of jewelery at a pawn shop in Staines. He had done this by the simple expedient of opening each of the Squad's office doors in turn and enquiring if anyone had heard of a villain with a heart and arrow tattooed on the back of his left hand.

"Hang on a mo', guv," said Kate Ebdon. "That rings a bell."

"You know him?" asked Gilroy.

"Might do." Kate looked pensive. "Give me a few minutes, guv'nor, and I'll make a call to my old nick."

A quarter of an hour later, Kate Ebdon tapped on Gilroy's office door. "Thought I knew him, guv," she said, "but I couldn't remember his name. But my old buck at Leman Street remembered him. He's called Glass, Bert Glass, and he's got form as long as your arm."

"Got an address?"

"The PNC has him in Whitechapel, sir, but that was a year ago."

"What the hell was he doing in Staines then?"

"Maybe he's moved," said Kate with a cheeky smile and turned to leave the office.

"Not so fast, Kate," said Gilroy. "You started it, so you can finish it. Take Joe Bellenger with you and find this Glass. If he does anything sussy, bang him up and give me a bell."

*

76

"I flashed the photos of Skelton and Povey around the staff at the Agincourt Hotel, sir," said DI Evans.

"And?"

"And nothing, sir. None of them recognized the picture of Skelton, and one or two thought they may have seen Povey. But they weren't sure."

"Tremendous," said Fox.

*

Detective Constables Joe Bellenger and Kate Ebdon were no strangers to the sort of sleazy hostelries frequented by the villainry of London. They started their search for Bert Glass in his usual haunt, a pub in Whitechapel High Street. The arrival of the Australian woman detective, whom they thought had gone forever, alarmed the habitues, but when they discovered that she was looking for Bert Glass, they promptly surrendered him. It seemed the easiest way to get rid of the woman who had haunted them and harried them relentlessly during her tour of duty at Leman Street. Remarkably, Glass was said still to be living at his old address in a street east of Brick Lane.

The Indian landlord who owned the run-down house in which Glass had a room was more than willing to assist the police, for the same reason as the customers at Glass's favorite pub had been. He allowed the two detectives to wait in Glass's room, having first been cautioned that warning Glass of their presence could have dire consequences.

The room was a tip. In one corner there was an unmade bed. A newspaper-covered table had on it several dirty dishes and a cup of cold brown liquid. "Looks like his staple diet's corn flakes, baked beans and instant coffee," said Kate. Thin and dirty curtains hung, half-drawn, across filthy windows and a broken-down armchair sat forlornly in front of a small television set. And there was an overpowering stench of unwashed flesh. "Nice place," she added. Neither of the detectives sat down.

An hour after they had arrived, the door of the room opened and Glass entered. He wore jeans, a dirty white sweatshirt and a herring-bone jacket with worn-out elbows. Seeing Kate Ebdon, he stopped and turned, but Joe Bellenger had heard the man coming up the creaking staircase and was behind the door.

"Hallo, Bert," said Kate as Bellenger slammed the door shut, cutting off Glass's escape.

"I ain't done nothing," said Glass. He had a hunted look about him.

"We've got a warrant to search your room, Bert."

"What for?"

"Where have you just come from?"

"I've been out Staines way."

"What for?"

"Bit of business." Glass looked unhappy. "Who's he?" he asked, nodding at Bellenger. It was a pointless question.

"Flying Squad," said Bellenger.

Glass looked ill. "What d'you want then?" he asked.

"Turn out your pockets, Bert," said Kate.

Reluctantly, Glass emptied his pockets on to the table.

"Well, well, what have we here?" Bellenger gazed down at the jewelery that Glass's pockets had just yielded. "I suppose you've got an explanation for this, Bert?"

"It's not mine, it's a friend's," said Glass unconvincingly.

"That's what I hoped you were going to say," said Bellenger. "You're nicked, my old son."

*

Detective Sergeant Percy Fletcher had traveled from Scotland Yard to Piccadilly Circus by underground train. He knew that there was no point in trying to park a car in the West End of London, and he knew also that his quest for information would take him from one place to another.

Fletcher began his search at premises tucked away in an alley off Berwick Street in Soho. Politely known as an all-day live strip show, it entertained a succession of libidinous patrons who paid exorbitant sums of money to see young ladies taking off their clothes. The owner of this establishment was Janet Mortimer. Now about fifty years old – although no one knew her age for certain – she had lived in Soho all her life, most of which had been spent on the fringes of illegality. And she was in constant fear of the police, mainly because she also ran a brothel in the upstairs rooms that she thought the police knew nothing about. In all probability, the local police did not know about it. But Percy Fletcher knew. However, Percy Fletcher had more important things to do than to prosecute willing young ladies for selling their sexual favors to willing old men. In all honesty, he could see little harm in it.

Fletcher pushed open the door of Janet's office and almost collided with a young brunette wearing a sequin-covered bikini, black tights and very high-heeled shoes.

"Hallo, Janet," said Fletcher.

"I, er, oh, hallo, Sergeant Fletcher. Wasn't expecting you." Janet Mortimer was attired in a black satin dress, high at the neck, and her platinum-blonde hair was piled on top of her head in a fashion that was intended to make her seem younger. Ironically, it actually made her appear older. "You haven't met Marlene, have you?"

"No," said Fletcher. "Member of your stable, is she?" He grinned at the brunette as she wiggled her way out of the office, doubtless to warn the inhabitants of the upper rooms that the Old Bill had arrived.

"Have you seen this bloke around at all, Janet?" Fletcher tossed a photograph on to Janet Mortimer's desk. "His name's Kevin Povey."

Janet studied the photograph carefully and pursed her lips. "Don't think so," she said and looked up. "Villain, is he?"

"And some," said Fletcher. "We reckon there's three toppings down to him."

Janet nodded slowly. "I'll put the word out, Mr Fletcher," she said. "And if I hear anything, I'll give you a bell."

That afternoon, Percy Fletcher made several other visits to various establishments around Soho. Some were as dubious in character as the one he had just left. Others, up-market by anyone's standards, were those where Fletcher knew such influential people as head waiters, hall porters and security officers. By the time he had finished, he knew that the word was indeed out for Kevin Povey. All he had to do now was go back to the Yard and wait. At least, that was the way it was supposed to work.

Ten

Fox received the news OF Glass's arrest with mixed feelings. "You know, Jack," he said, "This damned enquiry is getting further and further away from the murder of Wally Proctor. Now we're involved with some petty toe-rag from Whitechapel who's been hawking diamonds around Staines. The man must be mad. I ask you, Jack, where's the logic in all this? I mean, do people actually wear diamonds in Staines?"

"You're right, guv'nor," said Gilroy. "It's not really the sort of trivial rubbish you need to bother yourself with. Leave it to me. I'll pop down to Leman Street and have a word with this Glass finger." Gilroy knew that there was not a cat-in-hell's chance of Fox passing up the opportunity to lean on a villain.

"You're probably right, Jack..." For a moment, Fox sounded as though he might acquiesce. But then his overpowering desire to interfere at every stage took command. "On the other hand, ten grand's worth of tomfoolery is quite a lot." He closed the file on his desk and slung it on the high pile of dockets that threatened to smother his pending-tray. "I think perhaps I will have a look at this fellow. Just in case." He stood up. "Be silly to overlook him if he holds the key to our murders, wouldn't it? If there's nothing in it, we can leave it to young Kate Ebdon to sort out," he added.

Gilroy grinned. "Shall I get Swann to get the car up, sir?" he asked.

"What?" Fox looked up from the piece of paper he had just found in his in-tray.

"The car, sir. D'you want the car brought up?"

"Oh, er, yes, Jack. Not going to walk to Leman Street." Fox glanced back at the piece of paper in his hand. "By the way, Jack, you're on a promotion board on Tuesday week. Good luck!" He initialed the slip of paper and tossed it into his out-tray. "Bit pointless, though. I hear they're going to abolish chief inspectors."

"And chief superintendents, sir," said Gilroy. "So I've heard."

*

Bert Glass was forty-two. And he had experienced prison life for fifteen of those years, once in Malta. His occupation was still shown on the Police National Computer as merchant seaman, and the tattoo which had betrayed him had been acquired in Hong Kong when he was a callow youth of eighteen. But it had been many years since Bert Glass had put to sea.

By the time that Fox arrived at Leman Street police station, Glass had recovered some of his self-confidence and, in his naivete, imagined that he could talk his way out of his latest bit of grief. But he had never been interrogated by the head of the Flying Squad before.

"Well, well, well," said Fox. He smiled benignly at the prisoner as he sat down in the chair opposite him. "We seem to have a bit of a problem, Bert."

"We do?" This was the last sort of approach Glass had expected.

"Indeed. Let me explain. I am Detective Chief Superintendent Thomas Fox... of the Flying Squad, and I think you might be in a position to help me."

"I want my solicitor," said Glass. He knew his rights.

"*Your* solicitor. Or *a* solicitor? Frankly, Bert, old son, you do not strike me as the type of villain who retains his own mouthpiece."

"All right. A solicitor. Or my social worker."

"Your what?" Fox turned to Gilroy. "Did I hear aright, Jack? The man wants his social worker."

"I think he means his probation officer, sir," said Gilroy, trying hard to hide his amusement. "He's on probation."

Fox carefully selected a cigarette from his case and lit it. "It's amazing, isn't it, Jack. Here we have a villain with a criminal record a mile high and some idiot puts him on probation." He peered closely at the prisoner. "And what, Bert, were you put on probation for?"

"It was all a mistake," said Glass.

"Usually is," said Fox. "Tell me about it."

"It was a case of mistaken identity," said Glass. "Me and two other blokes got nicked for thieving. Except I wasn't there. The Old Bill just come round my drum and nicked me. And I went down."

Fox shook his head. "Most unfortunate, Bert, but it does happen from time to time. However..." He picked up the plastic property bag containing the jewelery that had been found in Glass's possession and placed it in the center of the table. "Where did this come from?"

"Found it, didn't I?"

"Really?" Fox affected great interest in this statement. "Where exactly?"

"Can't remember."

"Oh dear!" Fox would dearly have loved to jog Glass's memory by giving him a quick rap in the mouth, but he knew that this fictional method of interrogation never worked. "Why then, Bert, did you not hand it into a police station?"

"'Tain't worth nothing."

"How d'you know that?"

"The geezer in the—" Glass stopped suddenly, appreciating that he was in danger of talking himself into a verbal cul-de-sac.

"The geezer in the pawn shop in Staines, I think you were going to say, told you they were paste. Yes?"

Glass stared sullenly at Fox. "Yeah. Well he's, like, an expert, ain't he. So, if the gear ain't worth nothing, you can't nick me for it, can you?"

"On the contrary, Bertie, old dear, these sparklers are not paste."

"What they worth then?"

"To you, Bertie, about five years, I should think," said Fox, "but on the open market..." He pretended to give the matter of the jewelery's worth some close consideration. "About ten thousand pounds."

Glass appeared positively sick at this revelation. It was a portrayal of mixed emotions, deriving from the knowledge that the pawn shop assistant had lied to him and thus deprived him of acquiring a small fortune, and because he now knew that he was in serious trouble. "Oh!" he said.

"But that is a minor matter," said Fox loftily.

"It is?" Glass's tortured mind failed to grasp how the police could possibly regard the unlawful acquisition of ten thousand pounds' worth of jewelery as a minor matter.

"Yes, indeed, Bertie. You see, dear boy, my detective inspector here..." Fox indicated Gilroy with a flourish. "My detective inspector has been making enquiries since your arrest, and he has learned that this jewelery is part of the proceeds from an audacious confidence trick perpetrated on two, possibly three, harmless little old ladies."

"Oh!" said Glass again. He had decided that his responses were best confined to monosyllables, not that he would have been able to define it thus.

"Don't keep interrupting," said Fox. "But the real problem, as far as you're concerned that is, is that two of the villains involved in the said scam have been murdered."

Glass drew breath sharply and was about to say something when he remembered that Fox had told him not to interrupt.

"Now, given that whoever topped those two icemen probably had it away with this little lot..." Fox tapped the property bag with his forefinger. "That someone has a lot of explaining to do."

Glass had been involved in petty crime all his adult life – and for a lot of his juvenile one, too – but he had never been party to a crime of violence. "I don't know nothing about no toppings," he said vehemently.

"Alas, Bertie," said Fox, "I fear that your denial is not sufficient of itself to row you out of this aggravation." He banged the top of the table so violently that Glass jumped. "Now where did you get them from?"

"I done a drum down Notting Hill." Glass knew when the odds were against him and his brain, such as it was, went into top gear. And he did not much care for this mocking policeman opposite him. A policeman who looked as though he could get quite violent, despite his dandified clothing.

Fox adjusted his top-pocket handkerchief and lit another cigarette. "Where in Notting Hill?"

"Don't rightly know."

Fox leaned forward menacingly. "Well you'd better start remembering."

Glass's face crumpled as his rarely used thought processes came into play. "I got out at Notting Hill Gate." He glanced up at Fox. "Off the Tube, like."

"Yes?"

"And I walked down as far as the nick—"

"Notting Hill nick?"

"I s'pose so."

"I would have thought you'd have known every nick in London, Bertie," said Fox mildly. "But do go on. It's fascinating."

"And I turned right, up a street called…" Glass lapsed into silence once more.

"Ladbroke Grove," prompted Fox.

"Yeah!"

"And then what?"

"Well then I threw another right—"

"Not a right hook, I trust," murmured Fox.

"And went along until I reached a bit of grass. There was some flats off of the other side, like, and I done a bit of drumming—"

"Perhaps you would explain 'drumming' for the benefit of the tape recorder, Bertie," said Fox in a tired voice.

"Well, like, ringing door bells till I found one when there was no answer."

"And you eventually found one?"

"Yeah."

"What number?"

"I dunno." Glass frowned as though genuinely sorry that he could not assist.

"What floor was it on?"

"The top floor."

Fox turned to Gilroy. "What d'you think, Jack?"

"Almost certainly Robin Skelton's drum, guv'nor," said Gilroy, smothering a grin.

But Fox laughed out loud. "D'you know, Jack, there is a certain irony about a tenth-rate villain like this one here—" he waved at Glass. "—screwing the drum of a sophisticated iceman like Skelton and having it away with ten grand's worth of gear that has already been nicked once." He swung back to concentrate on Glass, to whom most of the conversation between Fox and Gilroy had been unintelligible. "When did you carry out this burglary, Bertie?"

"Few days ago, I s'pose," said Glass, unwilling to commit himself.

"Tell me, why go to Notting Hill? Bit off your manor, isn't it?"

"I'm, like, an importunist," said Glass.

"I think you mean opportunist," said Fox.

"I know what I bleedin' well mean," said Glass churlishly. Fox raised his eyes to the ceiling. "But it seemed like a good place for a screwing,"

Glass went on. "Lot of pricey motors round there, see. You can always tell."

"That, you prat," said Fox, "is because they park there before hopping on the Tube at Notting Hill Gate to go to central London."

"Don't matter, do it? I done all right." Glass nodded sorrowfully at the property bag of jewelery. "Well, nearly," he added.

Fox laughed and stood up. "Where's Kate Ebdon, Jack?"

"In the canteen, sir," said Gilroy.

"Let her listen to this tape and then tell her to charge our friend here with burglary, will you?" said Fox.

*

"Mr Fletcher?"

Percy Fletcher recognized Janet Mortimer's husky voice immediately. "What is it, Janet?"

"Is it all right to talk?"

"Yes."

"Listen, I was talking to one of my girls today."

"One of your strippers?" asked Fletcher flippantly, intent on having a bit of fun at the woman's expense.

"You know what I mean, Mr Fletcher." In addition to the strip joint and brothel she ran in Soho, Janet Mortimer was also responsible for a number of high-class call girls who operated in West End hotels and pieds-a-terre. They were discretion personified, these girls, and never a whisper of their activities had reached the ears of either the police or the popular press. That was probably because Janet Mortimer vetted the girls' clients and knew that a scandal would result in prosecution for her and ruination for them.

"What have you got then, Janet?"

"It's nothing very much, but one of my girls was entertaining a gentleman last night and happened to mention the name you mentioned to me. lust on the off chance."

"And?"

"Well, like I said, it's nothing much, but this trick said he once knew a Povey, but a Gordon Povey. He's dead now, apparently, but he was in the diamond trade, years ago. Did very well out of it, so the punter said. Even had a yacht in the South of France. Cannes apparently."

Fletcher had been scribbling down the details as Janet Mortimer had been speaking. "Is that it?"

"Sorry, Mr Fletcher, but that's the best I can do. If anything else crops up, I'll let you know."

"Thanks, Janet, you're a treasure," said Fletcher and replaced the receiver. For a few moments, he studied his notes. Two words struck him as possibly relevant to the enquiry into the deaths of Proctor and Skelton. One was "diamond" and the other was "Cannes". He stood up and made his way, thoughtfully, to Fox's office.

*

Detective Constable Kate Ebdon had been left behind at Leman Street police station to deal with the mass of paperwork that was involved in the arrest and charging of Bert Glass. She had listened to the tape of Fox's interview with the petty criminal and had come to the conclusion that Glass was lying. And Kate, being a resourceful sort of hard-nosed detective, rather like a brasher, younger, female version of Tommy Fox, decided to have another go at Glass.

She strode into the interview room and stood in front of the table behind which Glass was lounging, her hands on her hips. She wore tight blue jeans and a white poplin shirt, and her flame-red hair was tied back with a bow. "You're a lying little bastard, aren't you, Glass?"

Glass had jousted with Kate Ebdon before and did not relish doing so again. She had none of the suavity of the man who had recently interviewed him, and Kate's aggressive Australian accent unnerved him. "Aren't you supposed to switch that on?" he asked lamely, pointing at the tape recorder.

"Too right, mate," said Kate. "And I will, once you start telling the truth."

"I told that other copper all that I—"

"Balls!" said Kate. "I've just listened to the tape and that was a load of moody if ever I heard it."

"It's the God's honest truth, Miss Ebdon, so help me."

"You just listen to me, bastard-features, before I start kicking you all round this bloody interview room."

"I want a solicitor—" Glass began plaintively.

"You'll need a bloody team of paramedics if you don't wind your neck in." Kate was not at all angry but she knew how to put the frighteners on tuppenny-ha'penny toe-rags like Glass.

"What's got your dander up, then, Miss Ebdon?"

"I don't like it when you try to have me over, Glass, that's what. All this crap about screwing a drum in Notting Hill. You were bloody hand-in-glove with Robin Skelton, weren't you? You were his runner, weren't you?"

"How did you know that?" Glass suddenly realized that there was no deceiving this woman officer. But he was unaware that she had taken a gamble in making such a wild allegation.

"Because Skelton wasn't the sort of stupid bastard that you are. D'you honestly think that a bloke who'd gone to all the trouble of nicking a load of ice and other assorted gear off some rich old bird is going to leave it lying around his pad so that the likes of you could nick it?"

"What else could I say? The bloke's been snuffed out, ain't he? That other copper would have had me for the topping if I'd told him what had happened."

"Well I've got news for you, Glass. You're going to tell me all about it. And if you miss anything out, I'll kick you in the balls. Got the message?"

Glass nodded resignedly. "All right," he said, "I'll tell you what it's all about."

"Good," said Kate and switched on the tape recorder. "This interview, at Leman Street police station, is commencing at 3.10 p.m. on Tuesday the twenty-ninth of June." She turned to face the miserable Glass. "Now, Mr Glass," she said, "I understand that you have asked to see me because you have further information to offer about the possession of certain items of jewelery for which you have been arrested. You are not obliged to say anything, but anything you do say…"

*

"Mr Fox? It's Spider here."

Fox groaned. "What is it?"

"I think I might have something for you, Mr Fox. Can we make a meet?"

"See you in the Albert in half an hour," said Fox. "Don't be late."

Eleven

"I know it's a lot to ask, Janet, but I really do need to talk to the punter who your girl was speaking to about this Gordon Povey." Fletcher had told Fox of Janet Mortimer's information about the deceased diamond merchant who had once owned a yacht in Cannes. It could be a coincidence – coincidence featured in police work more than most people realized – and there might be no connection between Gordon Povey and the Kevin Povey that Fox was so anxious to interview. But it was not a lead that could be overlooked. However, both Fox and Fletcher appreciated that it would be very difficult to persuade Janet Mortimer to reveal either the identity of her call girl or the name of the man she had entertained.

Janet Mortimer leaned back in the tatty chair in the equally tatty office of her Soho strip-joint and smiled. "D'you know what you're asking, Mr Fletcher?"

"Yes, I know, Janet, and I wouldn't be asking if it wasn't very important. This Kevin Povey has almost certainly murdered three people. The first was five years ago, the other two quite recently."

"And I suppose if I don't play ball, you're going to arrange to have this place ripped apart by the Vice Squad."

"You know me better than that, Janet," said Fletcher. "All I'm asking for is a little co-operation. I couldn't care less about what you do here. After all, it's between consenting adults, isn't it?" He grinned at the blowsy madam.

Janet Mortimer smiled too. "I don't know, Mr Fletcher. I'll have to talk to the girl. If she says no, then that's it."

"Fair enough, Janet."

*

"Hallo, Mr Fox." Spider Walsh was already installed in the darkest corner he could find at the Albert public house in Victoria Street. "I don't not like being seen so near the Bladder, you know."

"Whether you like being seen near the Yard or not is of no interest to me, Spider," said Fox. "You said that you'd got something for me."

"It's dry old work, Mr Fox," said Walsh.

"You drive a hard bargain," said Fox, placing a five-pound note on the table. "Get me a large Scotch and a pint of stout for yourself."

Walsh grabbed at the note and made for the bar. Minutes later he was back with the drinks. "There's your change, Mr Fox," he said, putting the money on the table and sitting down again.

"Right then, what's this earth-shattering information you have for me?"

"I heard a whisper, like, Mr Fox," said Walsh, once he had taken a mouthful of his Guinness. "And it seems this Povey what you was asking about has been seen up West."

"Where up West? And when?"

"'Bout a week ago, so my contact tells me."

"And who's your contact?" asked Fox, knowing that there was no chance of his being told.

"Now play fair, Mr Fox, you know I can't reveal my sources."

Fox grinned and took a sip of whisky. "Get on with it then."

"The word is that he was seen round about the time that Proctor got topped. You know, the geezer in the flounder. In and out of one or two clubs, like. But he ain't been seen since."

"What were the names of these clubs, Spider?"

Walsh shrugged and pulled his raincoat around his scrawny figure. "Don't rightly know, Mr Fox. My sources never let on like."

"Is that it, then?"

"Well, it's better than sod-all, Mr Fox, ain't it?" said Walsh nervously.

Fox picked up his change and put it in his pocket. "D'you know, Spider," he said, "on the basis of value for money, you're the most expensive snout I've got."

Walsh grinned a lop-sided grin. "Knew you'd be pleased, Mr Fox," he said.

*

"Got a minute, sir?" asked Kate Ebdon, catching Fox as he strode along the corridor.

"What is it, Kate?"

"It's about Bert Glass, sir."

"Better come in." Fox led the way into his office and closed the door. "Charged him, have you?"

89

"Yes, sir. And I got him remanded into police custody for questioning. Just in case you want to have another go at him."

"Why should I want to do that?"

Kate grinned. "I listened to the tape after you and Mr Gilroy had left the nick, sir," she said, "And I didn't believe a word of what he'd said. I know Glass of old and he's a lying little tosser." Fox nodded knowingly. "So I decided to have another go at him."

"Exposed him to some of your feminine charm, no doubt," murmured Fox.

"Something like that," said Kate. "Anyhow, he's singing a different song now." She put a tape on Fox's desk. "D'you want me to play it through, sir?"

Fox shook his head. "No, just give me the gist of it."

"Well, sir, Glass now admits that he was Skelton's runner, and it's quite obvious that he was terrified of the man." "Hang on. Who was terrified of whom?"

"Glass was terrified of Skelton, sir." Kate had heard of Fox's occasional pedantry, but this was the first time that she had encountered it directly.

"Good. Go on then."

"Glass was used by Skelton to deliver bent gear. Skelton was always afraid of transporting the stuff himself because he'd got previous and he knew that if he got pulled by the Old Bill, he'd be nicked very smartly."

"Not very astute of him," said Fox. "Glass had form as well."

Kate grinned. "I think it was a sort of insurance," she said. "Glass didn't say so, but I reckon that Skelton took the view that if he lost a consignment on its way to the fence, that was bad luck, but at least he'd live to thieve another day. And Glass was so frightened of getting topped if he opened his mouth that he'd've stayed shtoom and done porridge rather than grass on Skelton."

Fox nodded. "That I can understand," he said. "So how come he screwed Skelton's drum at Notting Hill? If that was what he did. After all, there was no sign of a break-in, but I suppose he could have 'loided it."

Kate Ebdon knew all about 'loiding, as forcing a door with a credit card was known, but she also knew that it had not happened on this occasion. "He went in with a key, sir," she said. "He now says that he went to the flat in Bayswater in response to a telephone call from Skelton, to pick up some gear—"

"Where the hell did Skelton get that from then? When Jack Gilroy searched that flat and the one at Notting Hill, he took possession of all the jewelery that was there."

"No idea, sir," said Kate. "Perhaps he'd had it in a safety deposit box, or at another flat we know nothing about, and got it out while he was on bail. Anyway, the important thing was that when he got there, at around three in the afternoon, he found Skelton dead. So, not wishing to miss out, Glass took the key of the Notting Hill flat and went straight down there. He claims that he was lucky enough to find the ten thousand pounds' worth of jewelery that Joe Bellenger and I found him with later. The same stuff he was hawking around Staines, I suppose."

"Saucy little bastard," said Fox. "Well done, Kate. I think that I'll have to go and have another chat with Master Bertie Glass." He stood up. "And you can come too. Get hold of Swann, will you?"

"Is that the idle sod who drives you, sir?" asked Kate with a grin.

"You've met him, then," said Fox.

*

Bert Glass looked distinctively nervous when Fox strode into the interview room accompanied by Detective Constable Ebdon.

"So you went 'drumming' until you found an empty flat, did you, Bertie?"

Glass ran a hand round his mouth. "I didn't want to get into no trouble," he said, his eyes still fixed firmly on Kate Ebdon.

"Got a funny way of going about it, Bertie," said Fox. He sat down and took a cigarette from his case. "One of the worst offences in my book is to waste the time of the head of the Flying Squad." He lit his cigarette. "And I've just convicted you of that offence." He let a thin layer of smoke drift into the air above Glass's head. "So you were Skelton's runner, were you?"

"Well, I done a bit for him, yeah. But only from time to time."

Fox leaned forward and studied the small-time villain's face. "I don't think you realize the seriousness of your situation, Bertie, old thing," he said. "Theft from a dwelling is one thing, but obstructing a murder enquiry is a very dangerous thing to do. There are some very worldly people about, and even some judges, who might think that you actually committed this murder in order that you could steal the jewelery for which you stand charged." He leaned back and let out another thin stream of tobacco smoke.

"Gawd blimey, guv'nor," said Glass, the anguish clear on his face. "I never had nothing to do with that topping, so help me. That'd be asking for trouble, wouldn't it?"

"In the field of asking for trouble, Bertie," said Fox with a grim smile, "I'd say you were a front runner."

"I swear I never had nothing to do with it, sir." Glass had now got to the theatrical stage of wringing his hands. It had no effect on Fox. "Like I told the lady, guv—" he shot an imploring glance at Kate Ebdon, who grinned insolently back at him. "—when I got to the Bayswater gaff, Rob was dead."

"How did you know he was dead?" asked Fox. "You a qualified medical practitioner, are you? Among your other skills."

"Strewth!" Glass stared at Fox unbelievingly. "You only had to look at him. Eyes wide open and holes in his chest with all blood oozing out." He shook his head. "It was horrible."

Fox was unmoved. "How did you get into Skelton's flat if he was already dead then?"

"I had a key, didn't I?"

"You have the bare-faced cheek to sit there and tell me that Skelton trusted a toe-rag like you with a key to his flat?"

Glass grinned. "Not exactly. I sort of acquired it."

"Oh, you acquired it, did you? How?"

"Well, he'd left his keys lying about one day when I got there. He'd just had a shower like, and he let me in and told me to wait while he put his duds on. His keys was on the table, so I took a pressing."

Fox shook his head. "D'you mean to tell me that you carry a bar of soap around with you on the off chance of finding a key you want to copy? Pull the other one, Bertie."

"It's the truth. 'Cept it wasn't soap." Glass grinned at the detective. "That's old hat these days. Nah, I had some of that Blu-Tak in me sky, didn't I. It's good for that sort of thing. Anyway, I got a copy made by a mate of mine what's in the business."

"What business is that, Bertie? Burglary?"

"No, nothing like that. Anyway, like you said the other day, I'm a bit of an importunist."

"I said that you were an—" Fox broke off. Even he realized the futility of trying to educate Bert Glass. "Never mind," he said and leaned forward to stub out his cigarette in the tin lid that served as an ashtray. "What did you do with the pistol you used to kill Skelton, Bertie?"

The blood drained from Glass's face as he realized that all his smart talk – he thought it was smart, anyway – had had no effect on Fox. "I never had no gun," he said. "I ain't never had a gun. Them's dangerous."

"True," said Fox. "They tend to kill people."

"I tell you, he was dead when I got there."

"Did you ring the bell when you arrived?" asked Fox.

"Yeah, course I did. Didn't want Rob to know I'd got a key to his drum, did I? That's be asking for aggro, that would."

For the moment, Fox appeared to believe Glass's story, although in all honesty he did not think that Glass had had anything to do with the killing. "All right," he said, "tell me the names of the fences you took this stuff to."

Glass gasped at the enormity of Fox's question. "I can't tell you that," he said.

"Oh. Why not?"

"Look, guv'nor," said Glass, leaning forward confidentially, "I know I'm going down for thieving the tomfoolery."

"Very foresighted of you," said Fox.

"Well, I don't know if you know what it's like in stir—"

"Oh, indeed I do, Bertie. Some of my best customers are in prison."

"Well, if I grass on these receivers, I'll get done in the nick for sure."

"And if you don't, Bertie, old fruit, you'll likely get done for Skelton's murder."

Glass's chin dropped on to his chest as he considered the predicament in which he now found himself. After a moment or two of deep introspection, he looked up again. "Can you like keep it to yourself, if I tell you, guv'nor?"

"Names?" said Fox brutally.

Glass sighed. "Sailor Pogson," he said.

Fox laughed outright. "Sailor Pogson?"

"It's the truth, so help me," said Glass, fearful that his latest statement had also been disbelieved.

"Oh, I believe you, Bertie. I haven't had such good news in years. And now you can tell me who Skelton's other associates were. Apart, that is, from your good self."

"What?"

"Who did he run with, Bertie?"

"You're asking me to get topped meself," said Glass miserably and again, he lapsed into a mood of deep depression.

"I think you'd better start putting the papers together for the Crown Prosecution Service, Kate," said Fox, turning to the woman detective who throughout the interview had been sitting in a chair slightly behind Fox, and watching Glass carefully. "Think about the murder of Robin Skelton. For a start." He turned back to Glass. "I hope you don't regard that as a threat, Bertie," he said. "I was merely giving instructions to my detective constable here."

"I know he ran with Wally Proctor," said Glass hurriedly. "And there was some bloke called..." His brow furrowed as he did his best to recall the name of a man who had entered, briefly, into the business affairs of his late employer. "Got it. Some bloke called Povey. Kevin Povey."

"Never heard of him," said Fox, betraying no sign of the interest he had in the man whom Glass had just mentioned. "Who was he then?"

"Dunno really. But he was a bent bastard."

"How unusual," murmured Fox, "That you should be mixing with such people."

"Well, he was Australian, wasn't he," said Glass and shot an insolent grin at Kate Ebdon, well knowing that he was out of danger now. At least, as far as she was concerned. "You watch your mouth," said Kate.

"Australian, was he?" asked Fox. "How did you know that?"

"Well, he talked like her," said Glass, nodding in Kate's direction.

"Where did he live?"

"Dunno. I never went there. But I think Rob said he had a pad down Clapham way. Stockwell maybe."

"But you don't know the address."

"No."

"Or his phone number, perhaps?" asked Fox.

"No. Well, I never had nothing to do with him, see. I met him the once, down Rob's place."

"And when exactly was this?"

Glass looked thoughtful. "Must have been just after Wally Proctor copped it."

"You don't happen to know whether this Povey was an engineer, do you, Bertie?"

Glass looked puzzled. "An engineer, guv? Nah! He was into nicking tomfoolery, wasn't he. Same as Rob and Wally."

*

"Mr Fletcher, it's Janet Mortimer."

"Hallo, Janet. What news?"

"I've had a word with my girl, Mr Fletcher, and she's very unhappy about all this."

"Understandable," said Fletcher.

"But she's willing to have a chat with you. I've told her you're straight and she's got nothing to worry about."

"All right, Janet. Where and when?"

"I don't want her coming round here," said Janet. "Nor you too often. I've booked a room in a hotel. You can meet her there. Here," she added, "I don't suppose your firm'd be willing to pay for it in the circumstances, would they?"

"The room or the girl?" asked Fletcher with a chuckle.

"The room, of course." Janet laughed too.

"I'll see what I can do."

"And another thing, Mr Fletcher. She don't want none of your women detectives there."

"Don't worry, I'll bring another man, Janet. And you'd better be there, too."

"Don't worry about that, Mr Fletcher. I'm not letting her out of my sight."

"Right then, shall we say about seven this evening?"

"That'll do fine," said Janet. "By the way, it's the Agincourt Hotel in Park Lane. Room 203."

"Is it indeed," said Fletcher. "Well, well,well."

95

Twelve

Matthew Hobson was a seasoned detective constable who had been on the Flying Squad for four years. Despite the strict rule regarding postings after three years, he had somehow managed to avoid the notice of the personnel department. But he had resisted the temptation to sit the promotion examination for fear that being made a sergeant would most definitely result in his transfer. Consequently, he was quite happy to get involved in whatever the criminal fraternity, or Tommy Fox, threw at him. But this evening, it was Detective Sergeant Percy Fletcher who had called on his services.

The two detectives made their way to Room 203 at the Agincourt Hotel and Fletcher tapped lightly on the door.

"Hallo, Mr Fletcher, come in." Janet Mortimer, wearing another of her black satin creations – this one had acquired a slightly "rusty" look about it – closed the door firmly behind them.

"This is Matt Hobson, detective constable of this parish," said Fletcher and glanced at the raven-haired girl who was sitting on the bed, leaning back on her hands with her legs crossed.

"Nice meeting you, Mr Hobson, I'm sure," said Janet, sounding more like the wife of a provincial mayor than the madam she was. "This is Karen." The girl on the bed was about nineteen and soberly dressed in an elegant black suit. Her skirt reached to mid-calf and her white silk blouse was buttoned high to the neck. She wore black stockings and good-quality high-heeled shoes. She was not, Fletcher thought, the sort of girl to be found in Shepherd Market, much less in the King's Cross area. This, undoubtedly, was an expensive whore.

"Hallo." Karen spoke listlessly. She had obviously not been looking forward to this encounter and, by the nature of her profession, was apprehensive of the police.

"Evening, Karen." Fletcher held out his hand.

After hesitating briefly, Karen shook hands with the detective. "I don't like this, you know," she said.

"There's nothing to worry about," said Fletcher. He was surprised at the girl's cultured, educated voice. "I just wanted to have a chat with you about this bloke you were with the other night."

"Yes, Mrs Mortimer told me." Karen toyed with her gold bracelet and looked down at the carpet.

"I don't suppose you'd be prepared to give me his name, Karen." Fletcher gave the girl a reassuring look.

Karen glanced at Janet Mortimer as if seeking her permission. "Well, I don't know," she said. "I mean, he'd know who'd told you, wouldn't he?"

"Not necessarily." Fletcher moved an upright chair from under the writing table, swung it round and sat down so that he was facing the girl, but not too close. He knew about the intimidating effect of invading someone's personal space and, right now, he wanted the young prostitute's confidence. "We would make discreet background enquiries about him and only interview him when we had something other than Gordon Povey to talk about. Then we would get him to volunteer the information." He smiled. "We're quite good at it, you know. There's no way that he'd link our visit with you."

But still the girl hesitated. Then she looked at Janet.

"What d'you think, Mrs Mortimer?" she asked.

"I've known Mr Fletcher for a long time, Karen," said Janet. "He's not like ordinary coppers. I'm sure he won't let us down."

"Are you the only girl who's been with him, Karen?" asked Fletcher.

"No," said Karen. "He's been with two or three of us, but he always asks for me. Only I'm not always available. We don't like him much. He's an oily little creep. As a matter of fact the girls call him the Fat Luvvy."

"What does he do for a living? Any idea?"

"He's a company director of some kind, I think. He's got a big BMW and wears expensive suits. He's very generous, though, and always gives us a little something extra."

"How d'you know he's got a big BMW, Karen? I thought you only met him in places like this."

"Yes, I do normally, but sometimes he gives me a lift afterwards."

"I see." Fletcher leaned forward, linking his hands together between his knees, and waited. He was an expert interrogator and knew that a young girl like Karen, when asked to reveal information that to a prostitute was sacrosanct, would need time.

"His name's David Rice." Karen spoke softly, almost as if hoping that she would not be heard.

"How old is he?"

"About fifty, I should think."

"And have you any idea where he lives?"

"I can give you all that," said Janet Mortimer. "At least, a phone number."

Fletcher nodded. "Fine," he said. He knew that Janet had known the man's identity all along. But he also knew that Karen's madam respected the girl's professional status and if the information was going to be given to the police, it had to come from the prostitute's own lips.

"Thanks, Karen," said Fletcher, standing up. "We won't let you down, but I expect that Mrs Mortimer told you how important it is that we should speak to this man."

"Yes, she did."

"Well, perhaps I can buy you both a drink."

"You can buy me one, Mr Fletcher," said Janet, "but Karen's got an appointment."

Karen stood up too. "Don't remind me," she said. "It's Moby Dick again, isn't it?"

"Why d'you call him Moby Dick?" asked Fletcher, a grin on his face.

"Because he's from Wales and he's got a big willy," said Karen, and for the first time since Fletcher and Hobson had arrived, she smiled.

*

Fox strolled back and forth across his office, humming a little tune as he read the statement which Kate Ebdon had taken from Bert Glass following their latest interview with him.

"Excellent. Oh, excellent." Fox dropped the sheaf of statement forms on his desk and smiled at Kate. "That, I think, is good enough to stitch up Master Pogson," he said and rubbed his hands together. "I'm looking forward to this," he added.

"Are we going to nick him, sir?" asked Kate.

"Most definitely," said Fox. "But he's a crafty bastard, is Sailor. I think we'll do this by the book. Nip down to Bow Street, Kate, and get warrants for Pogson's arrest and, to be on the safe side, search warrants for his office and his address in…" He paused. "I think he's got a drum in Bromley. Sounds right. Bit of a social climber, our Sailor. But check it before you go for the briefs. Oh, and ask DI Evans to see me, will you?"

*

A subscriber check on the telephone number that Janet Mortimer had provided for David Rice revealed that the man Karen called Fat Luvvy had a flat in Pimlico. Fletcher called the number once or twice during the day, but there was no answer. And no answerphone. Enquiries continued.

He had told Fox about the interview with Karen in the hope that the detective chief superintendent might have allocated resources to set up a surveillance on the girl's client. But DI Henry Findlater was still engaged at Barnes, attempting to discover the identity of Julie Lockhart's boyfriend, the man Rosie Webster and Kate Ebdon had seen when they had called on the dentist's wife. Consequently, Fletcher had been left to solve the problem himself.

He and Hobson found the flat in Pimlico where British Telecom had said Rice's phone was installed and kept watch. At about seven o'clock, they saw a man fitting the description of Rice get out of a large BMW and let himself in.

Two hours later, they saw Karen alight from a taxi and knock at the door. She did not emerge again until a quarter past seven the next morning. Having assessed the girl as a high-quality tom, Fletcher came to the conclusion that Rice had a lot of money. A night with Karen, he reckoned, would have cost upwards of five hundred pounds. At eight-fifteen, Rice came out, got into his car, and drove the short distance to Fulham. He parked in a reserved bay in the forecourt of an office block and strode in, cheerfully acknowledging the salute of the doorman with a wave of his *Daily Telegraph*.

"Got the bastard," said Fletcher.

*

Fox sent DI Gilroy and his team to Bromley and had taken Denzil Evans's team with him to Sailor Pogson's office near City Road. The two raids had been timed to coincide.

Fox mounted the stairs, two at a time, followed by Evans, Kate Ebdon and two or three other Squad officers, and pushed open the door of Pogson's office so violently that it hit the filing cabinet behind it.

"What the bloody hell—?" Pogson leaped up in alarm.

"Hallo, Sailor. I'll bet you didn't expect to see me again so soon."

Pogson surveyed the head of the Flying Squad and the officers who stood behind him. "What the hell's going on, Mr Fox?" he asked.

"I recently had a long and interesting conversation with a man called Bert Glass," said Fox.

"Should that name mean something?" Pogson sat down again, trying his best to look unconcerned at the sudden invasion of his office by the Heavy Mob.

"Oh yes." Fox looked around the office with apparent interest before turning his gaze on the accountant. "He was Robin Skelton's runner."

"Am I supposed to know all about Skelton's staffing arrangements then?" Pogson's outward bravado did its best to disguise his innermost feelings of panic. Something told him that his days as Fox's informant were over.

"Mr Glass has made a statement in which he says that on several occasions he delivered items of jewelery to you at the said Skelton's behest. Stolen jewelery. Furthermore, he says that you took it from him without question and placed it in your peter." Fox glanced significantly at the large safe standing in the corner of Pogson's office.

"Does he really? Tell a lot of lies, does he, this man Glass?"

"Yes, lots," said Fox, "but on this occasion I happen to believe him, Sailor. Therefore, it would greatly oblige me if you would open that safe of yours so that we could see if you're holding any stock of questionable ownership."

Pogson smiled. "I'm afraid that won't be possible," he said. "You see, it contains clients' confidential papers."

"Thought it might," said Fox and produced a sheaf of forms from his pocket. "Here we have," he continued, "a search warrant issued by the Bow Street magistrate this very morning, Sailor, together with – and this will be of paramount interest to you personally – a warrant for your arrest."

That news clearly disturbed Pogson, but he did not intend to give in easily. "I'm afraid that an ordinary search warrant doesn't cover such things as my clients' confidential papers," he said. "You see, Mr Fox, the Police and Criminal Evidence Act, with which I'm sure you're familiar, specifically excludes such documents."

"So it does." Fox withdrew another sheet of paper from his pocket. "I almost forgot," he said. "I envisaged the possibility that you might have such papers mixed up with unlawfully acquired goods, Sailor, so I sent Detective Inspector Evans here to see a circuit judge. One of the more understanding circuit judges, I may say, and he very kindly granted Mr Evans a warrant to search for what is called excluded material."

"Oh!" said Pogson and threw a bunch of keys on to the desk. "I hope you know what you're doing."

"Practice makes perfect, Sailor," said Fox, "and I've had a lot of practice." He picked up the keys and handed them to Evans. "By the way," he went on, "the same magistrate and the same circuit judge also issued warrants for the search of your house in Bromley."

"What?" Once again, Pogson rose from his chair, his face suffused with anger. "But my wife will—"

"Your wife will be quite safe, Sailor." Fox paused. "If, of course, my officers find any stolen goods there, the question will arise of whether your wife had guilty knowledge." He waved a hand airily. "But that's a matter for the courts, as I'm sure you understand." He turned towards the officers who now had the safe and the filing cabinet open. "How are we doing, lads?" he asked.

"I think you might be interested in this, sir," said Detective Sergeant Roy Buckley, handing Fox a bulky docket that he had just removed from the bottom drawer of the filing cabinet. "Seems to contain a few familiar names."

"And there are these, sir," said Denzil Evans, emptying the contents of a large brown envelope on to the desk.

Fox gazed at the jewelery now sharing the desktop with a dirty cup and saucer, a pot of ballpoint pens, a diary and heaps of files. "Isn't that amazing?" he said. He glanced at Pogson. "And there was I thinking that you were an accountant, Sailor." He shook his head in wonderment and addressed Evans. "Where's the nearest nick, Denzil?"

"City Road, sir."

Fox sniffed. "I don't like City Road," he said. "Take Sailor to Charing Cross. You meet a better kind of custody officer there."

By comparison, the search at Pogson's house in Bromley revealed very little. The first estimate of the property taken from Pogson's City Road office was twenty thousand pounds, but the safe at the Bromley house yielded only a necklace that was unlikely to net more than about a thousand. Mrs Pogson swore it was hers, and was promptly arrested. But as Fox frequently said, it is not possible to come first in all contests.

*

"Well," said Fox when Sailor Pogson had been placed in a cell at Charing Cross police station, "a very successful morning's work."

"Want me to charge him, sir?" asked Evans.

"No, not yet, Denzil. I am by no means satisfied that the jewelery we found in Sailor's possession had been unlawfully obtained."

"But, sir—"

Fox held up a hand. "No, Denzil, be fair to the chap. He may have a perfectly acceptable explanation for it being in his safe. And Mrs Pogson did say that the necklace found at Bromley was hers, according to Jack Gilroy, anyway. No, Denzil, We must make further enquiries. In fact, I think I'll tell Sailor that. He may just feel inclined to assist us in those enquiries."

"What enquiries, sir?" asked Evans, by now completely mystified.

"Into the whereabouts of one Kevin Povey, Denzil. Who else?"

Thirteen

Sailor Pogson did not appear to have enjoyed his brief sojourn in Charing Cross police station and he glared malevolently at Fox when the detective entered the interview room. Fox smiled, promptly switched on the tape recorder and cautioned the bent accountant.

"Why haven't I been granted bail?" Pogson demanded.

"Because I need to talk to you, Sailor." Fox sat down and gazed at Pogson. "And, apart from anything else, I thought you might run away if we let you out."

"I've sent for my solicitor." Pogson was sitting with his arms folded and a truculent leer on his face.

"Very wise," said Fox. "If ever I saw a man who needed a solicitor, it's you."

"And what about my wife?"

"Oh, we released her without charge."

"I should bloody well think so, too," said Pogson angrily.

"I think she saw that she was heading for trouble, Sailor." Fox selected a cigarette from his case and spent some time getting his lighter to work. "Probably worked that out not very long after she married you, but then women are strange creatures, don't you think?"

"What d'you mean, heading for trouble?" Pogson sat forward slightly, suddenly taking a keen interest in what Fox was saying.

"My officers found a necklace in the safe in your bedroom at Bromley. Didn't amount to much. Probably a grand at best, and that's on a good day. However, your good lady claimed that it was her property."

"It is," said Pogson rapidly.

"So my officers arrested her. But, lo and behold, Sailor, when they got her to the nick, she had a change of heart. Quite amazing really. Said she'd never seen it before, that it was yours, and that she knew nothing about it, or the jewelery in a briefcase in the loft, which she kindly pointed out to us." Fox smiled at the accountant who had now slumped in his chair.

"The silly cow," said Pogson. "Why the bloody hell couldn't she keep her mouth shut?"

"She's probably wondering why she didn't do that the day she said 'I will', Sailor," said Fox. "However, there might be a way in which you can assist me."

That comment clearly interested Pogson, and he resumed his upright position. "What exactly are you suggesting?" he asked, his eyes narrowing.

"Don't get too excited, Sailor, old sport, but it has been known that those who assist the police are sometimes treated more benevolently by the courts than those who are hostile. Got the idea?"

Pogson took out a handkerchief and polished his rimless spectacles. Then he put them on again. "What's it worth?" he asked bluntly, his accountancy training never far beneath the surface.

"I am very interested in talking to a man called Kevin Povey. I think that he might just be able to assist me with my enquiries into two brutal murders. Namely, those of Wally Proctor and Robin Skelton."

"I've never heard of him," said Pogson.

"Oh dear!" said Fox. "That's what you said the first time I mentioned Robin Skelton."

"I don't know any Kevin Povey." Pogson spoke earnestly and with a note of regret. Having had a sort of lifeline thrown him by Fox, he was disappointed that he had no information to offer about someone who was dearly of interest to the head of the Flying Squad. "I could put out a few feelers, I suppose."

"Not from in here, you couldn't," said Fox, waving a hand around the interview room.

"Well then, what about bail?" Pogson had driven hard financial bargains all his life, and he found no difficulty in applying the same techniques to any other transaction.

Fox raised a hand. "Let's not run before we can walk," he said. "The gear we found in your office and at your place at Bromley. Where did it come from?"

"I don't know."

"What d'you mean, you don't know?" Fox afforded Pogson one of his best cynical looks. "Did this jewelery just materialize, as if by magic? Did you open your safe one day and find this small mountain of valuable tomfoolery, and say to yourself, Goodness me, where did that come from? Is that the form, Sailor?"

Pogson sighed. "It came through the post."

"Did it really? When?"

"It was two days after Wally Proctor was murdered. This package arrived at the office. Wasn't even registered. A small cardboard box, addressed to me. I opened it and there it was."

"And how much jewelery did this magic box contain, Sailor?" Fox had a half smile on his face, as though disbelieving the whole story.

"The stuff you found at City Road and at Bromley."

"Including the necklace?"

"Yeah, including the necklace. I'd given that to the missus. She's always been on about wanting one of that sort. As a matter of fact, I was going to buy her one when this lot turned up."

"Good gracious," said Fox, "how fortuitous. I don't suppose for one moment that you still have the box and the wrapping in which this mystery prize arrived, have you?"

"Yes, I do, as a matter of fact," said Pogson.

"Really? Where?"

"It's in a safety deposit box."

"Why the hell did you keep the jewelery in your office and at Bromley, but put the wrapping paper and the empty box in a vault, Sailor? Have you gone barking mad in your old age?"

"It was insurance," said Pogson. "I knew that if you lot came sniffing round, you'd never believe a story like that."

"How true," said Fox.

"So I hung on to it, so that you could examine it forensically."

"Scientifically," murmured Fox. "However, none of that explains away Bert Glass's allegations that he frequently delivered stolen jewelery to your office."

Pogson smiled a tired smile. "D'you honestly believe the word of a tuppenny-ha'penny thief like this Glass person, of whom, incidentally, I have never heard?"

"If you've never heard of him, Sailor, how d'you know he's a tuppenny-ha'penny thief?"

Pogson paused for only a moment. "Got to be, hasn't he? After all, you said that he's admitted to taking stolen jewelery to people's offices."

DI Henry Findlater scored at last. For five days now, he and his small team had kept watch on the Lockhart house to see if lover-boy would return. Each day, Peter Lockhart would drive the short distance to his surgery and return home at about six. But on the morning of the fifth day, Lockhart emerged from his house holding a suit-carrier and an executive briefcase and got into a hire-car that had been waiting for about ten minutes.

Playing a hunch, Findlater had telephoned the Special Branch unit at Heathrow Airport and asked them to watch for a dentist called Peter Lockhart. Two hours later, he received a radio message to say that Lockhart had boarded an aircraft for Amsterdam along with several other dentists, all of whom were attending a one-day conference there.

At two o'clock the same afternoon, the man accurately described by Rosie Webster parked his car a hundred yards away and was admitted to the Lockharts' house by Julie Lockhart. She appeared to be wearing a black diaphanous gown of some sort, and warmly embraced her visitor.

The watching officers noted the registration number of the man's car and, to be on the safe side, waited until he left at five o'clock that afternoon and followed him to a house in Wimbledon.

*

At seven o'clock the same evening, Fox received a telephone call from Dickie Lord, the ex-DI now operating as an independent insurance investigator.

"I thought you might be interested, Tommy," said Lord. "I've just had another enquiry drop on my desk. A forty-five-year-old widow living in Brighton has put in a claim for the loss of jewelery."

"How much?" asked Fox.

"About fifty grand's worth," said Lord.

"Brighton's outside the Metropolitan Police District," said Fox.

"I know that," said Lord. "The question is, do the villains know it?"

*

Detective Sergeant Percy Fletcher had spoken to Janet Mortimer on the telephone and received her assurance that none of her girls was entertaining David Rice that evening, either in a hotel or at his pied-k-terre. What Fletcher and DC Matt Hobson had not allowed for, however, was that Rice might have used a different "agency". But that was exacdy

106

what had happened. When they knocked at the door of the Pimlico flat at eight o'clock, it was opened by Rice wearing a dressing gown and clutching what appeared to be a very large gin and tonic. And he looked extremely embarrassed. But he looked even more disconcerted when Fletcher told him who he and Hobson were, and produced his warrant card.

"I, er, I have someone with me at the moment," said Rice.

"That's quite all right, sir," said Fletcher reassuringly. "This is not a confidential matter. At least, I don't imagine it is."

"You'd better come in then." Rice led the way into the sitting room of his small flat. "Er, this is Mrs Rice," he said, indicating the barefooted girl reclining on the sofa. She was about twenty-seven and her attractive shape was barely disguised by the black satin wrap she was nearly wearing. To Fletcher's expert eye, she was clearly a prostitute and to her experienced eye, he was obviously Old Bill.

"These gentlemen are from the police, darling," said Rice. "I don't think we'll be very long." He looked hopefully at Fletcher, then back at the girl. "So perhaps if you were to have your shower now..." He glanced at the two detectives. "We're going out shortly," he added, as if to encourage them not to take up too much of his time; time for which he was obviously paying dearly. Fletcher wondered idly if Rice's libido would run out before his money did.

The girl swung her legs off the sofa and stood up, gathering her robe around her. "Okay, honey," she said, and with a seductive grin and a wink at Fletcher, she went through into the bedroom and closed the door behind her.

"Now, gentlemen, what can I do for you?" Rice was clearly more relaxed now that the girl had left them. He was on the short side, perhaps no more than five feet nine, and was overweight, his fleshy, florid cheeks undoubtedly the result of an excessive addiction to alcohol. And he was sweating. Fletcher could quite understand why Janet Mortimer's girls called him the Fat Luvvy.

"Bit of a mystery really," said Fletcher, as he and Hobson accepted Rice's invitation to sit down. He took a piece of paper from his inside pocket. "The police recently recovered a stolen car," he began, "and we found this piece of paper in it, among other things."

"Oh, really?"

"The odd thing about it, Mr Rice, is that it has your name, address and telephone number on it."

"Good Lord!" Rice seemed genuinely surprised, as well he should. Fletcher had scribbled the name and address only minutes before calling at Rice's flat. "I don't understand that."

"Nor do we, Mr Rice. That's why we're here." Fletcher smiled and adopted a puzzled expression.

"Whose car was it, do you know?"

"Not at the moment, no. It bore false plates and, as yet, our lab people haven't been able to bring up the numbers on the engine block and the chassis." Fletcher offered the piece of paper to Rice, who studied it with great interest. "We do believe, however, from other evidence found in the car, that it probably belonged to a diamond merchant." Fletcher continued convincingly with his fictitious tale. "And frankly, Mr Rice, that worries us. You see, we are currently investigating the murders of two jewel thieves that have occurred in London in recent weeks. Furthermore, we are looking again at a murder that took place on a houseboat in Shepperton five years ago."

Rice looked extremely concerned at this revelation. But it was not the reaction of a guilty man, more the response of someone who had only ever read about murders. And now, here were the police making enquiries about a piece of paper that had his name and address on it. "I really can't explain it," he said, handing the scrap of paper back to Fletcher. "Diamonds, eh?" He shook his head.

"You have no idea how your name and address came to be in a stolen car then?" Fletcher raised his eyebrows enquiringly.

"No, no idea at all, officer."

"We have reason to believe that a man called Kevin Povey may be implicated." Fletcher dropped the name casually into the conversation. "I suppose that name doesn't mean anything to you?"

"Good grief!"

"I see it does, Mr Rice." Hobson decided to enter into the charade.

"Well, no, I mean, not Kevin Povey, but Gordon Povey does. I suppose that Povey is not too uncommon a name, but the odd thing about it is that the Gordon Povey I knew was a diamond merchant."

"Really?" Fletcher looked suitably astonished.

"Perhaps you can tell us where we could find him, Mr Rice," Hobson asked.

"I'm afraid he's dead. Died about five years ago, I think."

"Oh, well, that rules him out," said Fletcher. "But can you tell us anything about him?"

"My wife and I got to know the Poveys in the South of France..." Rice looked across the room, a reflective expression on his face. "Must have been about ten years ago. Our yachts were moored alongside each other in Cannes. We seemed to be there at the same time each year and we got into the habit of having dinner together. But that was all. Just the odd dinner a couple of times a year, sometimes on our yacht, sometimes on theirs, and occasionally in Cannes itself."

"Sounds like a coincidence, Mr Rice," said Fletcher. "I take it from what you were saying that Mr Povey was a legitimate diamond merchant?"

Rice nodded. "Rather different from the sort of confidence tricksters we're talking about." Fletcher grinned as if to dismiss Gordon Povey as being beyond reproach.

"Oh, absolutely," said Rice.

"And the name Kevin Povey doesn't mean anything to you?"

"No, it doesn't. I believe the Poveys had a couple of children, but we never met them. They were grown up and had long since left home, so I understand." Rice paused, wondering whether to tell the police about a further coincidence. "It's very odd, but I heard this name only the other day."

Fletcher frowned. "Oh?"

"Yes. I heard a young lady mentioning Kevin Povey. Very strange, that. Twice in a week."

"And who was this young lady, Mr Rice? It would obviously be helpful if we could talk to her."

Rice looked away. "I really have no idea," he said vaguely. "We were in a club somewhere – I can't even remember where – and this couple were at the bar next to us. No idea who they were, but the woman mentioned Povey. Not to us, of course, but I just happened to overhear their conversation and the name rang a bell."

Fletcher grinned. "A West End club, was it?"

"Yes, it was, as a matter of fact, but, as I said, I can't remember which one."

"Oh, that's easily explained," said Fletcher. "We've been mentioning his name around the clubs in the West End for about a week now, in the hope that someone might know where we can find him. Happens all the time, you know. Detectives will often push out a name in places that a suspect has been known to frequent. We call it casting bread on the waters." He stood up. "Well, we'll just have to put this piece of paper down to some extraordinary coincidence, Mr Rice," he said, patting his pocket. "These things happen, but we always have to follow up leads, you know. I should forget all about it if I were you." He smiled amiably and then paused. "I suppose your wife wouldn't recall any more about this Gordon Povey, would she?" he added, glancing meaningfully at the closed bedroom door.

A look of apprehension crossed Rice's face. "Er, no, not possible," he said and gave a nervous laugh. "Different wife, you see. Got divorced."

Fletcher gave an understanding nod. "Oh, I see. Well, thank you for your time. I hope we haven't held you up for too long."

"Oh, er, no, not at all."

"Do have an enjoyable evening then."

"What?"

"You said that you and your wife were going out, Mr Rice," said Fletcher, and glanced once more at the bedroom door.

"Oh, yes, of course," said Rice, and gave another nervous laugh.

*

The man whom DI Findlater and his team had followed to Wimbledon from Julie Lockhart's house was called Jeremy Ryan. By examining the electoral roll, the detectives discovered that his wife's name was Beverley. Armed with that information, they next visited St Catherine's House and searched the marriage records. Fortunately for Findlater, they were married, almost something of a novelty these days. Using as a guide the ages of the couple at the time of their wedding, and the wife's maiden name, they found the Ryans' dates of birth in another section of the General Register Office.

Back at New Scotland Yard, DC March fed this information into the Police National Computer. "Bingo!" he said.

"Known?" asked Findlater.

"Yes, sir. Jeremy Ryan has one previous conviction for theft from an office, three years back. Nothing on Beverley Ryan."

"Good," said Findlater. "Draw the file."

Jeremy Ryan's criminal record showed that he had been convicted of stealing documents from the office of an insurance broker in Chelsea and had been placed on probation for two years.

"How very interesting," said Fox when this information was laid before him. "Henry, go and see this insurance broker and find out exactly what documents this Ryan stole. Oh, and as young March is so good at doing searches at St Catherine's House, get him to see if he can find anything on a Gordon Povey. Percy Fletcher's come up with some information that he was a diamond merchant. Might be a coincidence, but we'd better do a bit of digging, I suppose. Died about five years ago, so Perce says. Tell March to work back from there. Gordon Povey's supposed to have had two children. Never know, one of them might be called Kevin."

Fourteen

Reluctantly, Fox decided that he would have to go to Brighton. Dickie Lord's information that a forty-five-year-old widow was claiming for the loss of fifty thousand pounds' worth of jewelery interested him. Admittedly, people were losing jewelery almost every day of the week, but this was a substantial amount and the woman was a widow. And it might just be that she had fallen victim to a trickster in the same way as Mrs Ward, Mrs Bourne and Mrs Harker.

Fox and Gilroy were driven to Brighton by the ever-complaining Swann who was only really happy when seated in the drivers' room at Scotland Yard with a hand of cards. Preferably a good hand.

It was a neat, detached house in the Preston Park area. The woman who answered the door was wearing a white trouser suit and had several gold chains around her neck. She was a blonde, though obviously not a natural one, and had a ready smile.

"Mrs Elaine Carter?"

"Yes."

"Mrs Carter, I am Detective Chief Superintendent Thomas Fox... of the Flying Squad." The woman looked slightly puzzled. "At New Scotland Yard." Fox produced his warrant card.

"Oh! Perhaps you'd better come in. I'm in the conservatory at the moment. Is that all right?"

"Perfectly, madam," said Fox, wondering why it should not be.

"Well, er, are you sure it's me you want to see?" Elaine Carter's face still bore the puzzled frown that had greeted Fox's introduction of himself.

"If you are the lady who's lost a substantial quantity of jewelery, Mrs Carter, yes."

"Ah, now I see. But I thought the local police were dealing with that, here in Brighton."

"I'm sure they are, Mrs Carter, but we in London are looking into several similar thefts. Thefts which appear to be connected with at least two murders."

Mrs Carter put her hand to her neck. "Oh, good heavens. You surely don't think—"

"There is no need to alarm yourself," said Fox. "The victims were not those who had lost their jewelery. It's more of an internecine war among those who did the stealing."

"Like gang warfare, you mean?" Mrs Carter looked quite excited at the prospect of being involved in the sort of drama she had only ever seen on television. "Well, well."

"I wonder if you could perhaps tell Detective Inspector Gilroy and me about this burglary…"

"Oh, it wasn't a burglary," said Elaine Carter.

"Not a burglary?"

"Oh no." Mrs Carter lowered her eyes and then looked up with a guilty expression. "I'm afraid I was the victim of a confidence trickster. I think that's what you call them, isn't it?"

"It might be," said Fox. "Would you care to explain?"

"I'd better begin at the beginning then."

"That would be helpful," murmured Fox.

"I was widowed about two years ago. A car accident on the M1. My late husband was a director of an insurance company and he left me very well provided for."

"I see." Fox had already deduced, from the quality of the furnishings in a house that would have fetched at least two hundred and fifty thousand pounds, that Mrs Carter was not exactly on the breadline.

"There were one or two people who told me that it wasn't easy to adjust to widowhood," said Elaine Carter, "but I wasn't prepared to accept that, so I made a determined effort. After all, I was only forty-three when it happened, and I was damned if I was going to sit at home and mope."

"Quite right," said Fox admiringly.

"So I went out and got myself a job with a yacht chandler in Brighton. My husband and I used to do a bit of sailing and I've always loved the water. It wasn't very strenuous work. Taking supplies and spare bits and pieces out to yachts in the marina, that sort of thing. I didn't need the money, but I wanted something that would enable me to meet people. I started a new life really." Elaine Carter sounded very enthusiastic about it.

"And you're still there?"

"Too true. It's only two or three days a week, but I wouldn't miss it for anything. There's not much going on in the winter, but in the summer it can get quite hectic, you know. I had determined to put the past behind me and meet people. I started going to parties and I got invited out to dinner by all sorts of people. I'm even being taken to Cowes Week this year."

"Delightful," said Fox half-heartedly. He did not share Elaine Carter's enthusiasm for sailing and was unhappy in any form of vessel that did not have an engine in it.

"And then I met this man. He seemed a very nice type..." Elaine Carter paused. "One is a bit choosy after a happy marriage that has lasted twenty-two years, but he was very kind, very considerate. He said he understood because he had lost his wife some years previously and he knew the trauma it caused."

"And so you got to know this man better, did you?"

"Better?" Mrs Carter laughed. "We had an affair," she said. "He was quite a bit younger than me and we had some riotous times."

"And how long did this last?"

"For about four months after he'd moved in. Oh sure, he would disappear for a few days from time to time. On one occasion he was gone for nearly a fortnight, but he always came back."

"Until the last time, I presume," said Fox.

"I suppose you think I was crazy to trust him?"

"It happens, Mrs Carter, I'm afraid."

"Yes, I suppose it does, but it shouldn't have happened to someone my age."

"And when this man left, he took your jewelery with him. Is that it?"

Mrs Carter nodded sadly. "'Fraid so," she said. "And now it looks as though the insurance company is not going to pay out."

"Really?" Fox knew that from his conversation with Dickie Lord.

"They're working on the principle that because he was living with me, it's much more difficult for me to prove that he actually stole my jewelery. They seem to have convinced themselves that I must have given him permission, or something ridiculous like that. As I said, my late husband was in the business and I know that insurance companies will do anything to avoid paying out." Mrs Carter smiled ruefully. "But

I'm going to fight it, even though it is Jim's old company that I'm insured with. If I'd been dishonest, I'd've told them I'd been broken into." She sighed at the apparent unfairness of life.

"What was the name of this man, Mrs Carter?"

"Don Fortune, he called himself. Should have been fortune *hunter*."

"Would you have a look at some photographs, Mrs Carter?" Fox took the prints that Gilroy produced from his brief-case and handed the first one across. "Have you seen him before?"

Elaine Carter examined the photograph of Wally Proctor and shook her head immediately. "No, that's not him."

"This one then." Fox handed over a copy of Robin Skelton's photograph.

Again, the woman shook her head. "Nor him," she said.

Finally, Fox produced the print of Kevin Povey, a print the police knew to be at least five years old. "Is that him?"

Mrs Carter stared at the photograph for some seconds before handing it back. "That's him," she said. "But he looked older. Was that taken some time ago?"

"Yes, it was, Mrs Carter. Tell me, did this man own a yacht?"

"I don't know if he owned it, but he was certainly on a yacht, the first time I met him. I'd taken a couple of cleats out to him and he invited me below for a drink. He could have been a professional crewman, I suppose, there are a lot of those about. They take yachts from one part of the world to another, you know."

"I suppose he didn't have an Australian accent, did he?" asked Fox, remembering what Bert Glass had told him.

Elaine Carter nodded thoughtfully. "Yes, he did, but it came and went. I'd forgotten that. When I asked him if he was Australian, he just grinned and said he'd spent some time there, but that'd he'd been back about three years." She paused. "Yes," she said, "I'm sure that's what he said." She looked up at Fox with a quizzical expression on her face. "Does this mean you've caught him?" she asked.

"Unfortunately no, but it's only a matter of time." Fox debated briefly whether to tell this lone widow what the police knew of Kevin Povey, but then decided that it might only serve to frighten her. There was no chance of his returning to Elaine Carter, not unless he brought the jewels with him, and Fox could think of nothing less likely than that. "I very much doubt that you'll see him again, Mrs Carter, but if you do, perhaps you'll let me know, or the local police." He paused. "But if I were you, I wouldn't let him into your house again."

"I can assure you, Mr Fox, that there's no chance of that," said Elaine Carter vehemently.

*

The insurance broker whose offices were in Chelsea was called Browning. He had a beard and wiry gray hair, and he remembered Jeremy Ryan very clearly. "I only took him on because business was well up that year and I needed some help," he said. "He wanted to learn the business, so he said. I must have been feeling charitable that week." Browning grinned. "Most unusual for an insurance broker," he added.

"And how long was he here, Mr Browning?" asked Henry Findlater.

The broker stood up and walked across to a filing cabinet in the corner of his cramped office. "I can tell you exactly," he said. "I'm very hot on keeping accurate records. Have to be in this business." He produced a file and opened it on top of the cabinet. "Yes, here we are. Three weeks." He replaced the file and slammed the door shut.

"And it was at that point that he stole some of your records?"

Browning sat down behind his desk and nodded. "Yes," he said. "It was the week that the photocopier broke down. Bloody nuisance. The engineer came round, looked at the damned thing and then said he'd have to get a spare part. Didn't see the sod again for a week."

"Are you suggesting that Ryan might have photocopied other records then?" asked Findlater.

"He did. Your chaps found them when they searched his house. After all, there's no point in stealing files if there's a copier standing in the corner, is there? I reckon it goes on all over the place. I mean to say, Inspector, how often does anyone in an office ask an employee specifically what they're copying? It's all done on trust and you don't have time anyway."

"So it was the week the photocopier broke down that you found Ryan taking documents, is that it?" Findlater was jotting down notes as he spoke.

"Yes. And it was pure luck that I found out then. Wasn't very lucky for Ryan. He was going out to lunch and he'd got one of those flashy executive briefcases with him. But as he got to the door, the case fell open and all these files went across the floor. If I hadn't been in the outer office, I wouldn't have known anything about it. Anyhow, I challenged him and asked him what he was doing."

"What did he say to that?"

Browning stroked his beard and grinned. "Not a lot he could say. He started to spin me a yarn about going out to see a client. Well, for a start he hadn't got any clients, and secondly, the files he'd got were all policies that were up and running." He smirked. "So then he changed his story and said that he had one or two friends that he was meeting for lunch and thought that they might put a bit of business his way and he was taking these files with him to show these prospective clients how it was done. Well, that didn't stand up for a moment, so I called the police."

"Did the police at Chelsea take a note of the subjects of these files?" asked Findlater.

"I suppose so. I don't really know. They let me have them back the very next day because I said I might need them."

"Is it possible for you to give me the names of the clients who were the subjects of the files he took and the ones he copied?" Findlater looked up from his pocket book, an expectant look on his face.

"Well, I don't know about that," said Browning. "They are confidential, you know."

"I realize that," said Findlater, "and we will, of course, treat the information in confidence, but we think that this theft may have been a part of an ongoing conspiracy to defraud insurance companies." He did not think that at all, but he knew that the mere suggestion of it would strike home.

"Oh, that's different," said the broker. "Why didn't you say so?" He opened a drawer in his desk and produced a handwritten list which he handed to Findlater. "There you are, Inspector."

Findlater ran his eye down the list. Two of the ten names were of women who had already excited the interest of the Flying Squad: Mrs Audrey Harker of Chiswick and Mrs Linda Ward of Earls Court. Findlater wrote down all ten names.

*

"It's bloody obvious," said Fox. "Ryan was going through Browning's files to find anyone who could provide rich pickings for our three icemen: Proctor, Skelton and Povey. And Chelsea would be a good place for it. He would pass this information on and then one of the three would make the acquaintance of a rich widow, chat her up and have her jewelery away."

"Looks like it, sir," said Findlater, peering through his owl-like spectacles at his notes. "It was just bad luck that the photocopier broke down that week. He might still have been doing it."

"He probably still is," said Fox gloomily. "I doubt that he would have stayed at Browning's for too long, even if he hadn't been caught out. Once he'd milked his files, he'd have been off somewhere else. What's he doing now, Henry, any idea?"

"No, sir."

"Well, I think you'd better find out. Put some of your lads on him. See where he's working now." Fox opened his day-book, the unofficial record he kept of things to do. "Any joy from young March? He was supposed to be finding out about Gordon Povey."

"Don't know, sir. Shall I get hold of him?"

"Do that, Henry." Fox glanced at the clock. "Christ!" he said, "Is that the time? Tell him I'll be gone in five minutes." Moments later, DC March tapped on Fox's office door and entered, nervously.

"Come in, Ted, I shan't eat you," said Fox. "What have you to tell me?"

"Gordon Povey, sir." March shuffled through the handful of papers he had brought with him. "Sergeant Fletcher's informant was right, sir. Povey did die five years ago. Heart attack, according to the death certificate." He exchanged that sheet of paper for another. "Married thirty years ago in Maidstone to a Rachel Carey."

"Is that it?"

"Yes, sir."

"Did you do a birth search to see whether they'd had any children? This bloke that DS Fletcher saw reckoned they'd had two."

March shook his head. "I went right the way through, sir," he said. "From the date of the Poveys' marriage to the date of Gordon Povey's death. Nothing, sir."

Fox nodded. That looked like another promising lead that had come to nought. "I suspected that Kevin Povey was a bastard," he said. "I think you've just proved it."

"Anything else, sir?" asked March.

"Yes. Mrs Elaine Carter of Brighton said that Don Fortune, the ratbag who nicked her jewelery, and whom we now know to have been Kevin Povey, claimed that he had been widowed some years ago. Have a poke about in the divorce register and see if you can find anything." Fox stood up and adjusted the collar of his jacket. "But as he's a lying bastard, I don't suppose that was true either. But you never know your luck, Ted."

"No, sir," said March whose idea of luck did not include hours spent in the dusty archives of the General Register Office.

*

"I'm not very good at buying flowers," said Fox when Jane Sims opened the door of her Knightsbridge flat, "but I hope these will do." He handed the girl a bunch of carnations. "I warned the seller thereof that he would be in trouble if they didn't last at least a week."

Jane smiled. "That's very sweet of you, Tommy," she said. "Come in and pour us some drinks while I put these in water."

Fox poured the whisky and lit a cigarette, leaving his case open on the occasional table. Jane smoked only occasionally, but he always offered her one.

"And how are all your murders going, Tommy?" Jane placed the vase of flowers on top of the television cabinet and sat down on the settee opposite Fox.

Fox shrugged. "They're not," he said. "Every time we come up with something that might be useful, it seems to peter out. And all the time we're getting further and further away from the real nub of the thing. I've almost forgotten that we're supposed to be dealing with a bloke who got shot in a cab at Hyde Park Corner."

"I'm sure you'll solve it, Tommy." Jane tucked her legs up on the settee. "Your men speak very highly of you, you know."

Fox glanced at her, a sceptical look on his face. "How d'you know that?" he asked. "They're right, of course," he added with a grin.

"They were talking about you after dinner at the Yard the other night. After you'd gone, of course. They obviously think that you're terrific." Jane took a sip of whisky. "And so do I," she added softly.

"You don't want to believe a word they say," said Fox. "Who in particular was giving you all this claptrap?"

"Jack Gilroy for the most part."

Fox scoffed. "Well, he would," he said. "Up on a promotion board next week. Wants to keep on the right side of me, just on the off chance that I'll put in a good word for him."

"But he is a good detective, isn't he?" asked Jane.

Fox nodded. "Yes, he is, but don't ever tell him I said so. He might slacken off."

Jane laughed. "God, Tommy Fox, you're a hard man," she said.

"Anyway, they're bound to butter you up," said Fox.

"Why?" Jane raised an eyebrow and smiled.

"Because you're the daughter of an earl, and that impresses my lot. And because you're an attractive woman."

"D'you think so?" Jane smiled as she fished for the compliment.

"Well, that's what Jack Gilroy told me," said Fox, "And, as I said, he's a good detective."

Jane laughed and threw a cushion at Fox. "You can be an absolute bastard at times, Tommy," she said.

"Not all the time. I came here specifically to take you out to dinner." Fox glanced at Jane's casual attire. "But not in that rugby shirt," he said, "so go and put on a frock and we'll find a decent restaurant somewhere."

Fifteen

Detective Inspector Henry Findlater's motley crew of surveillance officers discovered what Jeremy Ryan purported to do for a living within an hour of setting up their observation. At nine o'clock in the morning, Ryan left his house and drove to a one-roomed office over a shop in the center of Wimbledon. Just inside the street door, at the foot of the stairs, there was a small sign which stated "Jeremy Ryan, Insurance Broker".

Fox smiled archly when Findlater reported this information to him. "Be interesting to discover how many of his clients have had their jewelery stolen, Henry," he said.

"The only way I can think of is to get a search warrant, sir," said Findlater.

"And that'll have to be from a circuit judge, I suppose," said Fox. "Yet again. No, Henry, there's an easier way. At least, to start with."

Findlater looked slightly puzzled. "There is, sir?"

"Yes, indeed, Henry. Go and have a word with the local VAT office. If you talk to them nicely, they may well tell you what Master Ryan is about. Unofficially, of course."

"But he may not be registered for VAT, sir."

"Highly likely, Henry. Highly likely." Fox grinned. "But in my experience of VAT officers that minor problem merely serves to whet their appetite. And they will be able to tell us the state of his business."

"Right, sir."

"If he appears to be doing very little, then we'll pounce. With a warrant." Fox gave Findlater another evil smile. "I've got a feeling about this, Henry," he said.

*

"Kevin Povey, sir," said DC March.

"Have you arrested him, Ted?" Fox beamed expectantly at the young detective.

"No, sir," said March nervously. "I've been at St Catherine's House."

"Yes, I know. Any joy?"

"I'm afraid not, sir. There's no trace of Kevin Povey having been divorced either in that name or in the name of Don Fortune."

"Doesn't surprise me," said Fox gloomily. "Anything else?"

"Just for good measure, sir, I went through the marriage records and he doesn't seem to have been married either."

"That would account for his not having been divorced then, I suppose."

"And there's no trace of his birth either, sir. I went back fifty years, and there's nothing."

"Perhaps he doesn't exist," said Fox hopefully. For a moment or two, he reposed in deep thought. "Ask DS Crozier to see me, will you?" he said at last.

Detective Sergeant Ron Crozier had once let it be known that he spoke French. He had also let slip that he had been an actor, albeit unsuccessful, before joining the Metropolitan Police some twenty-four years previously. As a consequence, Fox always picked him for any job that required one or other of these attributes. Today, it was Crozier's linguistic ability that had influenced Fox's decision to select him for a distant enquiry.

"You wanted me, sir?" Crozier approached Fox's desk with apprehension.

"Ah, Ron. D'you remember that job we had in the South of France?"

"In the South of France, sir?" Crozier looked genuinely puzzled. He knew that Fox tended to ignore constabulary boundaries when it suited him, but the South of France was stretching the limits of his authority a bit far.

"Yes, yes. That job where we found the wrong body in a coffin somewhere, following a jewelery heist in the West End. Surely you remember that."

"Oh, yes, sir. Of course."

"I went over there and made contact with some Frog copper in Nice, and then you went over and brought back some woman. Jane somebody, yes?"

"Yes, sir. I remember now. It was *Inspecteur Principal* Pierre Ronsard."

"That's the fellow. Pop over and have a word with him, will you? See what he knows about the French police interviewing the Poveys after the houseboat murder at Shepperton. When this enquiry started Mr Semple at Eight Area said that the Poveys were on their yacht in Cannes when it happened."

"But Cannes is about thirty-two kilometers from Nice, sir," said Crozier.

"Really? What's that in English, Ron?"

Crozier calculated quickly. "Twenty miles, sir."

"Well, there you are then, Ron. Go and see what you can find out."

"But Ronsard was at the *Police Urbaine* in Nice, sir. It'll have been someone in Cannes who did the enquiry."

Fox nodded in agreement. "I'm sure you'll sort it all out, Ron." He glanced at the clock. "I reckon you could get over there in time for dinner." For a moment, he paused before adding his usual caveat. "And don't spend too much of the Commissioner's money, Ron."

*

Detective Inspector Denzil Evans had been deputed to accompany Sailor Pogson to his safety deposit box and recover the wrappings in which the mysterious parcel of jewelery had arrived at the accountant's office. Being cautious enough to think that it might one day be required as evidence, Pogson had sealed it in a plastic bag, but when it was examined by the forensic science laboratory at Lambeth, the experts there were unable to find anything that might further Fox's investigations. The box and the paper in which it had been wrapped were of a common brand and easily obtainable from almost any stationer. There was nothing that would enable the police to trace the supplier. Needless to say, there were no fingerprints on either the paper or the box, and the only indication of the parcel's source was that it bore a Maidstone, Kent, postmark.

"Interesting, that, sir," said Evans when he reported the laboratory's findings to Fox. "I understand that the Poveys were married in Maidstone. I wonder if there's a connection."

"Only if the parcel's been lost in the post for thirty years, Denzil," said Fox. "Or was that another of your Welsh jokes?"

*

Henry Findlater was shown into the office of the principal in charge of the Wimbledon VAT office and explained his problem, emphasizing, as Fox had told him to, that his enquiry was very likely connected with three outstanding murders.

"I thought about joining the police when I left school," said the VAT officer.

"Really?" said Findlater without much enthusiasm. "What stopped you?"

"Don't like working nights. Now then, you wanted to know about Jeremy Ryan." The civil servant opened a slim file. "Well, there's not much here. We followed up an advertisement that Ryan had put in a local paper, offering competitive insurance rates. So we paid him a visit..."

"And?" Findlater took his pocket book out.

The VAT officer grinned. "You won't need that," he said. "Ryan was in such a poor way of business that it was a miracle he was surviving. He'd had practically no business at all. And we went through his books from the day he'd set up."

"And when was that?"

"About three years ago." The VAT officer closed the file. "Incidentally, we had queries from two or three of our other offices around the country. It seems that Ryan had advertised in their local papers too, and they wondered if he was on some sort of fiddle. They thought that he might have been advertising away from home so that we wouldn't notice." He grinned and closed the file. "Have to be sharper than that to avoid the Revenue, I can tell you, Inspector."

*

Detective Sergeant Ron Crozier had not bothered Pierre Ronsard at Nice, despite Fox's suggestion that he should do so, but had telephoned the *Police Urbaine* at Cannes direct.

When his aircraft touched down at Nice Côte d'Azur Airport, an *Inspecteur Principal* Victor Lasage of the *Sûreté Urbaine* was waiting to meet him and drive him the twenty miles to Cannes.

Lasage spoke excellent English and Crozier vowed not to tell Fox that, in this case, his ability to speak French was not required. Despite his apparent reluctance whenever he was assigned a task by his chief – a standard police reaction – Crozier enjoyed the rare occasions when he could escape to France. And from Fox.

However, the moment that Lasage and Crozier arrived at the former's office the following morning, a detective held out the handset of a telephone. "There is a flying fox on the telephone for you, m'sieur," he said. "I think." The man looked utterly baffled by the experience of receiving a call from Fox of the Flying Squad, an experience not aided by the fact that he spoke little English and Fox spoke no French.

"Crozier, sir."

"Ah, Ron, it's you. Fox here."

"Yes, sir."

"I've just spoken to some half-wit who didn't understand a word I said. He seemed to be speaking some foreign language."

"Most of them do over here, sir."

"Yes, well. Now then, how are you getting on?"

"I'm just about to start on the paperwork, sir."

"Good heavens," said Fox, "What have you been doing?"

"Getting the lie of the land, sir. Background stuff. Looking at the harbor. That sort of thing." In fact, Crozier and Lasage had spent the whole of the previous evening over dinner. In common with most Frenchmen, eating was a near-religious experience for Lasage and nothing, save the most dire cause, was allowed to interfere with it.

"Good, good," said Fox. "Well, don't waste your time, Ron. There's plenty for you to do back here." There was a click and the telephone went dead.

"Trouble, Ron?" asked Lasage.

"It's my guv'nor," said Crozier. "He's mad."

The Frenchman gave a Gallic shrug. "It's the same in France," he said. "Now then, you want to know about Gordon Povey, yes?"

"Yes," said Crozier. "About five years ago, you were asked by Scotland Yard to interview Mr and Mrs Povey on their yacht here in Cannes."

Lasage nodded. "Perhaps," he said. "What about?"

"Their son, a Kevin Povey, was wanted for questioning in connection with a murder which took place on a houseboat in England. At a place called Shepperton."

"I was not here at that time," said Lasage, "but I will look in the records." The French inspector turned to a junior detective and issued a string of instructions. Minutes later, the man returned and laid a file on Lasage's desk.

"Here we have it," said the *inspecteur* and flicked open the docket. For the next few moments he turned pages, scanning each one rapidly. Then he turned to face Crozier. "It is as you say. A request was received from

Scotland Yard to interview Gordon and Rachel Povey on their yacht in Cannes harbor. They were on holiday…" He paused and smiled. "But it was a long holiday. They had been here for some months, avoiding the English weather, *n'est-ce pas*?"

"Very sensible if you can afford it," said Crozier.

"Oh, I think they could," said Lasage. "The officer who interviewed them said they seemed to have plenty of money." He shrugged again. Lasage did a lot of shrugging. "But then if you own a yacht in Cannes harbor, you have to have plenty of money."

"What was the outcome?"

"Gordon Povey was fifty-two years old and looked very ill, according to the officer. He told our man that he had heart trouble and was taking much medication."

"That would be right," said Crozier. "He died shortly afterwards of a heart attack."

"*D'accord*," exclaimed Lasage. He pulled out a packet of Gauloise cigarettes and offered one to Crozier.

"No thanks," said Crozier. "But did he know anything about his son Kevin?"

"Not according to this." Lasage dropped ash on to the open file and brushed it off, leaving a smudge on the page. "He said that he had not seen him for some years, and that even when he and his wife…" He paused and looked up. "That is Gordon Povey and his wife. Even when they were in England, they did not see him. The detective said that they did not seem to know about the murder and were visibly upset…" He paused again. "That is the right expression, Ron?"

Crozier laughed. "I should think it probably is," he said.

"Mrs Povey began to cry when she heard the news and the officer said that they started arguing, but that they were speaking so fast that he didn't understand what they were saying. He seemed to think that Mrs Povey was blaming her husband for what had happened to their son."

"Did the officer ask them how long exactly it was since they had last seen their son?"

"Yes." Lasage glanced at the file again. "They merely said two or three years."

"We have been told that Gordon Povey was a diamond merchant. Is that confirmed?"

Again, Lasage looked at the file and eventually nodded. "Yes, that is so. But he had retired two years before because of his ill health."

"And that's about it, I suppose."

"That, as you say, Ron, is about it." Lasage closed the file with a gesture of finality. "Time for a glass of pastis, I think," he said, and stood up.

*

"Jack, have you had any luck with the Brighton police about Povey?" asked Fox.

"No, sir, not as yet." Gilroy had been confronted by Fox in the corridor outside his office. "I had a word with the local DC I down there and he was going to make some enquiries around the marina, but I somehow doubt that Povey's still in the area. Knowing that Mrs Carter frequently visited yachts, he'd have to be mad to stay there."

"Or cocky, Jack," said Fox. He straightened a notice about the Flying Squad dinner-dance that was pinned to the social activities board. "I hope that Lady Jane doesn't get to hear about that," he said.

"Too late, sir. The commander mentioned it to her at the senior officers' dinner the other night."

"Wonderful!" Fox looked displeased.

"She said that she would try to persuade you to take her, sir." Gilroy grinned.

"Is that so? Well, Jack, if the Brighton police don't come up with something about Povey, you and I might be down there that night. Making some local enquiries at the marina."

*

"How the hell did you spend this much?" Fox looked up from the expenses claim that Crozier had submitted on his return from France, a contrived look of horror on his face. "And all we got for that was what we knew already."

"I suppose we could have found that out by making a phone call, sir," said Crozier.

"Yes, we could," said Fox. "You should have thought of that." He signed the form and tossed it into his out-tray. "You used to be an actor, didn't you, Ron?"

"Yes, sir," said Crozier, sighing inwardly.

"Good. Got a little job for you. The story is this. You are a very rich man." Fox paused. "Well, you will be when that comes through." He waved a hand at the expenses form. "And you are seeking to insure your valuables. Trot down to Wimbledon and see this Ryan finger and tell him all about it. Make up some fanny about all this jewelery you've got, and your expensive car. Ryan advertises competitive rates for insurance, and I'm anxious to see what he comes up with. Mr Findlater has been making enquiries of the local VAT office and they seem to think that Ryan's existing on fresh air and little else. I suppose he's living on his wife's income. Apparently she's a departmental manageress at some big store in central London."

Sixteen

Detective Sergeant Crozier had done his homework. He had obtained from Henry Findlater details of the newspapers in which Jeremy Ryan had advertised his services, and had selected one that circulated in the Chelsea area. Armed with the newspaper, and a carefully prepared cover story, he visited the Wimbledon office of the insurance broker.

"Can I help you?" Ryan looked up from some papers that were spread out on his desk and gave Crozier a reassuring smile.

"I wanted to see Mr Ryan," said Crozier. He had examined the surveillance photographs that Findlater's team had taken of Ryan, but did not wish to appear too well informed about the man's identity.

"That is I," said Ryan. He stood up and shook hands. "Do take a seat, Mr...?"

"Crozier, Ronald Crozier." The detective looked around the office as though assessing the probity of its tenant.

"And what can I do for you, Mr Crozier?"

"I'm looking to insure my mother's flat," said Crozier. "But I'm astounded at the high rates of insurance these days."

"Ah, yes." Ryan shook his head sadly. "The rising crime rate, hurricanes, floods..." He reeled off a list of recent disasters. "All pushed the rates up, you know. But we do our best to find an underwriter who gives credit to those who take care. After all," he went on, warming to his subject, "why should you pay for the carelessness of others?"

"Absolutely," said Crozier, although he failed to understand how being the victim of a hurricane, for example, could be regarded as carelessness. "My mother has been living in France for the past ten years," he continued. "But now that she's into her seventies, she wants to move back here, and I think I've got her a flat in Chelsea."

"In Chelsea, eh?" Ryan nodded approvingly and tapped his teeth with his bail-point pen. "Problem with Chelsea," he said, "is that it's in a high crime area." He dropped the pen and, opening a drawer in his desk, took out a bulky folder. "However, we'll see what we can do." He drew a printed form towards him. "What's the address of this flat?"

Crozier gave Ryan details of a flat that was to let in a modern block in Chelsea, which he had found in the same paper as Ryan's advertisement. "It's not confirmed yet, of course. My mother still has to see it, but she's a widow and quite willing to leave all this business to me."

"She's very lucky to have a son who's so caring," said Ryan patronizingly. "Now, what sort of value are we talking about? Contents, that is."

Crozier looked thoughtful for a moment and then quoted a figure that would indicate a rather rich old lady. "And then there's her jewelery," he added.

"Oh!" Ryan glanced up sharply.

"Is that a problem?" asked Crozier innocently.

"Not a problem, but it does tend to push the rates up, depending on the value of the jewelery in question, of course."

Again, Crozier appeared to be thinking. "I suppose it must be about thirty thousand pounds," he said eventually. "But it might be more. I really ought to get her to have it valued. I've tried, several times, to persuade her to put it into a safety deposit box at the bank, but she won't hear of it."

"Always a difficult thing to do," said Ryan.

"What is?"

"Persuading elderly people not to keep their valuable possessions at home with them." Ryan sighed. "But there we are." He referred to the folder and, after punching a few figures into a calculator, scribbled an amount on a scrap of paper. "I think that's the best I could offer you, Mr Crozier," he said. "It's very difficult getting the rate down when a substantial amount of jewelery is involved, particularly in an area like Chelsea."

Crozier glanced at the figure that Ryan had written down. It was a good fifteen per cent above the rate that a detective sergeant on the Fraud Squad had obtained for him from a reputable underwriter. "It is a bit high," he said.

Ryan nodded understandingly. "I can only advise you to shop around, Mr Crozier," he said, standing up and holding out his hand. "I like to see clients getting the best deal, even if it is with another broker. But if you can't do any better, do come and see me again, or give me a ring. Obviously, we can't do anything until you can confirm that your mother's actually moved in, but once she has, I can offer immediate cover from that very moment." He made it sound as though he was doing Crozier a favor.

*

"I gather from the DAC on Eight Area that the Squad's virtually taken over this Proctor enquiry, Tommy." Commander Alec Myers gazed at Fox through a haze of cigarette smoke.

"Much of the enquiry is centerd here now, sir," admitted Fox reluctantly. He knew what was coming next.

"Apparently Jim Semple's been complaining that you've left him with nothing to do."

"First time anyone's ever said that about me, sir," said Fox, a look of regret on his face.

"Right then, that's it," said Myers. "I'll tell DAC Eight Area that he can release Semple and you can move the incident room here. How's the damned enquiry going, anyway?"

"We're getting there, sir," said Fox, by no means certain that that was the case. "But it's not really a job for the Squad."

"If that's a last-ditch attempt to shunt it back to Eight Area, you can forget it, Tommy," said Myers. "It's yours and you're stuck with it."

"It is rather holding up everything else."

"Simple answer to that," said Myers. "Solve the bloody thing."

*

"I'm going to take a chance on this one," said Fox to the assembled Flying Squad officers. Several of his audience quietly confided to each other that there was nothing new in that. "It's looking increasingly likely that the murders of Proctor and Skelton are down to Kevin Povey, who's also in the frame for the Shepperton houseboat job. Now we have another runner, namely Jeremy Ryan, self-professed insurance broker. I say self-professed because he doesn't seem to want any business. Ron Crozier went to see him yesterday on a fanny. Ron, you have the floor." Fox made a sweeping gesture to indicate that the detective sergeant should join him at the front of the room.

Crozier stood up. "The quote he gave me for my fictitious widowed mother's fictitious flat and fictitious jewelery," he began and received a few sarcastic comments, "was way above anything else on the market. A mate of mine on the Fraud Squad told me that I could have got a lower rate almost anywhere else. The obvious conclusions are that Ryan has set up this so-called business as a front simply to glean information about rich widows with a fair amount of tomfoolery. At a guess, I'd say that he passes that information on to the likes of the late Proctor and Skelton, and possibly even Povey, who then do the business. And I've no doubt that Ryan gets a cut of the profit once the gear's been unloaded on to a fence."

"Thank you, Ron," said Fox, resuming center stage as Crozier sat down again. "Anyone got any points?"

"Why don't we set up this flat that Ron propped to Ryan, guv'nor," said Percy Fletcher, "and see if we get a bite?"

"What, act as *agents provocateurs*, Perce?" said Fox. "What a positively disgraceful suggestion."

The audience dissolved into laughter and young Ted March asked his neighbor what the joke was.

"No, Perce, it would take too long, and it might not come off at all. Well, it might, but it would probably net the wrong fish. Povey must know he's in the frame for the Proctor and Skelton toppings, and he's probably lying low until the dust settles. We've wasted enough time on this already and I don't want to tie up a team staffing an empty flat in Chelsea, just to see if some smart Alec comes knocking at the door. Even if he did, he's only got to say that he's called at the wrong address and it's a blow-out. Our clever little friends in the Crown Prosecution Service would wet their pants if we suggested that that amounted to a conspiracy to commit murder and other nefarious offences." Fox's audience laughed again, long and loud.

"What's the plan then, sir?" asked Kate Ebdon.

"The plan, Kate," said Fox, smiling at the Australian detective, "is that we spin Mister Ryan's drum for him, and his office. Rattle him a bit and see what drops out. I've a feeling that he has one or two files in his possession that will tell us a lot."

*

It took forty minutes of persuasive argument in chambers before Fox was able to convince a circuit judge that his application for a warrant to search Ryan's office was justified. Even so, the judge was only just convinced and granted the warrant with a certain measure of reluctance.

"All this talk of people being murdered in taxi-cabs and on houseboats, and stolen jewelery arriving anonymously through the post, is all very well, Mr Fox," said the circuit judge, "but it seems to me that you're embarking on a fishing expedition and that you don't really have any evidence with which to charge this man Ryan."

"Good heavens, Your Honor," said Fox, "No thought was further from my mind. The facts of the matter—"

"Ah, some facts, at last," said the judge mildly.

"The facts, Your Honor, are that the man Ryan purports to trade as a broker offering competitive rates of insurance. It would appear, however, that he has no intention of selling a policy, but has merely set himself up for the purpose of gleaning information about those better-off members of our community who are naive enough to consult him, with a view, subsequently, to robbing them of their hard-earned possessions."

"Yes, yes, you've said all that several times, Mr Fox, but how do you know this?"

"One of my officers, a Detective Sergeant Ronald Crozier..." Fox leaned across the desk and prodded one of the sheets of paper that were spread out in front of the judge. "His statement is there, Your Honor. Crozier visited Ryan on the pretext of seeking insurance cover. The quote he was given was about fifteen per cent above the going rate, a clear indication in my view that Ryan has no intention of selling insurance."

"But that is speculative—" began the judge.

"And furthermore," Fox went on hurriedly, "I am reliably informed that VAT officers visited Ryan's office and found that he appears not to have made sufficient money even to pay the rent."

"And how do you know that?"

"Information received, Your Honor," said Fox vaguely.

"Mmm!" The judge toyed with the papers. "And how long has he been trading, Mr Fox?"

"Approximately three years, Your Honor," said Fox, and then put in the poison. "In fact, since the date of his last conviction."

The judge smiled blandly. "You shouldn't have mentioned that really, Mr Fox, but now that you have, perhaps you should tell me about it."

"He was convicted of stealing documents from an insurance broker for whom he worked, briefly. Two of the documents were records of policies issued to widows, one in Chiswick, the other in Earls Court, who were subsequently relieved of jewelery to the collective value of one hundred thousand pounds."

"I see," said the judge, and unscrewed the cap of his fountain pen.

*

Most detective chief superintendents would have assigned a detective inspector to carry out the search of Ryan's office, but Fox did not count himself among the majority of his colleagues. Consequently, he decided to join Jack Gilroy, DS Crozier, and DCs Bellenger and Tarling in their examination of the insurance broker's dubious business.

"Good morning," said Fox, as he pushed open Ryan's door.

"Good morning to you, sir," said Ryan, rising from behind his desk and flashing a confident smile at his visitor. But the smile changed to a look of concern as the remaining members of Fox's team followed him in. "Er, what exactly...?" he began and then caught sight of Crozier. "Oh, it's Mr Crozier." He gave the detective a puzzled glance.

"Detective Sergeant Crozier as a matter of fact," said Crozier and grinned as the broker's jaw dropped.

"My colleagues and I have a warrant to search these premises," said Fox, casting an interested gaze around the small office, "but it looks as though there are too many of us. Never mind, we'll take it in turns."

"What's this all about?" asked Ryan, doing his best to put a brave face on the sudden arrival of the police.

"What this is about, Mr Ryan," said Fox, "is that we have been granted a search warrant by a circuit judge who shares my apprehension about your business and the reasons for its existence."

"Who are you then?"

Fox smiled. "I am Detective Chief Superintendent Thomas Fox... of the Flying Squad," he said.

"But I don't understand," said Ryan, still attempting to maintain an air of injured innocence.

"Don't worry, Mr Ryan, we'll explain it all as we go along." Fox turned to Gilroy. "Right, Jack, see what you can find."

"Just a minute," said Ryan. "Can I see this warrant?"

"Of course." Fox held out his hand and waited until Sean Tarling had produced the document from his pocket. "There you are, Mr Ryan. Impressive, isn't it?"

"But I still don't understand." Ryan sank down into his chair and shook his head.

Fox turned to Crozier. "See what you can do with that, Ron," he said, pointing to Ryan's personal computer. "Not that I think Mr Ryan's likely to have recorded anything incriminating on it."

Sean Tarling opened the bottom drawer of the office's sole filing cabinet and took out a locked deed box. "You got the key for this?" he asked Ryan.

"You don't really want to see in that, do you?" asked Ryan. "It's only personal stuff. Letters I don't want my wife to see." He winked. "Know what I mean?"

Tarling leaned threateningly over the broker and glared at him. "Hand it over, mister," he said in his rich Irish brogue, "unless you want me to strip-search you."

Ryan gulped and put his hand in his trouser pocket. "It's that one," he said, singling out a small key from the ring he handed Tarling.

The detective put the box on the desk and unlocked it. Inside were about seven or eight files unlike any of the others that the police had found in Ryan's office. He riffled through them quickly and then turned to Fox. "These might be of interest, guv," he said.

"Yes, they might indeed," said Fox. "Pop down to the nick and make a few phone calls. You know what we're looking for, don't you?"

"I reckon so, sir," said Tarling with a broad grin and raced away to the police station. By the time he returned, the remainder of the team had finished their search and were waiting for him before leaving.

"Well?" Fox stood up and raised an eyebrow.

"Have a word, sir?" said Tarling. "Outside."

"What have you got, Sean?" asked Fox when they were at the bottom of the stairs by the street door.

"Out of the eight names and addresses on these files, sir, three have been the victims of theft of jewelery in the last year or so. Same MO as those we've already looked at, or so it seems. Inexplicable burglaries with no sign of forcible entry."

"What an extraordinary coincidence," said Fox and retraced his steps to the office on the first floor.

By now, Ryan had recovered much of his composure.

He had sensed that the police had found nothing incriminating, but then he did not know what they were looking for. "Satisfied?" he asked truculently as Fox entered the office.

"I am now," said Fox. "Mr Ryan, I am arresting you for conspiring with others to steal jewelery. Anything you say will be given in evidence."

"What on earth are you talking about?" Ryan stood up, an anguished expression on his face. "I don't know anything about any jewelery." He pushed his hands into his trouser pockets and stared at the group of police officers. "I warn you," he said. "I'm going to sue you for every penny you've got."

"It's actually every penny that the Commissioner's got," said Fox. "You see, he trusts me implicitly and he always pays my bills if anything goes wrong. However, on this occasion you may find that this is regarded as an Act of God. I should read the small print, if I were you." And with that he turned to Gilroy. "Show Mr Ryan to the car, Jack, there's a good fellow."

"Which nick, sir?" asked Gilroy.

"Charing Cross, of course, Jack. I've always found that at this time of year Wimbledon nick tends to get full up with bustle-punching clergymen who have tired of watching the tennis."

Seventeen

Fox had been driven to Charing Cross police station in his own car and he had detailed Crozier and Tarling to escort Ryan. Since his brief exchange with Tarling, Ryan had been apprehensive of the brash Irish detective, and the journey was completed in total silence.

At the police station, the custody sergeant had filled in the plethora of forms that result from an arrest and then placed Ryan in one of the interview rooms.

His salesman's bonhomie abandoned, Ryan had become surly. He had been arrested once before and even though his appearance at court had resulted in his being placed on probation, it was not an experience he wished to repeat. "I want to know what this is all about—" he began.

"So do I," said Fox with a disarming smile as he sat down and lit a cigarette. "Perhaps you'll tell me."

"I've got nothing to say."

"Oh dear," said Fox, "I've just lost my bet."

"What?" Ryan looked puzzled by the detective chief superintendent's comment.

"I bet Mr Gilroy here that your very first utterance would be a demand for a solicitor."

"What do I need a solicitor for? I've done nothing wrong."

"How original," said Fox. "But, Jeremy, old fruit, what about these?" He produced the eight files that had been taken from Ryan's deed box, and spread them on the table.

"What about them?"

"You didn't insure any of these people, did you?"

"That's not a crime, is it?" asked Ryan with a sneer. "A lot of people consult me but don't take out policies."

"I've noticed that," said Fox. "Rather strange, isn't it?"

"Happens all the time," said Ryan.

"Then why did you keep these files and lock them in a box that you were disinclined to allow us to see?" Fox smiled benignly at the bogus insurance broker.

"I keep lots of files about people who never took out policies."

"Yes, but they were in the ordinary filing cabinet in your office, and they were indexed on your computer. But these weren't." Fox indicated the eight files with a sweep of his hand.

Ryan hesitated as his brain searched furiously for a convincing excuse. "They had details of substantial amounts of clients' jewelery," he said. "Not the sort of thing to leave lying around the office."

"But they weren't clients, Jeremy, old thing. On your own admission, none of these people took out a policy, so why not destroy the files? Much safer even than keeping them in your deed box."

"I'd forgotten they were there," said Ryan churlishly. "I'd been meaning to have a clear out, as a matter of fact."

Fox grinned. "What a shame you hadn't done so before we arrived," he said. "It's now much more difficult for you, isn't it?"

"What d'you mean?"

"What I mean, Jeremy, is that of these eight clients – or non-clients, I suppose you'd call them – three have lost the substantial amounts of jewelery which you've recorded."

"Just as well I didn't arrange for them to be underwritten then, isn't it?" snapped Ryan.

"When you worked for the broker in Chelsea..." Fox changed the subject with a swiftness that alarmed Ryan, "And were nicked for thieving some documents—"

"That was all a mistake."

Fox ignored the interruption. "Two of the documents which you nicked related to widows in Chiswick and Earls Court respectively." He stubbed out his cigarette and leaned back in his chair. "And would you believe, they both had jewelery stolen. They were quite substantial amounts too. About one hundred K to be precise."

"What's that got to do with me?" Ryan was unhappy at the direction the questioning was taking, and he began to realize that this sarcastic detective opposite him appeared to be well informed.

"I don't like coincidences," said Fox and glanced at Gilroy. "That's a well-known fact among the criminal fraternity, isn't it, Jack?"

Gilroy nodded gravely. "It is indeed, sir," he said.

Fox returned his gaze to Ryan. "And I began to wonder how it was that a total of five rich widows, all of whom had files which you either held at your office, or which you saw during your brief period of employment at Chelsea, should all have had their sparklers nicked. Funny business, isn't it, Jeremy, dear boy?"

"You can't prove anything."

"That's a pious hope," said Fox mildly. "I'm very good at proving things. You ask around when they bang you up in the Scrubs, or wherever else Her Majesty is pleased to have you sent."

Ryan did not like the sound of that. "I want a solicitor," he said.

"Ah!" said Fox. "I thought you said you'd done nothing wrong."

"I haven't," said Ryan, "but you're trying to stitch me up."

Fox scoffed. "Stitch you up?" he said. "I haven't even begun yet." He leaned forward confidentially. "What I really wanted to talk to you about, Jeremy, are the murders of Wally Proctor and Robin Skelton."

Ryan's face paled quite dramatically. He somehow knew that the police would get around to that eventually. "I've never heard of them," he said.

Fox nodded, a serious expression on his face. "I see," he said. "D'you mean to tell me that you don't read a newspaper or watch the television news, Jeremy?"

"Sometimes."

"And you know nothing about the man who was murdered in a cab at Hyde Park Corner?"

"Oh that!" Ryan sounded unconvincing. "Yes, I saw something about that."

"Well, there we are then." Fox brushed lightly at his sleeve. "Now I know that you passed information to both Proctor and Skelton about rich ladies who had unwisely responded to your advertisements and innocently told you all about their jewelery. And Messrs Proctor and Skelton later paid you for that information." It was a guess, but Fox was certain that it was not too wild a guess.

"Rubbish!" responded Ryan.

"But that doesn't interest me too much, Jeremy, because I have much greater worries than that."

"So?"

"Let me outline my theory to you, if you've got a minute to spare, that is. You had been feeding these two icemen with this very useful information, without which, I may say, they would have been unable to steal all this lovely jewelery—"

"That's a pack of lies," said Ryan.

"No, no, do let me finish, Jeremy. But you suddenly decided that they weren't paying you enough for all your hard work. So you decided to murder them." Fox sat back and smiled.

"You're bloody mad," said Ryan, jerking upright in his chair. "I didn't kill anyone. For Christ's sake, d'you think I'm crazy or something?"

"Well, if you didn't, who did?"

"How the hell do I know?" Ryan's face was working with anguish now.

"How about Kevin Povey?"

"Who?"

"Oh, don't ponce about, Jeremy," said Fox. "You know perfectly well who I'm talking about."

"I've never heard of him."

Fox appeared to mull over this piece of information for some time. Then he lit another cigarette. "Oh, I'm sorry, do you?" He pushed his cigarette case towards Ryan.

"No." Ryan shook his head.

"I find that very odd, you know," said Fox eventually.

"What, that I don't smoke?" asked Ryan sarcastically.

"No, that you've never heard of Kevin Povey."

"Well I haven't."

"D'you mean to say that Julie Lockhart's never mentioned his name?"

Ryan looked stunned. "What?" he muttered. "Who?"

"What an appalling memory you do have, Jeremy. Let me refresh it for you. Julie Lockhart, *nee* Strange, is the dentist's wife who lives at Barnes, and you, old son, take advantage of his absence to give her a seeing to. And she was the woman who witnessed the murder of one Jason Bright on a houseboat at Shepperton about five years ago by a man police firmly believe to be Kevin Povey. Do you still say she hasn't mentioned the incident to you?"

"How d'you know all this?"

"Because, Jeremy, two of my officers were interviewing Mrs Lockhart when you made an unheralded appearance in her sitting room, wearing nothing more than a dressing gown. Furthermore you were seen warmly greeting Mrs Lockhart, who at the time was wearing next to nothing, shortly after her husband had departed for Amsterdam a few days ago."

"Have you been following me?" Ryan leaned forward, an expression of fury on his face.

"My word, you do catch on fast," said Fox. "But I repeat the question. Did Mrs Lockhart not mention Kevin Povey to you?"

"No," said Ryan and slumped back in his chair.

Fox turned to face Gilroy. "I think we'd better send Sergeant Webster down to Barnes again, Jack," he said. "Get her to ask Mrs Lockhart if she's ever mentioned Kevin Povey to our Mr Ryan here. And while she's at it, tell her to pop in and see Peter Lockhart, explain the situation and ask him if he's ever met Mr Ryan and whether he's heard of Kevin Povey." He turned back to Ryan. "Now, where were we?" he asked.

"All right, all right," said Ryan. "So she did mention him, but that's all. I never met the guy."

"Oh well, that resolves that," said Fox and stood up. "Oh, one other thing. When were you last in Maidstone?"

"Maidstone? I've never been to Maidstone in my life," said Ryan.

"Good. You can go then."

"Go?"

"Yes," said Fox. "Why not? I shall admit you to bail to return to this police station in twenty-eight days' time. Unless, in the meantime, you hear from us that your attendance is not required." He waved a hand airily in the direction of the door. "The sergeant will deal with all the paperwork. Bit like the insurance business, really. Everything has to be written down."

"Can I have my files back?" asked Ryan, pointing at the documents still spread on the table.

"Don't push your luck," said Fox.

"Was that a wise move, sir?" asked Gilroy, once Ryan had left the station.

"No option really, Jack." Fox stacked the files into a neat pile and handed them to Gilroy. "That's pretty flimsy stuff to base a charge on, much less to get a remand in custody."

"Are you just going to let him go then, guv'nor?"

"Not quite, Jack. Henry Findlater and his merry men were waiting outside the nick for Ryan's departure. Just to see what he does next."

"Couldn't we get an intercept put on his phone, sir?"

"For a dodgy conspiracy to steal, Jack? There's no chance that the Home Secretary would grant a warrant for that. Not unless we could prove that some MP'd had his tomfoolery lifted."

*

Lady Jane Sims had announced her intention of going shopping in the West End and she had asked Fox if he would go with her. "You're very good at picking clothes for me, Tommy," she had said.

"I can't just knock off to go shopping with you," Fox had said. "But I will meet you for lunch."

Now, at just past one o'clock, Fox and Jane were seated in an Italian restaurant within handy distance of Scotland Yard.

"It's a shame you couldn't come with me this morning," said Jane. "I wanted your advice."

"What about?"

"I've bought a new dress for the dinner-dance."

"What dinner-dance?" Fox furrowed his brow but, deep down, he knew.

"The Flying Squad one that Alec told me about."

"Alec Myers?" asked Fox with a pretence at innocence. Jack Gilroy had mentioned that Myers had told Jane all about the forthcoming function and Fox had sworn to himself that he would have words with his commander.

"Yes, of course. You will take me, Tommy, won't you?" Jane leaned forward, a pleading look on her face, and placed her hand over Fox's.

"I'd love to, Jane," Fox lied, "but it's very difficult to make firm arrangements when I've got so much on."

Fox detested the annual dinner-dance and had only attended it in previous years because he was the operational head of the Squad. And each year, he had taken a different partner, although there had never been any romantic attachment. But he had known Jane Sims for almost a year now, longer than any of his previous women friends, and felt disinclined to expose her to the sometimes bawdy environment of detectives at play.

But Jane was not going to accept a refusal without a fight. "When I first met you, Tommy, you said that I should never let work interfere with my social life. And, what's more, you said that you never did."

"But I've got two murders on my plate, Jane." Work had never stopped Fox enjoying himself before, but he was searching, lamely, for excuses.

"You had a murder on your plate then. My sister." Jane Sims looked sad as she recalled the reason for their meeting and wished she had not mentioned it. It was unfair.

"All right then." Fox capitulated. Although he was a hard-nosed detective, and scourge of London's villainy, he realized that he was fast reaching the point where he would happily give in to the woman opposite him. But he still wasn't sure whether he liked the idea of the permanent relationship that seemed to be developing. "But it'll be nothing like the hunt ball, you know," he said.

"I should bloody well hope not," said Jane and smiled.

*

"You remember Mrs Carter saying that she couldn't recall the name of the yacht that she had delivered cleats to, sir..."

"What the hell are you on about, Jack?" asked Fox Gilroy sighed inwardly. It was rare for Fox to forget anything, but he was quite often in a perverse mood. "Mrs Elaine Carter," he began patiently, "had her jewelery spirited away by Kevin Povey, calling himself Don Fortune."

"Yes, I know," said Fox.

"And she met him when she delivered some cleats to his yacht, or the yacht he was crewing on."

"Where's all this leading, Jack?" asked Fox with a tired voice.

"I decided to ring the yacht chandlers she worked for, sir, to see if they could trace the order—"

"And?" Fox suddenly looked interested.

"They found it, sir. The yacht's called *Windsong*."

"How original," said Fox. "There must be dozens of yachts called *Windsong*."

"There are, sir, but it was the name of the yacht which Gordon Povey owned and which was moored in Cannes harbor when the French police interviewed the Poveys following the murder of Jason Bright."

"Is that it?"

"Not quite," said Gilroy. "There is no central yacht register, but I made some enquiries in the yachting world through a mate of mine in Special Branch—"

Fox sniffed. "Wonderful," he said.

"And he was able to track down the *Windsong* that was owned by Gordon Povey."

"Was he now?" said Fox. "I take back that sniff about SB," he added with a grin. "What can you tell me about it? Where is it, for instance?"

"I'm waiting further particulars, sir, but I can tell you where the yacht is not."

"Oh?"

"It's not in Brighton Marina, sir. Not any more."

"Jack," said Fox, "you never cease to amaze me."

"I thought..." began Gilroy tentatively.

"Well, that's a start," muttered Fox.

"I thought that you might like to have a word with the navy, sir."

"Why should I want to talk to the navy, Jack?"

"Perhaps they could be persuaded to keep watch for it, sir. Let us know if they sight it. Their Provost Marshal is a lieutenant-commander, name of—"

"A lieutenant-commander?" Fox looked horrified at the suggestion. "I shall speak to an admiral, at the very least. What's the telephone number of the navy, Jack?"

Eighteen

"Did you manage to get hold of an admiral, sir?" asked Gilroy.

"Didn't bother eventually, Jack," said Fox. "I came to the conclusion that if their top brass is anything like ours, I'd've been wasting my time. So I spoke to a commander – one of theirs, not one of ours – who seemed to understand what I wanted."

The truth of the matter was that Fox had been unable to find his way through the labyrinthine Ministry of Defence switchboard. After a frustrating twenty minutes, he had eventually taken advice from a sergeant in the Murder Office who put him in touch with the naval officer who acted as liaison between the police and the Royal Navy. "The situation now is that *Windsong* is on the navy's list and any sightings they make will be reported to me. With any luck, we'll capture this bastard before he's very much older."

*

Jane Sims was already dressed when Fox arrived to take her to the Flying Squad dinner-dance. "I've poured you a Scotch," she said as they entered the sitting room of her Knightsbridge flat.

Ignoring the whisky for a moment, Fox kissed her warmly and then held her at arm's length. "Let's have a proper look at you then," he said.

Jane broke free, took a step back and turned round slowly. The halter neckline of her emerald green dress flattered her shoulders and emphasized her long neck. And the full, calf-length skirt showed off to advantage her slender, dark-stockinged ankles. Fox's sharp detective's eye recognized that the black velvet high-heeled shoes were those she had worn to the Squad dinner.

"Well?" Jane spoke quietly, holding her head on one side. As she moved, the light caught her diamond loop earrings.

Fox nodded approvingly. "My God, you scrub up well," he said with a grin.

Jane wrinkled her nose at him. "I suppose, coming from you, that's a compliment indeed," she said.

Fox took a sip of whisky. "No, seriously, you look great," he said moving closer to her and taking her left hand. "They are real diamonds then," he said, as he examined Jane's wrist-watch.

"D'you know," said Jane, "For one moment, I thought you were going to kiss me again."

Fox gave the girl a perfunctory peck on the cheek and then fingered one of her earrings with his free hand.

"Have you got an ear fetish or something, Tommy?" asked Jane, quite brusquely.

"Not particularly," said Fox, failing to sense her sudden hauteur. "I was checking the ice."

"The ice?" Jane looked confused. "What on earth are you talking about now?"

"Diamonds are known as ice in the trade," said Fox, stepping back and relinquishing his hold of her hand.

"Oh, I see. Well, thank you for adding to my criminal vocabulary." There was still a tiny element of sarcastic hostility in Jane's voice that Fox should bring his work into their personal life yet again. "Yes, they're diamonds all right. An eighteenth birthday present from Daddy."

Fox nodded slowly and thoughtfully. "Got much of it, have you?" he asked. "Jewelery, I mean."

"A fair amount."

"Where d'you keep it? Not here, I hope."

"Of course not," said Jane tersely. "Do give me some credit, Tommy. There've been far too many burglaries in this area for me to keep it at home. Most of it's in a safety deposit box at the bank. I keep one or two small items here, those I'm wearing this evening, for instance. But why all the questions?"

"I've had an idea," said Fox mysteriously and placed his empty glass on a side table. "Shall we go?"

"I suppose so," said Jane. Suddenly her earlier delight at the prospect of an evening's dancing seemed to have dissipated.

Since the senior officers' dinner, word had spread down through the ranks of the Flying Squad that Fox had found himself a girlfriend who was not only an absolute stunner, but an earl's daughter as well. The less prurient of Fox's subordinates suggested that his motive was financial, believing, in their naivete, that a title was automatically accompanied by great wealth. Whatever else his friendship with Lady Jane Sims had achieved, it had certainly resulted in an increase in the sale of tickets for the dinner-dance. Wives and girlfriends did not intend to pass up the chance of meeting someone whom several of them had described as "A lady in her own right".

Fox's table was in the center of the room opposite the band, and because he was head of the Squad, he was obliged, as a matter of duty, to share it with the Commissioner, the Assistant Commissioner, the DAC, and Commander Myers and their respective wives. Fox groaned inwardly as he acknowledged his dinner companions and accepted that the company, combined with Jane's inexplicable coolness, meant that it was not going to be a good evening. He almost hoped that an officer would rush in, in about ten minutes' time, to tell him that Povey had been arrested. But then, looking around the ballroom, he decided that he would rather not leave Jane to the mercies of this bunch of likeable hooligans who were called the Flying Squad.

*

The dinner-dance had finished at two o'clock in the morning, and Fox had accepted Jane's invitation to stay at her flat for what remained of the night. As a consequence, when he arrived at the Yard early the next day he was still wearing his dinner jacket – an occurrence which evinced no surprise whatever from his staff – and was not in the best of moods.

Detective Inspector Gilroy was waiting in his office. "Good morning, sir," he said.

"Matter of opinion," growled Fox as he began to change into the spare lounge suit which he always kept in his wardrobe at the Yard.

"Did Lady Guv enjoy herself, sir?"

"I don't know where she gets her stamina from, Jack," said Fox. "I think she'd have gone on all night, given the chance." He walked across the office to the door with the intention of bellowing for coffee just as his secretary entered with two cups on a tray.

"Thought you and Mr Gilroy might need some coffee, Mr Fox," said the woman, a whimsical smile on her face.

"Too right," said Fox and sat down behind his desk. "Well, Jack, I'm sure you haven't just dropped in to see how I'm feeling this morning."

"No, sir, we've had a signal from the Ministry of Defence about *Windsong*."

"What about it?"

"She was sighted in the English Channel about twenty miles north of Alderney at six-thirty this morning, proceeding westwards. It was seen by a naval helicopter from Culdrose apparently."

"Splendid," said Fox enthusiastically, his tiredness and his hangover forgotten. "So what's happening, Jack?"

"The navy are quite keen about it apparently, sir. They're awaiting your further instructions. Seems they're prepared to send a fast patrol boat from Portsmouth to intercept, if that's what you want."

"Too true it's what I want, Jack." Fox stood up and rubbed his hands together. "How long will it take us to get to Portsmouth?"

Gilroy looked horrified. Despite his apparent vitality, he too was feeling the effects of a late night and too much alcohol, and had hoped to get to bed early. "A good three hours, I should think, sir."

"Rubbish, Jack. Get hold of India Nine Nine. Be down there in no time at all in a chopper. Give the lads a day out, won't it?"

Gilroy yawned and stood up. "I'll get on to Lippitts Hill, sir," he said listlessly. Lippitts Hill, on the edge of Epping Forest, was where the Metropolitan Police based its helicopters.

"Yes, do that, Jack, and get hold of Swann. Tell him to stand by to take us to Battersea Heliport. That's where they'll be able to pick us up, I should think." Fox rubbed his hands together. "I can't wait to lay hands on Master Kevin Povey," he said.

*

The police helicopter touched down at Portsmouth Dockyard and a waiting car whisked Fox and Gilroy straight to the Royal Navy patrol boat which was standing by, ready for sea. Within minutes they were forging past Spithead and out into the Solent.

"Our latest information," said the young lieutenant who commanded the vessel, "is that *Windsong* is now about thirty miles south-west of Start Point, and under sail."

"Well, it would be, wouldn't it?" asked Fox, gripping the bridge rail.

"I mean she's not under power. She's not using engines." "Any sign of the crew?"

The lieutenant grinned. "The helicopter pilot reported sighting a young woman in half a bikini at the helm. Apparently, he circled two or three times just to make sure."

148

"Any reaction?" asked Fox.

"Yes, she waved."

"Any sign of a man on board?"

"Yes. One. The chopper pilot saw him come up on deck with a mug. He gave it to the girl and then went below again."

"Excellent," said Fox. "If only he knew."

The sea was calm and the sun high, and as the morning wore on, so it became hotter. Fox felt a little out of place wearing his dark suit, and regretted not having had time to collect his Herbert Johnson panama hat from his flat.

About an hour after the patrol boat had left Portsmouth, a signals rating appeared on the bridge with a message flimsy. The lieutenant glanced at it and handed it back to the seaman. "She's turned, apparently, and is making her way back towards us."

"Why should she be doing that?" asked Fox.

"God knows. Something to do with the wind, perhaps. I know I'm in the Royal Navy, but I don't know too much about sail." The lieutenant grinned. "Much prefer having a few powerful diesel horses under me," he added, and tapped the compass housing with the flat of his hand.

"Any idea where she might be making for?"

"No," said the lieutenant. "Your guess is as good as mine. Channel Islands maybe." He shrugged. "But the chopper will let us know if she changes course again."

"I hope this helicopter pilot of yours doesn't make himself too obvious," said Fox. "Don't want him to give the game away."

The lieutenant grinned. "Doesn't matter," he said. "*Windsong*'s not going anywhere where we can't intercept her. Your man might get away from you on land, but he can't escape the Royal Navy out here, you know." He glanced round. "Where's your inspector gone?"

"Downstairs," said Fox. "He's not feeling too well."

The lieutenant groaned. "I take it you mean that he's gone below," he said.

An hour later, the naval patrol boat encountered a stiff breeze and the white-capped waves began to look quite formidable. The lieutenant nodded sagely. "Forecast was right for once," he said. "They said that we might run into some heavier weather. Probably why *Windsong* turned. I should think she's crewed by a couple of amateurs." He laughed. "Might even finish up rescuing them."

But the choppy seas proved to be but a freak area and within forty minutes or so, the vessel was in calmer waters once more.

"Ah!" said the lieutenant, grabbing his binoculars, "I think that could be her." For a few moments, he concentrated his attention ahead.

"Is it her?" asked Fox, who could see nothing with the naked eye.

"Reckon so." The lieutenant handed Fox the binoculars. "Have a look for yourself."

Fox adjusted the glasses and peered through them. The yacht was approaching them under full sail, and now there were two people in the cockpit, a man and a woman. The man was stripped to the waist and, as the helicopter pilot had said, the woman was wearing half a bikini.

"Can we board her?" asked Fox.

"Too true we can," said the young lieutenant and, as they drew nearer, picked up a loud-hailer. "*Windsong*, this is the Royal Navy. Be so good as to heave to, please." And turning to the quartermaster, he issued a string of orders.

Within minutes, the naval patrol boat was alongside the yacht. "Is this bloke likely to be dangerous?" the naval officer asked Fox.

"If he's who I think he is, he's probably committed three murders," said Fox mildly.

"Jesus Christ!" said the lieutenant. "In that case, I'll just pick up my revolver. And we'll take a seaman with us."

"With a belaying pin?" asked Fox.

The lieutenant grinned. "You've been reading too much Hornblower," he said. "You going to bring your inspector with you?"

"No," said Fox. "Let him sleep it off, or whatever he's doing downstairs."

The young couple on the yacht looked thoroughly bemused as an armed naval officer and a tall well-dressed civilian swung aboard their craft accompanied by a stern-looking bearded seaman.

"Good afternoon." The lieutenant addressed the man and shot a quick glance in the girl's direction, disappointed to see that she had now donned the top half of her bikini. The man was about thirty, his girlfriend a few years younger. "This gentleman is from the police," said the naval officer, indicating Fox.

Fox knew instantly that the man facing him was not Kevin Povey. Although the only photograph the police had of Povey was at least five years old, there was no way that the yachtsman could have been the wanted man. Nevertheless, the yacht was called *Windsong*.

"I'm Detective Chief Superintendent Thomas Fox... of the Flying Squad," said Fox. "Who are you?"

"Geoffrey Cooper," said the man, holding out his hand. "And this is Sally Hughes." The girl in the bikini smiled.

"Are you the owner of this yacht?" asked Fox.

"Yes, of course. But what's this all about?"

"Have you owned it long?"

"About five years, I suppose. Why?"

"We have reason to believe that it was used, earlier this year, by a man called Kevin Povey who is wanted for questioning by the police," said Fox, holding on to a stanchion rail to steady himself against the slight swell. "Does that name mean anything to you, Mr Cooper?"

"Not a thing," said Cooper. "Never heard of him. And no one else has been aboard her, apart from friends of ours." He grinned at his girlfriend. "Must say this is all rather exciting, isn't it, old girl?"

"Yah!" said the girl and smiled again.

"Well, if that's it, you'd better come below and have a drink," said Cooper.

"No thanks," said Fox. "Tell me, Mr Cooper, was this yacht recently in Brighton Marina?"

"Good God no," said Cooper. He seemed offended by the suggestion. "We moor on the Hamble. Bloody expensive, mind you, but there you are."

"Would you mind telling me who you bought the yacht from then?" Fox was still unhappy, and he did not much care for Cooper or his Sloanish girlfriend.

Cooper ran his hand through his hair. "Ah, now you're asking," he said. "Damned if I can remember." He glanced at Sally Hughes. "Don't s'pose you can remember, old girl, can you?"

"Hardly likely," said Sally drily. "You were sleeping with that awful Virginia person at the time. I've only been your chief mate for a year. Or had you forgotten?"

Cooper laughed. "Yes, of course." He turned to Fox again and grimaced. "Bit of an own goal, what?"

Fox glanced at the naval officer who, throughout the exchange, had remained silent, but had been unashamedly examining Sally Hughes's figure. "Is there any way of checking previous ownership of this yacht?" he asked.

"Probably," said the lieutenant, "but none that I know of. I daresay it could be done through Lloyds or some organization like that. Not really my scene, I'm afraid."

"Look, old boy," said Cooper, "I'm not trying to be obstructive or anything like that, but I honestly can't recall the name of the woman I bought her from. Tell you what, though, if you let me have your number, I'll give you a ring the moment I get back to the Hamble and have a chance to look through my papers. Incidentally, *Windsong*'s a pretty common name for a yacht. In fact there are probably dozens of them about. Could be another one of the same name, eh?"

And Fox had to be satisfied with that. After apologizing for delaying Cooper and his girlfriend, Fox, the lieutenant and his seaman boarded their patrol boat again and headed home for Portsmouth.

By nine o'clock that evening, Fox and Gilroy were back at Scotland Yard.

"The next time you get a signal from the bloody navy, Jack," said Fox, staring gloomily into his empty whisky glass, "ask them to check the names of the crew before they ring us, will you?"

"Yes, sir." Gilroy had lost interest in the whole proceedings. He was not a good sailor at the best of times, and going to sea immediately after a late and somewhat alcoholic evening was not exactly his idea of fun. "I think I'll push off, sir, if that's it for today," he said.

"I was going for a quick pint at the Star, Jack," said Fox. "Fancy one, or are you going to finish early tonight?"

Gilroy glanced at the clock. It was twenty-five to ten. "I think I'll finish early tonight, guv'nor," he said. "If you don't mind."

Nineteen

Fox stood back to allow the Assistant Commissioner to enter the revolving doors of New Scotland Yard. But once inside, Pcter Frobisher paused. "Very good do the other night, Mr Fox," he said in his carefully cultivated drawl. "Thoroughly enjoyed it, and I must say that Lady Jane Sims is a charming girl."

"Yes, she is, sir," said Fox curtly. "I'm not sure that she enjoyed herself too much, though. Hardly her scene, coppers at play, is it? All a bit working class by her standards, I should think." He despised the Assistant Commissioner, and his superior attitude, and did not like being patronized.

"Well, she told me how much she liked the company." The Assistant Commissioner entered the lift and pressed the buttons for the second and fifth floors.

"She would, sir," said Fox. "She's very polite. It's the upper-class breeding, I suppose."

"Yes," said Frobisher. "I suppose so. She did have one tiny complaint, though."

"Oh?" The lift reached the second floor and Fox stepped out, holding the doors open.

Frobisher laughed. "She said that you were always talking shop. Still, my lady wife says the same thing. It's a failing among policemen."

Having been put in a bad mood by the Assistant Commissioner, Fox was not pleased to be confronted by his commander, Alec Myers, as he was about to enter his office.

"Thinking of transferring to Thames Division, Tommy?" asked Myers, a broad grin on his face.

"It was good information, sir," said Fox. "I can hardly be blamed for the bloody navy getting it wrong."

Myers laughed. "Well, I suppose it cleared your head after the dinner-dance. Incidentally, I think you ought to make it up with Lady Guv."

"Oh? Why?" Fox's eyes narrowed. He did not like the way that the Flying Squad had adopted Jane, and he did not much care for advice from senior officers about his personal life.

"She was having a bitch to my missus. Well, not a bitch really. She asked Daphne if policemen always talked about the job all the time. Said something about you giving her a crime prevention lecture just before you arrived."

"Really?" At last Fox began to understand Jane's coolness at the dinner-dance. "Well, I must get on, sir, if you'll excuse me."

"Of course, Tommy." Myers grinned. "I hope the Royal Navy isn't going to send us a bill for the use of one of its ships."

"They wouldn't dare," growled Fox.

Myers laughed and turned away. "Buy her roses, Tommy," he said over his shoulder as he walked away. "Never fails, believe me."

For some time, Fox sat at his desk, sifting moodily through the routine correspondence with which his in-tray had been overflowing. Then he reached for the telephone and tapped out Jane's number. "Jane?" he said, when she answered, "It's Tommy."

"Hallo." Jane sounded listless. "I tried ringing you yesterday. They said you'd gone to sea."

Fox laughed. "I had," he said. "But all in vain. Wrong boat. I'll tell you all about it when I see you."

"Thought you might," said Jane. She did not sound enthusiastic about the idea.

Fox realized that he had made the mistake of talking about his job again. "Are you free for lunch?" he asked hurriedly.

There was a pause. "Well, I am pretty busy…" Jane paused again. "Oh yes, why not? I'm only working on some boring designs for a shopping precinct."

"Good. I'll pick you up at about twelve-thirty. All right?"

"Make it twelve and we can have a drink before we go."

At half-past eleven, Fox strode into the Squad office. "Meeting an informant," he said. "Back about three, I should think."

"Very good, sir," said the duty sergeant and, waiting until Fox had closed the door, turned to his colleague. "And I bet I know which informant," he said. "Lucky bastard."

*

154

Fox had taken a taxi to Knightsbridge and alighted at a florist. Purchasing a large bunch of long-stemmed roses at what he regarded to be an exorbitant price, he then, somewhat self-consciously, walked round the corner to Jane Sims's flat.

Jane's face lit up the moment she saw the flowers. "For me?" she asked.

Fox bit back a retort about their being for Jane's cleaning lady and merely said, "Yes."

"Oh, how lovely." Jane took the roses in her arms and, leaving Fox to close the front door, walked through to the kitchen. "Perhaps you'd pour us a drink," she called. For the next few minutes, she busied herself cutting stems and finding vases to accommodate the two dozen blooms.

Suddenly, Jane's sitting room seemed to be full of roses. They were on the table, the sideboard and on top of the television cabinet. She surveyed them and then turned to Fox. Flinging her arms around his neck, she kissed him passionately. "They're wonderful, darling," she said. "Thank you so much."

It was the first time that Jane had ever addressed him as "darling" and Fox was taken aback by her sudden ardor. "It's no big thing," he said, slightly embarrassed that she should be so overwhelmingly grateful. "As a matter of fact, I think I owe you an apology."

"Whatever for?"

"I got the distinct impression that I'd upset you the evening of the dinner-dance, by talking about the job. In particular, about your diamonds."

"Oh that!' Jane smiled. "I was a bit cross at the time," she said, "but I shouldn't have been. It must be very difficult for you to leave it all behind."

Fox shook his head. "No," he said. "I was well out of order." He grinned. "I'll try not to do it again. Promise."

"Forget all about it. I should be giving you support, not criticizing," said Jane. "I really don't mind if you want to talk about…" She paused. "What is it you policemen call it? The Job?"

"Yes."

Jane smiled and took a sip of her whisky. "Funny expression," she said. She nodded towards the armchair where Fox usually sat. "Why don't you sit down? We've got a few minutes, haven't we?"

Fox realized that he was about to destroy the happier atmosphere that had been created by his gift of roses, but he had been nursing an idea ever since Jane had told him about her jewelry. He decided to take a chance. "Jane..." he said tentatively.

"Yes?"

"Look, I've had an idea, but if you don't like the sound of it, I'll say no more about it."

"What is it?"

"Well, it's connected with the job..." Still Fox was uncertain whether to go on.

"For goodness' sake, don't be afraid of mentioning it, just because of what I said." Jane gave him a reassuring smile.

"Well, when you mentioned your jewelery the other night, it occurred to me that you might be able to help with this murder enquiry of mine."

"Really? How exciting. What d'you want me to do?"

Fox remained silent for some time, reluctant to involve Jane in police business. But then he explained to her how Proctor, Skelton, and latterly Povey, had been relieving vulnerable women of their jewelery. "I was wondering," he continued, "If you would be prepared to ring this Ryan chap down at Wimbledon and ask him for a quote. Tell him what you've got in the way of jewelery and let him know that you're divorced and living on your own."

"What's the point of that?" asked Jane.

"With any luck, he'll pass that information on to Povey, who will then think of some way of scraping your acquaintance with a view to relieving you of your sparklers." Fox grinned.

"Isn't that a bit risky?' Jane looked a little apprehensive.

"No," said Fox firmly. "If you agree, there will be two very tough detectives here all the time, and I'll have the outside covered day and night. It'll only be until he makes his first contact. After that, he'll be locked up. For about thirty years with any luck."

"And who are these two tough detectives who'll be with me all the time?"

"A detective sergeant called Rosie Webster and a DC called Kate Ebdon," said Fox, and was amused to see that Jane appeared marginally disappointed.

*

156

"Blimey, sir, have you gone mad?" It was not often that Gilroy displayed any real criticism of Fox's plans, even the more hare-brained of them, but on this occasion he could not contain himself. "Surely you'd be putting Lady Guv at an unacceptable risk."

"Not with you in charge of the operation, Jack," said Fox mildly.

"But what about the job, sir? Involving innocent civilians in an operation to trap a bloke we think is a triple murderer is against all the rules. What will the commander say?"

"He won't say anything, because no one is going to tell him, are they, Jack?" Fox fixed Gilroy with a steely stare.

"But d'you honestly think that Ryan's going to fall for that, after we turned over his office and then nicked him?"

"Of course he is, Jack." Fox drew his hand across his desktop in a sweeping motion. "Jeremy Ryan's too cocky by half. He walked out of here straight back to his office in Wimbledon as though he hadn't got a care in the world. He thinks he's got away with it, you see."

"But he's still on police bail, sir."

"Not for much longer," said Fox. "I want you to go down to Wimbledon, give him his files back and tell him he's off the hook. Apologize profusely and tell him it was all a ghastly mistake. You know the form, Jack."

"And is he off the hook, guv?"

"Don't be silly, Jack. And don't forget to photocopy all those files before you give them back to him."

*

Jeremy Ryan reacted exactly as Fox had anticipated. He accepted Gilroy's apology – offered on behalf of the Commissioner – acknowledged that mistakes are made, and promised that he would not, after all, lodge a complaint. Once Gilroy had gone, however, Ryan vowed to himself that he would no longer keep records that might incriminate him. He was shrewd enough to realize that he might receive another visit from the Flying Squad at some time in the future. His one conviction, and now his recent arrest, had made him wise to the ways of the police and he was too canny to accept, at face value, Gilroy's assurance that he was in the clear.

It was at that point that he received a telephone call from a Lady Jane Sims.

Jane and Rosie Webster took to each other immediately but for once Kate Ebdon felt a little out of place. Admittedly, Jane Sims was attired in similar fashion to Kate – jeans and a sweater – but somehow she seemed to share Rosie's elegance rather than strike a common note with the Australian girl.

"Tell me again what happened when you spoke to Ryan," said Fox. "For the benefit of Rosie and Kate here."

"Let me get you all a drink first," said Jane.

Fox shook his head. "No thanks," he said. "These girls have got to be able to shoot straight if the necessity arises."

"Are you carrying guns then?" Jane glanced at the two policewomen, a disbelieving half smile on her face.

Rosie opened her handbag to display the blue steel of her revolver, and Kate pulled up her baggy sweater to show the butt of a holstered pistol nestling between the top of her jeans and her bare skin. "Too right, m'lady," said Kate with a grin.

"Well, what did Ryan have to say, Jane?" asked Fox.

"He was very interested," said Jane. "He took all the details and told me that he would get back to me. When he rang, an hour later, he gave me a quote that was well above the one you'd obtained for me, as you said it would be. I told him it was too much and that I'd look elsewhere."

"What did he say to that?"

"Didn't seem at all worried. He wished me luck and said he hoped that I'd find a cheaper policy. Very strange way to do business, I must say. In my experience in the building trade—" Fox smiled at the way Jane always described her architectural practice as the building trade. "—a salesman will always try to make a fight of it."

"Good," said Fox. "That's exactly what I expected." He glanced at the two detectives. "All we have to do now is to sit and wait." He turned back to Jane. "It may be some time before we get a bite," he said, "but Jack Gilroy's on the outside with a team and Denzil Evans will be covering the place by night. And now I must go," he added.

Jane saw Fox to the door and kissed him. "See you soon, darling," she whispered.

In the sitting room, Kate Ebdon grinned at Rosie Webster. "I guess the guv'nor's keen on her ladyship, don't you, skip?" she asked.

"Mind your own bloody business," said Rosie, "And concentrate on the job."

*

The following day, Detective Inspector Henry Findlater, who had been reassigned to watching Jeremy Ryan, saw him leave his office at about two o'clock in the afternoon. Findlater's team, skilfully "leap-frogging" with their cleverly disguised vehicles, were not surprised to see Ryan drive to Barnes. Although apprehensive that the police may have tapped his telephone, Ryan had not anticipated being under close surveillance. Not that he would have detected Findlater's professional followers. But, on this occasion, he did not stay very long with Julie Lockhart, the dentist's wife. Although, as DC Rex Perkins crudely put it, it was long enough for Ryan to "give her one".

Findlater passed this information to Fox who instructed the surveillance DI to split his team, leaving one half to follow Ryan and the other half at Barnes to see what Mrs Lockhart did. Not that Fox had much hope of discovering anything interesting. He was now convinced that if Julie Lockhart was still in touch with Kevin Povey, contact would be made by telephone.

Shortly after receiving Findlater's message, Fox got a telephone call.

"Is that Detective Chief Superintendent Fox?" asked the voice hesitantly.

"It is," said Fox.

"This is Geoffrey Cooper. D'you remember, you boarded my yacht, the *Windsong*, the other day in the Channel."

"Yes, I remember, Mr Cooper." Fox would have preferred not to be reminded. "What can I do for you?" Anticipating that Cooper might want to make a complaint about the fiasco in the Channel, Fox turned over a page in his private telephone directory ready to give the yachtsman the number of the Complaints Investigation Bureau.

"I've found the details of the woman I bought her from."

"Oh, good." Fox closed his phone book and drew a notepad towards him. He glanced at the clock, regretting that he had asked Cooper to telephone him with that information. In his experience, people rarely bothered to comply with requests of that sort.

"Yes. Are you there?"

"Yes. I'm still here, Mr Cooper."

159

"Right. Well the woman's name is Linda Ward. Mrs Linda Ward. And she lives in Earls Court. D'you want the full address?"

"Please," said Fox. But he knew that the address was already registered in the incident room.

Thoughtfully, Fox replaced the receiver of the telephone and walked through into the Squad office. "Find DS Fletcher for me," he said to the duty sergeant, "and tell him to see me as soon as possible, will you?"

"Right, sir," said the sergeant, his hand reaching out for the telephone. "Good do the other night, guv'nor," he added.

Fox glared at him. "I wish people'd stop talking about the bloody dinner-dance," he said.

"Christ!" said the sergeant when the door had slammed behind Fox. "Who's rattled his bars for him?"

"Probably Lady Guv," said the DC next to him.

Twenty

"Yes, sir?" DS Fletcher stood in the doorway of Fox's office convinced that whatever it was that the detective chief superintendent was about to lumber him with, it would involve walking or paper. Or both.

"Come in and close the door, Perce," said Fox. He handed Fletcher the slip of paper on which he had written Mrs Linda Ward's name and address. "This woman," he began, "is one of the losers who fell victim to Wally Proctor, better known to Mrs Ward as James Dangerfield. In fact, he saw her off for about seventy thousand pounds' worth of jewelery. It now transpires that Geoffrey Cooper bought the yacht, *Windsong*, from Mrs Ward. Given that Mrs Elaine Carter, the Brighton loser, met Povey on a yacht of the same name, it all seems too much of a coincidence. See what you can find out about Mrs Ward, will you? And, for that matter, her daughter, Michelle White."

"Yes, sir," said Fletcher.

"But discreetly, mind, Perce," said Fox.

"Yes, sir." Fletcher sighed inwardly, took the piece of paper and made his way to his usual starting point: the Police National Computer.

*

At five-thirty that evening, the telephone rang in Jane Sims's flat and for about the tenth time that day, Rosie Webster switched on the recording apparatus and donned the headphones. Then she signaled to Jane to answer the call.

Jane picked up the handset of her telephone. "Hallo?"

"Lady Jane Sims?"

"Speaking," said Jane.

"Oh, Lady Sims, I er—"

"It's Lady Jane, not Lady Sims," said Jane tersely.

"Of course. I do beg your pardon," said the voice on the telephone. Whoever he was, he was very smooth.

"Who is that?" asked Jane.

"You don't know me, Lady Jane, but my name's Laurence Bentley and I'm a security consultant."

"Oh?"

"I understand from a professional colleague of mine that you have quite a few valuable possessions in your home…"

"Who told you that?" asked Jane sharply.

"I have several colleagues in the insurance world, Lady Jane, among them Jeremy Ryan who, I understand, you recently consulted."

"Yes, I did. Not that I think that it concerns you." Jane smothered a laugh. This clown, she thought, made it sound as though she had consulted an eminent Harley Street surgeon.

"I hope you'll forgive me for appearing to interfere in your private affairs, Lady Jane, but very often you can obtain a lower rate of insurance if you have recognized and approved security devices fitted to your place of residence." Bentley seemed quite unabashed by Jane's slight show of hostility.

"I see," said Jane coldly. "In short, Mr, er, Bentley, you want to sell me some locks, and put bars on my windows. Is that it?"

Bentley laughed gently. "Security's a little more sophisticated than that these days, Lady Jane," he said. "But I can assure you that it will save you money in the long run."

Jane, on Fox's instructions, did not tell this Bentley person to go to hell, which would have been her natural reaction to a telephone salesman as unctuous as this one. "Well, I don't know," she said. "I think that I'm quite well provided for…"

"There's no obligation whatever, Lady Jane." Bentley went on quickly. "What I'm proposing, is that I carry out a survey of your premises and then provide you with a written report that would outline the weak points and then recommend the sort of alarms and other protective devices you may care to install."

"And then you'll try to sell them to me, I suppose?"

"Not necessarily. I do have contacts in the trade, of course I do, but I would merely offer advice. For a fee, naturally."

"Naturally," said Jane drily. She glanced at Rosie who nodded. "Well, I suppose there's no harm in that." Jane deliberately sounded reluctant. If she had not been acting as decoy for Fox, there was no way that the smooth-talking Bentley would have got past her front door. "When would you propose to do this, er, survey, Mr Bentley?"

There was a pause. "Just having a look through my appointments book," said Bentley. "Ah! I seem to have a free slot this evening. How would seven o'clock suit you?"

Jane paused too and then said, "Yes, that would be all right. But I do have to go out at about eight."

"No problem," said Bentley. "It should only take about forty minutes. Until this evening then."

The call had been traced to a mobile telephone and Rosie Webster knew that it would take time to discover the owner's address. But if Povey was the caller, it was likely to be false or, at best, an accommodation address.

"What happens now?" asked Jane Sims.

"We sit and wait," said Rosie. It was rapidly becoming a hackneyed phrase in the operation.

*

Fox had decided that he would bring in Denzil Evans and his team. Although Evans had been covering Jane's flat by night, it now looked as though that would no longer be necessary. By six-thirty that evening, some forty Flying Squad officers were stationed in the vicinity of Jane Sims's flat just off Knightsbridge. On foot, in cars – the closest of which were unrecognizable as police vehicles – and in shops and buildings nearby, they waited for the arrival of the man Fox was now convinced was Kevin Povey. Fox himself had joined Rosie Webster and Kate Ebdon inside Jane's flat.

There is an unwritten law – which no one has yet succeeded in repealing – that controls police operations of this sort. It says that, at some stage, something will go wrong. Sometimes it is a minor problem, easily resolved by officers at the scene. At other times, it can only be described as a monumental cock-up. In the aftermath of such occurrences, senior officers will seek to apportion blame which, by the same law, rarely falls upon themselves. On the other hand, the minions, who are on a hiding to nothing anyway, will attempt to shrug off the fiasco by blaming their superiors for not furnishing them with all the necessary information. On this occasion however, the fault rested with over-enthusiasm. In short, there were too many police officers.

Detective Constable Joe Bellenger, loitering at the far end of the street where Jane Sims lived, was the first officer to sight the target. Every member of the combined teams had been provided with copies of the only photograph of Povey the police possessed and Bellenger was in no doubt that the driver of the red Peugeot was him. Discreetly, he alerted the rest of the team by radio.

But Povey was a canny operator. He had, after all, been on the run for five years now and had become extremely wary. He reduced his speed and took careful note of the number of vehicles in the street. He saw, too, a number of pedestrians who seemed unusually casual in their progress, an uncommon sight in a city where normally everyone hurried. And he was not prepared to take any chances.

Suddenly, the red Peugeot shot forward as Povey hammered the accelerator pedal flat to the floor. A pedestrian leaped for his life as, tyres screaming and smoking, Povey threw the car round several corners with all the expertise of a racing driver. Eventually finding himself in Trevor Place, he shot the lights and turned left into Knightsbridge, narrowly avoiding a bus.

As Povey sped away, several of the more alert Flying Squad drivers set off in pursuit, leaving those officers still on foot in complete disarray. Gilroy snatched his radio from his pocket as he watched his driver hurtle away in the wake of the escaping Povey, and told Fox what had happened. Fox was not pleased. And was even less pleased when he later learned that one of the cars had collided with a taxi on the north side of Montpelier Square. The traffic inspector who reported the accident apportioned one hundred per cent of the blame to the police driver.

*

Detective Sergeant Percy Fletcher arrived back at Scotland Yard just after Fox had left for Knightsbridge and found Detective Superintendent Gavin Brace holding the fort.

"They're all out on this operation, Percy," said Brace. "Anything I can do?"

"No, sir, not unless you're in the picture on this Povey enquiry."

"Haven't a clue about it," said Brace thankfully, "but if you want Mr Fox, you can get him here." And he handed him a slip of paper bearing Lady Jane Sims's telephone number.

In the immediate aftermath of Kevin Povey's unpredicted flight, Fox was not best pleased to receive what he regarded as a routine call from

Fletcher. "What is it?" he asked testily. "I'm a bit tucked up here. Bloody Povey's taken it on the toes."

"It's about Mrs Ward, sir," said Fletcher, wedging the telephone receiver between his chin and his shoulder as he sorted through the bits of paper he had taken from his pocket.

"Can't it wait, Perce?"

"Might be relevant, guv," said Fletcher half-heartedly. He had spent nearly all day at St Catherine's House and he was not bothered whether Fox wanted the information now, later, or not at all.

"Well, make it quick," said Fox.

"I've found details of Michelle White's marriage to Paul White. She's Linda Ward's daughter and her husband's the property developer. They live at Chalfont St Giles."

"Yes, I know all that, Perce," said Fox impatiently. "Just get to the point, will you?"

"Michelle White's maiden name is Povey, guv."

"What?"

"Michelle White's maiden—"

"Yes, yes, I heard you," said Fox. "Did you do a birth search?"

"Yes, sir. No trace. And young March has already done one on Kevin Povey and that came up no trace as well."

"Yes, I know," said Fox thoughtfully. "Anything else?"

"Yes, sir. I then did a marriage search on Mrs Ward. That took me ages." Fletcher was determined to let Fox know how hard he had been working.

"I daresay it did, Perce, but did you find anything?"

"Er, yes, guv. Hang on." Fletcher shuffled a few pieces of paper and then deliberately took time over lighting a cigarette. "Ah, here we are. Mrs Linda Ward – incidentally, it's Rachel Linda Ward – was married to a Jonathon Ward about five years ago, bit less actually."

"How's she described on the certificate, Perce?"

"Rachel Linda Povey, nie Carey, a widow, sir."

"That rings a bell," said Fox.

"Yeah, it would. DC March did a search on Gordon Povey and came up with him marrying a Rachel Carey in Maidstone, thirty years ago."

"Yes, I know, but why the hell didn't he—?"

"Hold on, guv," said Fletcher, for once ahead of Fox's thinking. "He had no idea that Mrs Ward was Gordon Povey's widow. There was nothing to indicate that at all. I checked that marriage myself and she didn't call herself Rachel Linda Carey then. Just Rachel Carey. You can't blame March, guv."

Fox grunted, unhappy that he could not find fault with someone. "What about Ward? What did you say his first name was?"

"Jonathon, sir."

"Yes, Jonathon. Did you find a death entry for him?"

"No, sir," said Fletcher. "Either he died abroad or he's still alive. Somewhere."

"Tried the PNC?"

"Yes, sir. Nothing on Jonathon Ward."

"There wouldn't be," said Fox. "Is Ron Crozier knocking about up there? You are at the Yard, are you?"

"Yes, I am, sir, and no, Ron's not here. He's on some jolly at Knightsbridge, I believe," said Fletcher and winced as Fox crashed the receiver of his telephone back on its rest.

*

The Flying Squad had no idea of the route that Povey had taken and Fox ordered that details of the red Peugeot he was driving be circulated to all cars in the Metropolitan
Police District. A check on the PNC had shown that the registered keeper was Laurence Bentley, and gave an address in Battersea.

"Saucy bastard! I'll bet he's been living in Battersea ever since he came back from Australia." Fox had left Jane in the care of the two policewomen and was now standing in the street outside her flat holding court to those Flying Squad officers who had not taken off in pursuit of the errant Povey. "Denzil, take a team and get down to this address in Battersea as quickly as you can. I shouldn't think there's a cat-in-hell's chance that Povey will turn up there, not now he knows we've clocked his car, but get in there and see what you can find." He glanced around the group of assembled detectives. "Have we got anyone left who's tooled up?"

"Matt Hobson and I are armed, guv'nor," said Detective Sergeant Roy Buckley.

"Good," said Fox. "You go with Mr Evans."

"What about a search warrant, sir?" asked Evans.

"I have decided that the urgency of the situation does not allow for application to be made to a justice," said Fox loftily. "I shall therefore issue a superintendent's written order to search under the Explosives Act of 1875." He withdrew a printed form from his inside pocket and spread it on the bonnet of one of the Flying Squad cars. Borrowing a pen from Evans, he scrawled a few details and then signed the form with a flourish.

"But we don't think that he's got explosives, sir. Do we?" Evans always worried about the legal niceties, and Fox's maverick attitude to the law meant that the DI was in a state of constant anxiety.

"We know that he possesses, or has possessed, firearms," said Fox patiently. "And firearms contain bullets. And bullets contain explosive material. It's what makes them go bang, Denzil." Fox beamed confidently at Evans and handed him the written order. "So there you have it."

*

By dint of skillful driving, Kevin Povey had shaken off his Flying Squad pursuers, but he knew that the number of his car would now be in the possession of every police officer in London. When he reached the western end of the Cromwell Road, he parked the distinctive red Peugeot and locked it. Realizing that he was now in Earls Court, he hesitated as a thought entered his mind but, as quickly, he dismissed it. Remaining on the south side of the road, he walked to the next set of traffic lights and waited until a suitable car stopped on the red signal.

She was a young woman, probably no more than twenty-eight, and quite good looking. Povey opened the passenger door and slid into the seat beside her.

"What d'you think you're—?" began the woman, clearly alarmed.

Povey flourished his revolver. "Just drive and you won't get hurt," he said.

"But—"

"Do it!" screamed Povey.

Her face white with fear, the young woman released the hand-brake with a shaking hand, let in the clutch and drove off somewhat erratically.

*

Fox paced back and forth across Jane Sims's sitting room. He had already instructed DS Crozier to telephone Cannes in an attempt to persuade Victor Lasage to search for a record of the birth of Kevin Povey. But now, he did not know what to do next. There was no point in returning to Scotland Yard while there was a possibility of Povey being sighted somewhere, but there was nothing he could do immediately. For Fox, it was the most frustrating situation in which he could find himself.

"For goodness' sake sit down, Tommy," said Jane, "and have a drink."

"No thanks," said Fox, lighting another cigarette. "I wonder where the bastard's gone." He suddenly struck the palm of his left hand with the fist of his right. "Earls Court," he said. "It's all coming on top. If Michelle White's maiden name was Povey, and her mother was Linda Povey before she married this Ward bloke, it's an odds-on chance that Kevin Povey's her son." He grabbed at his personal radio and called Gilroy. "Jack, where are you?"

"Still outside, sir," said Gilroy. "It's where you told me to stay."

"Good. Is Swann there?"

"Yes, sir."

"How many men have you got there, Jack?"

There was a pause. "About ten, sir."

"Armed?" Fox's questions came out like the staccato fire of a machine gun.

"Four of us, sir. D'you want me to call SO19?"

"No. Don't want them posing all over the bloody place." Fox had no high regard for the operational members of Firearms Branch. "We're going to see Linda Ward."

"Linda Ward, sir?" Gilroy wondered what strange theory his chief was working on now.

"Yes. I'll explain on the way." Fox turned to Jane and, regardless of the presence of the two women detectives, kissed her. "Shan't be long," he said. "Take care."

"And you," said Jane, trailing him to the front door as he made a hurried departure.

"Told you, skip," said Kate Ebdon.

"And I told you, Kate. Mind your own bloody business."

Jane Sims returned to the sitting room and, indifferent to the niceties of the rank structure and the discipline that went with it, said, "Is Tommy always like this?"

"Only when he's got the bit between his teeth, m'lady," said Kate with a grin.

"For God's sake call me Jane. I can't abide all this m'lady business." Jane walked across to the drinks cabinet. "Well, I'm going to have a stiff whisky. You girls going to join me?"

Kate hesitated and glanced at her sergeant.

Rosie Webster stood up. "Oh, why the hell not. Thanks, Jane," she said. "I suppose you haven't got a gin and tonic, have you?"

Twenty-one

An armed detective stood on either side of the front door as Fox, Gilroy beside him, rang the bell.

"Oh, it's you again," said Linda Ward disdainfully. She clearly had no high opinion of the police.

"Are you alone, Mrs Ward?" asked Fox.

"Yes, I am. Not that it's any of your business." There was hostility in the woman's voice. "Have you come to return my jewelery?"

"Not yet, Mrs Ward. May we come in?"

"I suppose so."

Fox nodded to the two armed detectives. "All right," he said. "Wait here. Just in case."

Mrs Ward noticed the other two for the first time. "What exactly is going on?" she asked.

"I've come to see you about your son Kevin," said Fox as he and Gilroy entered the flat.

Mrs Ward turned sharply. "What d'you mean?" she demanded.

"Kevin Povey is your son, isn't he?"

"What if he is?" Linda Ward remained standing in the center of her sitting room and did not invite either of the police officers to sit down. She obviously did not intend that they should stay long.

"Mrs Ward, I think you know that Kevin Povey is wanted for questioning by the police in connection with a murder which took place in Shepperton about five years ago."

Mrs Ward sank into a chair and, with a limp wave of her hand, invited Fox and Gilroy to sit down also. "What has this to do with my jewelery?" she asked. She suddenly sounded tired, as though she had known that it would come to this one day, but had tried not to think about it.

"At the moment, I'm not sure," said Fox. In fact, he had a theory, but was not yet prepared to reveal it. "When did you last see him?"

Mrs Ward shrugged. "Ages ago," she said. "Perhaps a year. I can't really remember."

"Did he come here?"

"Good heavens no."

"How did he contact you then?"

"He telephoned."

"And do you have a telephone number for him?"

"No," said Linda Ward, glancing distractedly at her small bookcase. "I don't even know where he is."

"No idea?"

"I said no." Mrs Ward looked sharply at Fox. "I think he's abroad somewhere."

"You did know that he was wanted by the police, of course."

Linda Ward gave Fox a scathing glance. "Did I?" she asked.

"You were interviewed by the French police on your yacht at Cannes, about five years ago. The yacht was called *Windsong*, wasn't it?"

"I can't remember," said Linda Ward again.

"Which you sold to a Mr Geoffrey Cooper." Fox pursued his enquiry relentlessly.

"Yes. What of it?"

"Where is Mr Jonathon Ward, Mrs Ward?"

Again, Linda Ward seemed surprised at the depth of Fox's knowledge of her life, but refused to be coerced into answering his questions. "I haven't the faintest idea," she said.

"Is he dead?"

"I neither know nor care."

"I see. And you have no idea where Kevin Povey might be at this moment?" Fox thought it extremely unlikely that Mrs Ward, or anyone else, knew of the wanted man's present whereabouts.

"Of course not. Why d'you want to know?"

Fox thought that to be fairly obvious. "I wish to question him about the houseboat murder. And two others," he added quietly.

"Two others!" For the first time since the arrival of the police, Mrs Ward seemed disconcerted. She looked Fox in the face, and he was aware of a slight tic above her left eye that had not been apparent before.

"Yes, Mrs Ward. The murders of Wally Proctor, whom you knew as James Dangerfield, and a man called Robin Skelton. We also believe him to be implicated in a number of substantial jewelery thefts."

"My God!" Linda Ward was clearly shaken by this information.

For five years, she had been convinced that her son was innocent, but now the police were here, in her flat, telling her that he had lived a life of violent crime since that fateful moment of Jason Bright's murder. Her mind went back to the day when the French police came aboard *Windsong* seeking Kevin. And she recalled too, the furious argument that she and her husband had had afterwards about Kevin, and how they had raced back to England only for Gordon to die of a heart attack a day later. All his life, Gordon Povey had worked hard, building an international diamond business that had provided them with a lifestyle beyond her wildest dreams. A lifestyle that had furnished them with two beautiful houses, several cars – a Rolls-Royce included – a yacht in the South of France and a villa in the mountains behind Cannes at St Paul-de-Vence. Their two children, Kevin and Michelle, had been provided with the best of everything, but Linda Ward now realized that their own selfishness had left the two children without the caring warmth of a true family upbringing. Michelle was all right, or so it seemed, but Kevin had gone wildly off the rails. He had only to ask his father for money – for drugs, she suspected – or a new fast car, and he got it. Gordon would give the boy anything material, rather than devoting a few moments of his precious time to his fatherly duties. To Gordon Povey time had meant money, and by the time they had enough of it to relax, to take things easy, it was too late.

"Why d'you use the name Linda now, Mrs Ward?" asked Fox. It was not really pertinent to his enquiry, but Fox hated loose ends.

"I detested the name Rachel," said Linda Ward. "My first husband said he liked it and always insisted on using it, but when I met Jonathon, I started to use my second name."

"And where, as a matter of interest, did you meet your second husband, Mrs Ward?"

When Fox had first arrived, Linda Ward would have declined to answer that question. Would have told this arrogant policeman to mind his own business. But now, as the realization dawned upon her that her own shortcomings as a mother had probably contributed to Kevin's plight, she just answered him. "In the casino at Cannes," she said softly. "About a year before Gordon died."

*

According to the address on his vehicle registration, Laurence Bentley lived in one of the maze of streets south of Battersea Rise not far from Wandsworth Common. It was a terraced property, not in the best condition, and had net curtains at each of the windows facing the road.

Denzil Evans had brought half his team to a standstill some yards from the house. The remainder of his detectives he had sent along the adjacent street to enter the road from the opposite end. Now on foot they approached the house.

"Roy and Matt come with me," said Evans to the two armed officers. "The rest of you be ready to follow me in."

"Hold on, guv," said DS Buckley. "Matt and I have got shooters. We'll hammer on the door. Just in case."

"I'm the DI and I'll—" began Evans.

"Leave it out, guv'nor, please," said Buckley and strode up the short path to the front door, Matt Hobson right behind him.

The woman who answered the door was pretty, in a common sort of way. She was dressed in jeans and a tee-shirt beneath which it was clear she wore no bra. The tee-shirt bore a slogan that read HOW ABOUT NOW? in large red letters. She was barefooted and the scarlet varnish on her toenails matched that of her fingernails. Her hair, a golden brown, was long and fell straight to her shoulders. "Yes?" she said.

"Police," said Buckley and barged past the girl.

"Here, what d'you think you're doing?" Leaving the door open, the girl raced after Buckley. "You can't just come in here like that—" she began, but Hobson seized her by the shoulders and passed her back to Evans.

"Now just you hold on, miss," said Evans. "We're looking for Laurence Bentley."

"My husband's not here," said the woman. "If you'd asked politely, I'd've told you that." Despite her appearance, she spoke in cultured tones.

"Where is he then?" persisted Evans. It was a pointless question. In view of what had occurred in Knightsbridge an hour ago, it was unlikely that Bentley's wife had any idea where he was. As Fox had suggested, it was most unlikely that he would have returned home.

"Not here, guv," said Buckley, holstering his pistol as he came back down the stairs after he and Hobson had conducted a lightning search of the small house, the equally small garden and the shed.

"I just told you that," said Mrs Bentley. "What the hell's this all about?"

"Does your husband also use the name Kevin Povey, Mrs Bentley?" asked Evans. The DI and six of his officers were crowded into the tiny entrance hall, and Bentley's wife showed no signs of inviting them into the sitting room.

"Does he what?" Mrs Bentley laughed outright.

"Does he use the name Kevin Povey?" Evans patiently repeated the question.

"Of course not."

Evans sighed. "We have a warrant to search this house," he said. He had decided that to describe the superintendent's written order to search as a warrant would save complicated explanations.

"Have you indeed?" said Mrs Bentley truculendy. "And are you going to show it me, or do I have to take your word for it?" Clearly not in awe of the police, she stood defiantly, her hands in her pockets.

Evans withdrew the document and displayed it. "There you are, madam," he said.

Mrs Bentley glanced briefly at the order. "Well, I've never seen one before, so I suppose I'll have to accept that it's the genuine article," she said. "But why d'you want to search my house?"

"We have reason to believe that Laurence Bentley is Kevin Povey, who is wanted for questioning by the police."

"Is that so? And what for, may I ask?"

"For murder," said Evans. "Well, three murders, as a matter of fact."

Mrs Bentley threw back her head and laughed. "Are you seriously telling me," she asked, "That you suspect Laurie of committing three murders? You must be mad, the lot of you." Her gaze swept the six officers who were awaiting Evans's signal to get going. She noticed that young Ted March was gazing at her breasts and she promptly folded her arms.

"Yes, madam," said Evans and signaled to the others to make a start. "And now, I'd like a word with you. Shall we sit down?"

Mrs Bentley shrugged her shoulders and pushed open the door of the sitting room. She walked across to a settee and sat down, swinging her legs up and leaving Evans to select one of the armchairs. "Well, what d'you want to talk about?" she asked.

"Very nice." Evans gazed around the room. Although small, it was comfortable and the furniture was of good quality. On the deep pile carpet stood a large television set with a video recorder beneath it, and in a corner there was a Bang & Olufsen stereo unit. The three-piece suite was upholstered in black leather and the pictures which adorned the walls were a mixture of reproductions of well-known paintings and original watercolors.

"I don't imagine you came here to admire the fixtures and fittings," said Mrs Bentley, "so perhaps you'd explain what all this nonsense is about Laurie having murdered someone."

"What does your husband do for a living, Mrs Bentley?"

"Imports and exports," said the girl promptly. "And he's abroad at the moment, if you must know."

"Oh? Where abroad exactly?"

The girl hesitated for a moment. "France, I think," she said.

"You think? Don't you know?"

"I can't keep up with him," said Mrs Bentley, reaching out for a packet of cigarettes, but not offering Evans one. "It all depends what he's got on. If something crops up while he's in France, he might go on to Germany or Italy, or God knows where. I got a call from him once from South Africa. He was chasing an order or something of the sort." She sounded bored by the whole business.

"When were you married, Mrs Bentley?"

"We're not, but we've been living together for three years. Why?"

"And your full name?"

"Andrea Bentley. It's easier for me to use his name. But why d'you want to know all these things? I thought it was Laurie you wanted to talk to."

"Do you have any other places of residence?" asked Evans.

"Places of residence?" Andrea Bentley repeated the phrase in a bantering tone and gave Evans a mocking smile. "If you mean, have we got another pad somewhere, the answer's no. We're not made of money."

It was Buckley who made the first significant find. "Spare a minute, guv?" he said, poking his head round the sitting-room door.

"What is it, Roy?" Evans joined Buckley in the hall.

175

"A briefcase, guv, in the garden shed. It's had the bottom removed, but not very well. It looks as though Povey was experimenting, but it wasn't good enough. Could have been his first try at the one used to kill Proctor. And there are quite a few tools in there that you wouldn't normally associate with the usual stuff a bloke keeps." "Meaning what?" asked Evans.

"Well, most blokes keep hammers and screwdrivers, a couple of saws maybe, and possibly a wrench to change a washer on a tap. But this bloke's got quite a sophisticated set of tools that'd do credit to an engineer."

Evans nodded. "Tag the briefcase, Roy, but I'm not sure that the rest of the stuffs good enough to prove anything. Anyway, keep at it."

"Yes, sir," said Buckley.

"Does your husband do his own car maintenance, Mrs Bentley?" asked Evans as he returned to the sitting room.

Andrea Bentley looked momentarily mystified by Evans's question and then she laughed. "We might live in Battersea," she said, "but we don't have to behave like the other animals who live here. Of course he doesn't do his own car maintenance."

On his return to the tool shed, Buckley had continued his search. "Now there's a funny thing," he said as he sighted a pile of logs in the corner of the shed.

"What's funny about that, skip?" asked DC March.

"There are no fireplaces in the house, Ted," said Buckley. "They've all been taken out, probably when the central heating was put in."

With March's help, Buckley began to take down the pile of logs. As he did so, a metal box came into view. It was only small, no more than a foot by six inches by four inches, but it was secured by a padlock.

"Hand me that crowbar, Ted," said Buckley.

The young DC passed it across. "What d'you reckon skip?" he asked.

"Shan't know till we open it, shall we, Ted?" said Buckley with a grin, and wrenched the padlock off with the tip of the crowbar. "Well, now, and isn't that interesting?"

"What is it, skip?" asked March.

"Ammunition, my son." The metal box contained several small unopened boxes, each containing fifty rounds of ammunition, some of .38 caliber and one of .22. "And, would you believe, a pistol." Buckley turned to March. "Better get hold of Mr Evans, Ted. Let him have a look at this little lot."

While Buckley had been ferreting in the tool shed, DC Sean Tarling had been searching the Bendeys' bedrooms.

In the spare room, in a locked drawer which rapidly yielded to Tarling's violence, he found a small quantity of white powder that experience told him was cocaine. And a wash-leather bag containing a quantity of diamonds.

"Are these stones yours, Mrs Bentley?" asked Evans, displaying Tarling's find.

Andrea Bentley gazed wide-eyed at the diamonds that Evans had spread on the coffee table in the sitting room. "I've never seen those before in my life," she said. Glancing up at Evans, she asked. "Where did you get them from?"

"In a drawer in the spare bedroom," said Tarling.

"But that drawer's locked," said Mrs Bentley.

"Not any more it's not," said Tarling with a grin.

Andrea Bentley was about to protest when the telephone rang. Picking up the handset from its base, she extended the aerial and flicked the switch. "Hallo?" she said. Then she shot a nervous glance in Evans's direction. "Yes, they are. Laurie, what the hell's going on? What have you done?"

Evans grabbed the handset from the woman and spoke into it. "Bentley?" he said. But the line had gone dead. Slowly, he retracted the aerial and replaced the handset on its base station. "What did he want to know?" he asked gently.

Slowly, Andrea Bentley sat down on the settee, her head in her hands. "He wanted to know if the police were here," she said without looking up. "How on earth did he know you might be?"

Twenty-two

It was almost nine o'clock and beginning to get quite dark. Detective Inspector Henry Findlater was about to call it a day and send his surveillance team home when a Ford Mondeo drove into the road and turned on to the driveway of the Lockharts' house.

A man leaped from the passenger seat, ran around to the driver's side of the car and wrenched the door open.

"Christ, guv'nor," said the DC in Findlater's car, "I'm sure that's Povey."

With a pistol clearly visible in one hand, the man pulled a young woman from the driver's seat and forced her towards the house where he banged violently on the front door.

Within seconds, Findlater and several of his officers were out of their cars and running.

"Hey!" shouted Findlater. "Povey!"

The man leveled his pistol and fired. The round went harmlessly over the heads of the nearest group of policemen.

"Bloody hell!" said DS Crabtree, "He's got a shooter."

"So it would appear." Findlater, the dour Calvinistic Scot, was never given to exaggeration. He watched as the front door was opened by Julie Lockhart, and Povey forced his way in, pushing her and his hostage ahead of him. The door slammed and Findlater, pushing his owl-like glasses up to the bridge of his nose once again, returned to his car where he made an urgent radio call.

*

Fox had just left Linda Ward's flat and was getting into his car when the call came through. He leaped out again and shouted across the street to Gilroy. "Did you get that, Jack?"

"Yes, sir."

"Right, let's get down there. Fast."

With uncharacteristic speed, Fox's driver, Swann, affixed the magnetic blue light to the roof of the Scorpio and leaped back into the car.

"You mind you don't get a bloody hernia, Swann," said Fox. "Now get me to Barnes with all possible despatch."

"Right, guv," said Swann mournfully. With studied casualness, he moved the gear lever to "drive", flicked on the siren and accelerated away from Earls Court.

*

Findlater's radio call had brought several area cars into the vicinity of the Lockharts' house, together with the local territorial support group consisting of an inspector, two sergeants and twenty constables. Minutes later, Fox's Scorpio came into view.

"What have you got, Henry?" asked Fox, joining Findlater whose car had been withdrawn to a safe distance from the Lockharts' house.

Findlater related what had happened so far. "I've sealed off both ends of the road, sir—"

"I saw that," said Fox, who had driven through the white tapes at one end of the road.

"And the TSG is in the process of evacuating the houses on either side and opposite. And SO19 are on their way."

"Yes, I suppose they can't wait to get in on the act," said Fox, grudgingly admitting that, in the circumstances, the presence of officers from the Operational Firearms Branch was inevitable. "Have you spoken to him yet?"

"No, sir. It's obvious that he's not going anywhere, and he must know it if he's looked out of the window. I thought it best to wait for you, sir."

"What about a phone? Is there one anywhere?"

"We could try one of the houses on this side, sir, until we can get something of our own rigged up." Findlater glanced down the road as another police vehicle pulled up. "Ah, that looks like the Anti-Terrorist Branch."

"Who the hell called them? Povey's not a terrorist, for God's sake."

"I think they're alerted automatically to a thing like this, sir," said Findlater, who was far more in tune with modern methods than Fox would admit to being.

"Well, Henry, while we wait for the rest of the cavalry to arrive, we'll give Mister Povey a bell. See what he's got to say for himself."

The two officers walked down the road, further away from where Povey was holding his hostages, and knocked at the door of a nearby house.

"Good evening," said Fox, when a middle-aged man opened the door, "We're police officers. I wonder if we might use your telephone."

"Of course," said the man. "Come along in."

"What is it, dear?" asked a woman's voice from somewhere inside the house.

"It's the police, dear," said the man and turned to Fox. "My wife," he said, by way of explanation, and led the two detectives into a small room that was obviously used as a study. "There you are," he said, pointing to the telephone.

"Oh, hallo." The man's wife, a gray-haired woman, poked her head round the study door.

"Good evening, madam. Sorry to disturb you."

"That's all right, but what's going on? Martin and I saw all the police arriving. It's the Lockharts, isn't it?"

"It is, but you don't seem surprised."

The woman tossed her head. "Something to do with the dentist's wife, I'll be bound," she said. "A right madam, that. Just because her husband pulls teeth, she thinks she's something, that one. Always describes her husband as "medical", whatever that means. It's him I feel sorry for, you know, her carrying on. Poor man. She makes no secret of it, either. Men calling at the house when Mr Lockhart's away. Disgraceful I call it."

"I see," said Fox, non-committally. He turned to the man. "D'you have a phone book by any chance?"

"Yes." The man leaned down and took a telephone directory from a lower shelf of the bookcase. "We'll leave you to it, then," he said and left the room, closing the door after him.

Fox thumbed through the book until he found the Lockharts' home number. "There you are, Henry," he said. "D'you want me to ring him, sir?" asked Findlater.

"Of course, Henry. You know the rules. Junior officers negotiate because they can't make instant decisions."

"Very good, sir," said Findlater and dialed the number. At the end of a short conversation, he replaced the receiver. "That was Peter Lockhart, sir," he said. "Povey is holding them hostage—"

"Who is them?" asked Fox.

"Peter and Julie Lockhart and an unknown woman whose car Povey apparently hijacked."

"Is he making any demands?"

"He wants free passage out of the country, sir."

"I'll bet he does. Where to?"

Findlater smiled. "Brazil, sir."

Fox laughed. "If he thinks that Ronnie Biggs'll greet him like a long lost brother, he's got another think coming," he said and paused reflectively. "D'you know, Henry, I'm almost inclined to let him go. Povey obviously doesn't know that Brazil's not a safe sanctuary any more. The Brazilian law would probably take every penny he's got and then send him back. It's very tempting, I must say."

"What do we do now, sir?" asked Findlater.

"We get back to the center of things and sit and wait, Henry. That's what we do."

Outside, within an hour of Povey's arrival at the Lockharts' house, what is known as siege management was in place. An officer from Communications Branch had arranged with British Telecom for a line to be set up from the incident van which was staffed by Anti-Terrorist Branch officers. A catering van was serving hot drinks, sandwiches and hot dogs, with a promise of three-course meals to come. The press had started to gather, but had been held back by uniformed police at the taped-off ends of the road, where a press liaison officer from the Yard's Department of Public Affairs was talking to them. And the commander arrived.

"What's going on, Tommy?" asked Alec Myers.

Fox outlined the situation as he stared gloomily across the darkened street. "I've a bloody good mind to go in and get the little toe-rag myself," he said.

"Don't you dare, Tommy," said Myers. "There are procedures for this sort of thing. Leave it to the people who know what they're doing."

"And what's that supposed to mean, guv'nor?" asked Fox crossly.

"You know what I'm talking about, Tommy. You're very good at catching villains, but there are other departments at the Yard who are much better at this sort of thing than you are. You've had no experience of sieges. It's a very delicate situation, and there are three people's lives at stake. By the way, a negotiator's on his way."

"Bloody hell," said Fox gloomily.

*

At Scotland Yard, where the remaining officers of the Flying Squad had been retained on duty, Detective Sergeant Percy Fletcher took a telephone call.

"Is Detective Chief Superintendent Fox there?" asked the voice.

"No, he's not," said Fletcher in a tired voice. He had taken about six calls for the head of the Squad since the siege at Barnes had begun less than forty minutes ago. Each one was from a journalist seeking a short cut to information. "Who's speaking?"

"It's Geoffrey Cooper."

"What can I do for you, Mr Cooper?"

"Your Mr Fox came to see me a few days ago aboard my yacht. The *Windsong*."

"Yes, I know. What about it?" said Fletcher.

"I've just been watching the news on television. It mentioned a man called Laurence Bentley."

"Yes, it probably did," said Fletcher, wondering when Cooper was going to get to the point.

"Well, I know him, you see."

"Do you? Perhaps you'd tell me about it, Mr Cooper." Fletcher drew a pad of paper across the desk.

"I'm not sure that this is any good, but when Mr Fox came to see me, he asked if I'd ever taken *Windsong* to Brighton Marina, and I said no. But it's just possible that Laurence Bentley did."

"How's that then?" asked Fletcher wearily.

"I met him on the Hamble about a year ago, perhaps a little less, and got to know him quite well. At first I thought he was a commercial traveler—"

"Oh?" said Fletcher, "And what made you think that? Did he say he was?"

"No, not exactly, but he always had a clean shirt on a coat-hanger in his car."

Fletcher sighed and expressed an inward desire to be preserved from amateur detectives. "But he wasn't, I take it."

"No, he said he was in imports and exports, but that he was having a few weeks off and was spending them on his yacht which he said was moored there too."

"Did you see his yacht?" asked Fletcher. "Go aboard it at all?"

"Well, no, I didn't now you come to mention it. Anyway, when I told him that I had to go to the States for about six weeks, he offered to keep an eye on *Windsong* for me. Well, I was agreeable, of course. You'd be surprised how much stuff gets stolen from yachts these days, even in moorings like the Hamble."

"Yes, I probably would, Mr Cooper," said Fletcher, "but are you suggesting that Bentley may have taken your yacht to Brighton without your permission?"

"I don't know, but it's a possibility, isn't it? I just thought that I ought to let Mr Fox know, that's all."

"Thank you for your assistance, Mr Cooper," said Fletcher. He flicked up the switch on that line and pressed down the one next to it. "Flying Squad."

"Is Mr Fox there?"

"Who speaks?" asked Fletcher.

"It's Alec Clarke of the *Daily*—"

Fletcher flicked up the switch and lit a cigarette.

*

By one o'clock in the morning, the assembled police had settled in. There was little doubt that the operation would be a prolonged one. A detective chief inspector from Hounslow, a trained negotiator, had installed himself in the Anti-Terrorist Branch incident van alongside Fox, and had spoken to Povey several times.

"Well, what does he say now?" asked Fox as the DCI finished yet another conversation with the wanted man.

"He's accepted the trade, guv," said the DCI. "He'll let the unknown girl go, if we promise to have an aircraft standing by at Heathrow, fueled up and crewed, ready to go to Brazil."

Fox laughed. "These bastards will never learn," he said scornfully. "When's he going to release the girl?"

"Five minutes time, under instruction from SO19."

Fox groaned. "That means a lot of shouting from our macho friends," he said.

A ring of armed police was surrounding the Lockharts' house now, standing behind the battery of floodlights which illuminated it. Their leader, an inspector from Firearms Branch, put a loud-hailer to his mouth. "Right, Povey," he roared, "open the front door now. Slowly."

The front door opened and seventeen marksmen adjusted their sights as the girl whose car Povey had hijacked was pushed out. Then the door slammed. "Walk slowly towards me, miss," said the inspector. "There's nothing to worry about. You're quite safe."

"Prat!" said Fox. "She can't see him behind all those lights. Funny, that. I'd have said he was very strong on amateur dramatics. Should know about footlights."

The girl walked down the driveway and the moment she reached the darkness beyond the floodlights, she was seized by two policewomen who searched her thoroughly. It was not unknown in the annals of hostage-taking for an innocent victim to be fitted with an explosive device. Nevertheless, Fox thought that they were overdoing it a bit.

A uniformed constable approached the incident van. "Mr Fox?" he asked, looking enquiringly into its interior. "What is it?" said Fox.

"Mrs Ward's arrived, sir. She'd being held at the end of the road. What d'you want us to do with her?"

"I'll come and have a chat with her," said Fox. He had sent a police car for Linda Ward in the hope that her presence at the scene might induce Povey to give up his hostages and his crazy demands, and surrender to the police.

Keeping in the darkness, Fox strolled to the end of the road and slid into the back of the police car next to Povey's mother. "Sorry to bring you out so late, Mrs Ward," he said, "but it's possible that you may be able to help us." And he quickly outlined all that had happened since the first sighting of Kevin Povey near Jane Sims's flat some six hours previously.

Despite having been called from her bed, Linda Ward had taken great care with her appearance. She was dressed as if for a cocktail party, and her hair was immaculate. But there were obvious signs of tension. The tic above her left eye was working again, and her hands clutched her handbag tightly. "He's not a bad boy really, Mr Fox," she said. All her hostility towards the police had vanished. She was now conciliatory and clearly concerned about what was likely to happen to her son.

Fox decided that this was no time to make an issue of how much good or bad there was in Kevin Povey, and he put her comment down to maternal loyalty. "You said earlier, Mrs Ward, that you last heard from your son about a year ago when he telephoned you."

"That's right, but it wasn't true. We've spoken often on the telephone. He was living in Battersea with some girl. Andrea, I think her name was."

"Yes, I know," said Fox. Denzil Evans had briefed him fully on the result of his search at the Bentley house. "Did he know about the theft of your jewelery?" Fox posed the question lightly, in an offhand sort of way.

"Oh yes. I told him about it shortly after it happened."

"What did he say to that?"

"He was furious. I think he blamed himself really. He was always a caring boy, you know, and he seemed to think that if he'd kept a closer eye on me, it wouldn't have happened."

"Did he give any indication that he might do something about it?"

"He asked me all about James, James Dangerfield, that is, and I told him. He asked me to describe him, right down to the last detail. Then he said that he'd see what he could do about getting my jewelery back for me."

"Did he give you the impression that he knew this Dangerfield man,"The man we know as Wally Proctor?"

"Not really, no. But then he was always a secretive boy. When I told him all that I knew, he just said that I wasn't to worry. He said that he'd sort it out."

"I think he may have done," said Fox mildly.

Twenty-three

At two o'clock, Linda Ward's daughter, Michelle White, and her husband Paul arrived in their Rolls-Royce. Michelle White was, as one policeman put it, "dolled-up to the nines". Her straight, golden-brown hair was gathered into a pony-tail that hung down the back of her striking white trouser suit, her neck was adorned with an excess of gold chains, and several chunky bracelets fought for supremacy with her diamond-studded wrist-watch. Her husband wore a shell suit and a pair of Nike trainers. Minutes later, Andrea Bentley turned up, demanding to see her husband. All had seen the item about the siege on late-evening television news bulletins.

"Christ!" said Fox to the runner who had brought news of this impromptu gathering of Povey's kinfolk. "This is turning into a bloody circus. Keep them behind the tapes and tell them we'll send for them if we need them." He sniffed the air as the aroma of frying bacon wafted across from the mobile canteen. "And tell someone to get me a bacon sandwich," he added.

The detective chief inspector from Hounslow who was acting as negotiator was called Tony Kerby. He replaced the handset of the direct line that Povey had agreed to have installed, and turned to Fox. "He wants food sent in, sir," he said.

"Tell him to get stuffed," said Fox. Somewhere in the distance, the door of a police car slammed and there was a burst of laughter.

The negotiator grinned. He knew that he must never antagonize the man holding the two remaining hostages. And so did Fox. "What's the strategy, sir?" he asked.

"The strategy, eh?" Fox nodded sagely as he savored the words. Those who knew him better than the negotiator did would have detected the sarcasm. He detested the buzzwords that specialists in the police employed to give their skills some sort of mystique. "Tell him that we'll send in food if he releases his other two hostages, Tony."

"I'll give it a try, guv, but I think we'll be pushing our luck. Supposing he only agrees to release one?"

"Then tell him it'll have to be Julie Lockhart."

The DCI swung round on his chair and rang through to the Lockharts' house. "Kevin, this is Tony again. I've tried to persuade my bosses to send in some food, but they'll only agree if you release the hostages. I've done my best but that's what they say." Kerby held the handset away from his ear as Povey screamed an obscene response. "Kevin, listen to me. I'll try again, but supposing they say they'll settle for just one of the hostages? What d'you say to that?" He listened for a few moments more and then broke the connection. Turning to Fox, he said, "He's thinking about it, sir."

Fox yawned and tried, yet again, to solve the remaining clue in the previous day's *Daily Telegraph* crossword puzzle.

The telephone buzzed and Kerby gazed at it for some seconds before answering. It was all part of the negotiation techniques to impose elements of controlled stress on Povey. "Hallo, Kevin. Tony here," he said. There was a short conversation and then Kerby spoke again. "I don't think they'll wear it, Kevin," he said, "but I'll give it a try." And once more, he closed the line. "He'll release Peter Lockhart, sir, in exchange for food, but he won't let Julie go."

"We'll let him sweat for a while," said Fox and lit another cigarette. The DCI, a non-smoker, gazed balefully at the overflowing ashtray.

Fox allowed twenty minutes to elapse and then told Kerby to agree to providing a meal in exchange for Peter Lockhart's release, but that Lockhart had to come out first.

The Firearms Branch inspector went through his act with the loud-hailer again, and Peter Lockhart was bundled out of the door. For a moment, the dentist paused, blinking through his wire-framed spectacles at the bright floodlighting. He too was searched thoroughly when he reached the safety of the police lines.

An unarmed constable wearing bulky body armor walked slowly up the driveway with a tray. He reached the door and kicked a stone off the step before carefully setting down the tray.

When the officer was clear of the house, the front door opened and Julie Lockhart appeared, framed in the doorway. Around her neck there was a rope, one end of which was held by Povey. In his other hand, his pistol was held threateningly to the girl's head. There was silence, save for the hissing and humming of the Metro-lamps illuminating the macabre scene, as slowly, Julie stooped to pick up the tray and then moved backwards into the house. Once more, the door was closed.

"What's the situation like in there, Mr Lockhart?" asked Fox once the dentist had been given a cup of tea.

"That man's mad," said Lockhart. "He threatened to kill us all." His brow furrowed in anguish. "I'm desperately worried about Julie, but Povey said that if I didn't go, he'd kill me there and then." He looked up imploringly at Fox. "You've got to get her out of there," he said.

"We shall," said Fox. He sounded more confident of a successful outcome than he actually felt. An armed man holding a hostage always created a volatile situation, and

Fox knew that only skillful handling – and a big slice of luck – would resolve it satisfactorily.

"He's got some bee in his bonnet about Julie," Lockhart went on.

"Oh?"

"He keeps on about her having witnessed a murder, on a houseboat, years ago. God knows what he's on about, but he kept saying that if Julie said anything to the police, he'd kill her. What d'you think he means?" Lockhart suddenly recognized Fox. "You're the man who came to see me in the surgery, aren't you?" he said.

"Yes, I do believe I did come and see you," said Fox.

"And you showed me a photograph. D'you remember? It's him, isn't it? Povey. The man holding Julie."

"Yes, it is."

"D'you mean to say that you knew about him, even then?" Lockhart's voice rose slightly as he leveled the accusation.

"We've known about him for five years, Mr Lockhart, ever since he killed a man called Jason Bright on a houseboat at Shepperton." Fox paused. "Your wife was the only witness."

"For God's sake," said Lockhart.

"She never told you then?" said Fox.

"No. Not a word. Are you sure about this?"

"Your wife told us that she'd seen it, Mr Lockhart."

"Then why have you allowed this to happen? Why weren't we given police protection?"

Fox pondered whether now, while his wife was still held hostage, was the right time to tell Lockhart the whole story. Eventually he decided it might relieve the dentist's stress, rather than worsen it. "We have strong reasons for believing that your wife has been in touch with Kevin Povey quite regularly since the incident on the houseboat, Mr Lockhart," he said. "In fact, we are fairly certain that Mrs Lockhart has been acting as a go-between, passing information from a dishonest insurance broker called Jeremy Ryan to Kevin Povey in order that Povey could carry out a number of jewelery thefts."

With more violence than he had intended, Lockhart banged his teacup down on the narrow writing table in the police van that had been set aside for debriefing the hostages. "I don't believe any of this," he said angrily. "Are you trying to make my wife out to be some sort of criminal?"

"Not necessarily," said Fox mildly. "All I'm saying is that the evidence appears to point to that possibility." And he determined that Lockhart should not have it all his own way. "We have been keeping observation on your house for some time now—"

Lockhart scoffed. "I didn't see anyone hanging about in a macintosh and a trilby hat," he said, apparently influenced by the techniques of observation portrayed in second-rate American films.

"I'm very pleased to hear it," said Fox. "However, that does not alter the fact that my officers have seen Jeremy Ryan calling at your house. Always when you're out, either at work or away from home. As they did, for example, when you went to Amsterdam recently for your conference."

Lockhart opened his mouth and then closed it again. Then, eventually, he spoke. "Are you suggesting that this man's having an affair with my wife?" he asked.

Fox shrugged. "I don't know," he said, despite being convinced that Julie Lockhart had spent most of her time with Ryan in bed. "But visit her he did."

Lockhart leaned forward, his elbows on his knees and his head in his hands. He was obviously a naive man and the double blow of having his wife held hostage, and then learning that she had probably been unfaithful to him, looked as though it was going to engulf him. After some time, he looked up. Then he picked up the teacup, saw that it was empty and put it down again.

"Would you like another cup of tea, Mr Lockhart?" asked Fox.

"I suppose you wouldn't have anything stronger, would you?"

Fox grinned and taking a flask out of his pocket, poured a liberal measure of whisky into Lockhart's empty cup. "Try that," he said.

Lockhart took a hefty swig of the Scotch and nodded. "Thanks," he said. "You must have been a Boy Scout."

"No," said Fox. "I wanted to be a Girl Guide, but they wouldn't let me join."

For a moment, Lockhart took him seriously, then he laughed. For the first time since Povey had burst into his house.

*

Julie Lockhart's brief appearance in the doorway of her house, with a rope around her neck, had all been an act for the benefit of the watching police. Once the door had been locked, the two had settled down, side by side on the settee, to enjoy the meal which Fox had authorized. And they drank a bottle of wine from Peter Lockhart's meagre stock.

"What's going to happen, Kev?" asked Julie. "You know they're not going to let you out of here, don't you?"

Povey laughed. "They haven't got any choice," he said. "They've said that they've got a plane waiting at Heathrow to take us to Brazil."

"And you believe them?" Julie Lockhart was far more pessimistic about the outcome of the siege than Povey. "They're stringing you along," she said.

"Maybe." Povey finished his wine and glanced across the curtained room at the sideboard. "Has your old man got any brandy, gorgeous?" he asked.

"I think there's some in there," Julie replied listlessly. "But don't you think you're drinking too much?"

Prior to the meal, Povey had consumed half a bottle of whisky, but was showing no signs of being affected by it. He walked over to the sideboard and eventually found a quarter-bottle of Cognac. "Your old man's a bit of a cheapskate, isn't he?" he said. "No one buys quarter bottles of brandy any more." He held it up. "You having one?"

Julie shook her head. "No, thanks."

Povey poured a large amount of brandy into a glass and resumed his seat next to the girl. But instead of drinking it, he put the glass down on a table next to the settee. Then he leaned across and putting one arm

190

around the girl's shoulders, he pulled her towards him and started to fondle her breasts.

Julie pushed his hand away. "Not now, Kev," she said. "I couldn't."

"Well I could," said Povey, pulling her closer and putting a hand on her knee. "All this excitement turns me on." His hand moved higher. "I really need you now."

"I couldn't," said Julie again, attempting to stop the upward movement of his hand.

"Want me to force you, gorgeous?" asked Povey, a lascivious grin on his face. "Is that what turns you on? It always used to," he added.

But Julie Lockhart had never been able to resist the plausible Kevin Povey, who possessed all the playboy charm – however contrived – that her mundane husband lacked. Not for the first time, she wondered why on earth she had married the uninspiring little Barnes dentist. She stood up and started to undress.

But later, when they had finished, Povey's mood suddenly changed to one of suspicion. "How much did you tell the police?" he asked as he watched the girl putting on her underwear.

"I didn't tell them anything," said Julie, pulling her dress over her head and then running her fingers through her rich auburn hair. "My comb's in the bathroom. I won't be a moment," she added and moved towards the door of the sitting room.

Povey leaped from the settee and gripped Julie's wrists. "You're not going anywhere," he said. "I don't trust you."

"Kev, you're hurting me." Julie struggled to release Povey's grip.

"What did you tell them?"

"I told you, nothing."

"But they came here, didn't they?" Povey let go of the girl's wrists and pushed her down on the settee.

"Yes, but I don't know how they found out where I was living."

"What did they want to know?" Povey clearly did not believe Julie's protestations of innocence.

"They asked me about the night that Jason was killed."

"And what did you say?"

"What you'd always told me to say, that I didn't see anything. And that you'd threatened me."

Povey grinned at that. "Did you tell them precisely what I said I'd do to you if you grassed?" He had picked up his pistol from the floor and was playing with it. He had been toying with the weapon for most of the time since he had forced his way into the house. Firearms, like fast cars, gave Povey a feeling of supremacy. With him, it was almost a sexual thing.

"I do wish you wouldn't do that," said Julie. "I don't like guns. You know I don't."

"How did the police find Jerry Ryan then, if you didn't tell them where to find him?" Povey ignored the girl's concerns about firearms and continued to fiddle with his pistol, releasing the chamber, spinning it and then clicking it back into place.

"I don't know, do I? I suppose they have their ways. For God's sake put that thing down, Kev."

"They must have tapped the phone then?" Povey was not going to leave it until he was satisfied.

"I never telephoned him. I couldn't, could I? Peter used to go through the account with a fine-tooth comb, checking every number that appeared."

"Little tosser," said Povey. "How did Jerry get the information to you then?"

"He used to come here, when Peter was out."

Povey looked sharply at the girl beside him. "That was a bit risky, wasn't it?"

Julie smiled. "I've never known Peter come home early from the surgery in all the time I've been married to him," she said.

"And I suppose you and Jerry spent the afternoons in bed, screwing." Povey grinned. "Never could resist it, could you, you randy little cow." And he grasped her chin with his free hand and kissed her savagely.

Julie broke free. "Turn you on, does it?" she asked. "Thinking about me and him doing it."

Povey slapped the girl's face, hard. "Don't push your luck, gorgeous," he said. "Just think about Brazil. All that hot weather and those glorious beaches."

Julie still could not believe that the police would let them go. "And what about money, Kev?" she asked. "Have you thought about that?"

Povey grinned. "Swiss bank account," he said. "I've been stashing our ill-gotten gains away for nearly five years now. There's enough there for us to live on happily ever after."

The telephone rang again. With an oath, Povey leaned over the side of the settee and picked it up, at the same time leaving his pistol on the floor. "What do these bastards want now?" he said. "Are we ready to go?" he demanded of the negotiator. He listened for a few moments and then his face twisted in rage. "No," he screamed, "I don't want to talk to her. I won't, d'you understand? No way." He tossed the phone to the floor and picked up his pistol yet again.

"What is it, Kev?" Julie turned towards him, a look of concern on her face.

"My mother's here," said Povey. "Why the hell have they brought her, the bastards?" He was clearly disconcerted at this latest example of what he regarded as police trickery and delaying tactics.

"It wouldn't do any harm to talk to her, Kev." Julie laid a hand on Povey's arm.

"I'm not going to," said Povey angrily. "I know what they're trying to do. They're trying to get her to talk me into giving up. Well, there's no way. We're going to Brazil, you and me, and that's that." He leaned over the girl and began to undo the belt of her dress with his free hand.

"Not again, Kev, please," said Julie imploringly.

Suddenly, there was a loud report as the pistol went off accidentally, and Julie screamed.

Twenty-four

At the sound of the shot, Detective Chief Inspector Kerby leaped for the telephone and grabbed the handset. But Fox closed his hand over the negotiator's. "Hold it," he said. "Don't let the bastard think he's excited us."

"But supposing he's shot the girl, sir?"

"He won't have done," said Fox. "He's not going to throw away the only card he holds, is he?" He released the DCI's hand. "All right, now talk to him."

"Kevin, this is Tony." The negotiator spoke calmly when eventually Povey deigned to respond. "What happened in there?"

"Don't panic," said Povey insolently. "The bloody thing went off by accident."

"Is anyone hurt?"

"Nope!" said Povey and the line went dead.

Kerby turned to Fox. "What now, sir?" he asked, but before Fox could answer, the phone rang again. Kerby picked up the handset. "Yes?" he said.

"I'm bloody well sick and tired of waiting," said Povey. "If there isn't a car outside in ten minutes to take me and the girl to Heathrow, she's dead. Got it?"

"Look, Kevin, try and be patient. It's very difficult for us to arrange these things at short notice. It's all going ahead, I promise you, but it does take time."

"Shove it, copper," said Povey. "You've had hours to set it up and if there are any problems, they're your problems, not mine. Now then, listen good. I'm coming out in exactly ten minutes and there'd better be a car ready and waiting." And once more, Povey broke the call.

"I think we should see if his wife can persuade him, sir," said DCI Kerby.

Fox was not convinced of that, but he acquiesced to the negotiator's suggestion. "Get Andrea Bentley up here, fast," he said to one of the Anti-Terrorist Branch officers.

A minute or two later, Povey's live-in lover appeared at the steps of the incident van. "What's happened?" she asked. She still wore the jeans she had been wearing when Denzil Evans had interviewed her, but now she had a leather jacket over the tee-shirt with its provocative message.

"Would you be willing to talk to him, Mrs Bentley?" asked Fox. "He seems determined that he's going to Brazil. If he insists, there's no way we can stop him – for the sake of the girl he's holding – but it would be in everyone's interest for him just to give up peacefully." There was not the slightest chance of Povey going anywhere, much less Brazil, but it was unwise to tell Andrea Bentley that. If she was going to talk to Povey, she had to do so convinced in her own mind that he stood a chance of winning. Fox knew that the shrewd Povey would detect any doubt that existed in her voice.

Andrea Bentley nodded and then touched her forehead,, moving a stray lock of hair out of her eyes. "What shall I say?" she asked.

"Try to persuade him that he should release Julie Lockhart and then give himself up."

Andrea, now close to tears, bit her lip. In the space of a few hours, her life had been shattered. She had been completely unnerved by the arrival of the police at her house, the discoveries of ammunition and cocaine, and the later revelations that the man she had known for three years as Laurence Bentley had lived a life of crime and was wanted in connection with three murders.

Kerby made contact and then handed the phone across to the girl. "There you are, Andrea," he said. "Do your best for him."

"Hallo. Laurie, it's me, Andrea."

"What the hell do you want?" Povey snapped out his response in a voice that clearly betrayed the strain he was under.

"Darling, what's the matter with you?"

"The matter?" Povey laughed scornfully. "What d'you think's the matter, you silly bitch? The bloody law are trying to stitch me up, that's what the matter is. Now, be a good little girl, and piss off and mind your own business. You should have known that if you play with the big boys, you're going to get hurt."

Andrea Bentley threw down the handset and burst into tears. "He's never spoken to me like that before," she said, her voice distorted and muffled by her crying.

Fox sighed and signaled to a policewoman to look after the distraught girl. "Well, that was a blow-out," he said to Kerby as the WPC led the sobbing Andrea Bentley away to the mobile canteen.

"Got to try it all, sir," said the negotiator with a shrug.

"Well, Tony, you're the expert," said Fox, not meaning a word of it. "What comes next in your Boys' Own book of taking out armed hostage-takers?"

"There's no textbook way of doing it, sir," said Kerby patiently. "Every incident is different, obviously." Trained negotiators often met with hostility from investigating officers, due largely to the tension of the situation which affected not only the besieged gunman and his hostages, but everyone else involved in the operation too. And the longer it went on, the worse it got.

"Sorry," said Fox curtly and then grinned, "but I'm in need of a large Scotch." He had vowed, however, that alcohol and sieges did not mix, and had forborne from having anything stronger than tea since the operation had begun.

"His patience is going to run out quite soon now, sir," said Kerby. "I think we've tried everything. If we give him a car, we're merely allowing the problem to move outside our control and possibly put other people in danger. There's always the lesson of what happened at the Munich Olympics in 1972 when the Germans let them go to the airport, thinking that they'd be able to take them out once they arrived."

"There's no way that bastard's going anywhere," said Fox and lit a cigarette. "But we'll give him a car. Where's that inspector from SO19?"

"Here, sir," said a voice from just outside the incident van.

"Come in here and give me the benefit of your vast experience," said Fox, peering out of the door.

The Firearms Branch inspector, a bulky figure in flame-proof overalls and body armor with a pistol holstered at his belt, stepped into the van and removed his protective helmet. "Inspector Godley, sir," he said.

"Mr Godley," said Fox, swinging round on the swivel chair he had occupied for most of the night, "supposing we place a car in the road outside the house..."

"Yes, sir," said Godley impassively. He clearly had reservations about Fox's plan.

"You sound doubtful."

"I was going to suggest an assault on the house, sir," said Godley. "If my men go in at the back, armed with stun grenades, they could—"

"If your men go in with stun grenades, they're likely to get killed before they've got the pins out, Mr Godley," said Fox with thinly veiled sarcasm. "Povey is a shrewd operator. For years, he's been pulling jewelery thefts and robberies under our very noses, living not five hundred yards from where he was when we first started looking for him in connection with the Shepperton murder. And he's completely ruthless. There's no doubt in my mind that he murdered both Proctor and Skelton. Taking out a copper is not going to add one single day to his sentence and he knows it." He shook his head. "I'm not willing to risk policemen's lives even if you are."

Godley bridled at that. It was always the same with these macho Flying Squad officers. They thought they knew it all. "My men are experts, sir. They've trained with the SAS—"

"That's what worries me, Mr Godley," said Fox. "But I have to remember that there's an innocent woman in there, and the first noise that your officers make, like breaking a rear window, and he's going to top her, pretty damned quick."

Godley sighed. "What d'you suggest then, sir?" he asked.

"If we have a car put in the road outside the house, will one of your marksman be able to take him out if he attempts to take the woman with him?"

"Well, sir…" Godley looked thoughtful. "It rather depends on how—"

"Yes or no, Mr Godley?"

"Yes, sir," said Godley who disliked being pushed into a corner. "Provided my man gets a clear shot that is unlikely to endanger the woman."

"Well, I think we've got to try it," said Fox. "Mr Kerby here tells me that Povey is getting to the end of his tether and could well do something rash. In my view, and in the view of Mr Kerby, he might well decide to kill himself, having first killed Julie Lockhart." He glanced sideways at Kerby and received a nod of agreement.

"Very well, sir," said Godley reluctantly. "Give me a couple of minutes and I'll get my men in position."

"There goes an unhappy man," said Fox to Kerby as Godley stepped out of the van and made his way across to his own command post. "Have a word with our hero now, Tony, and tell him that things are moving. And tell him that further instructions will follow."

"Right, guv." Kerby picked up the phone again, for about the thirtieth time that night.

An unmarked police car moved into position opposite the entrance to the Lockharts' house and the driver got out, leaving the keys in the ignition. With an air of indifference that pushed his self-control to its limits, the policeman walked casually back to the incident van.

Kerby called Povey again. "Kevin, you can come out now. But do it slowly. Understood?"

There was no reply, but a minute later the front door of the house opened. Julie Lockhart appeared with Povey right behind her. The two started to move slowly down the drive, Julie shielding her eyes with one arm against the glare of the floodlights. Somewhere a policeman coughed loudly, breaking the intense silence of the night.

"Give that stupid sod a Meggazone," whispered Fox to no one in particular.

Povey had his pistol in one hand and his free arm was so tightly around Julie Lockhart's neck that she stumbled once or twice as she tried to walk ahead of him. But Povey stayed close to her, using her body to screen his own.

Then it happened. Julie Lockhart's body suddenly went limp. In the hours that she had been with Kevin Povey, her doubts about his reliability, even his sanity, had grown, and she knew that she was not going to go to Brazil with him, or anywhere else. Unable to fight him off, she had done the only thing possible: she had made herself a dead weight.

"Stand up, you stupid cow," Povey screamed at her, trying to pull her upright with the hand he had been forced to move from around her neck and the hand that held the pistol.

Behind the battery of floodlights, the police marksmen waited patiently, their rifles trained on the struggling pair. But still Povey did not present a clear target.

But then, as Povey persisted in trying to force the relaxed woman towards the waiting car that represented freedom, there came a sudden shout in the distance, to his left. Alarmed, Povey swung round, pulling Julie with him, and fired in the direction of the noise. "And the next one's for her," he yelled. By now, Povey and his captive had almost reached the car and he began to fire indiscriminately.

Fox, stationed immediately behind the floodlights, a mere six yards away, suddenly hurled himself forward and, regardless of his own safety, crashed into the couple. Julie Lockhart fell sideways, sprawling across the pavement, but Povey managed to stay upright, his pistol now pointing menacingly at Fox.

Then Povey fired, the noise deafening Fox as the round struck him, throwing him to the ground.

Two more shots rang out in quick succession and Povey staggered across the narrow pavement, clawing briefly at the side of the police car before collapsing. When a police officer reached him, seconds later, he was already dead.

*

Fox was propped up in bed, his left shoulder swathed in bandages. Midday sun streamed through the windows of his private room at St Thomas's, the "coppers" hospital. Sir James Gilmore, the Commissioner, had paid a flying visit to congratulate Fox on a successful outcome to the siege and to wish him a speedy recovery. And before departing had mildly admonished him for his recklessness.

Now, Detective Inspector Gilroy was seated beside Fox's bed, a sheaf of papers on his lap.

"Well, Jack," said Fox, "What happened?"

"Povey's dead, sir, and Ryan and Julie Lockhart are in custody."

"Really?" Fox sat up slightly and winced as pain lanced through his shoulder. "Charged?"

"Yes, sir. Conspiracy to rob for a kick-off. We searched the Lockharts' house after it was all over. We found technical drawings of the briefcase that was used to top Proctor, and the pistol that killed Skelton. At least, we're pretty sure it was the one. Julie Lockhart said it was anyway."

"Did she say anything else?" asked Fox.

Gilroy grinned. "She made a full statement, sir. She obtained information about rich widows from Ryan and passed it on to Povey. They'd been seeing each other ever since he came back from Australia. She'd been having an affair with him, and with Ryan, she said."

"Saucy little bitch," said Fox.

"Povey told her everything apparently. He'd been at it for years, moving in on defenceless and lonely women and taking them for all they'd got. Jewelery usually, but it's surprising how many of them succumbed to his charms and just gave him money. Then he'd bugger off."

"Why did he kill Proctor and Skelton?"

"He'd been working with them for a long time, a loose sort of conspiracy, I suppose you'd call it. But when Proctor had Linda Ward's sparklers away and passed them on to Skelton, Povey saw red. He had a very soft spot for his mother, according to the Lockhart woman." Gilroy grinned. "And hated his father apparently. Was delighted when he kicked the bucket. But he hated Jonathon Ward just as much, and when he appeared on the scene, obviously intent on milking Linda for all she was worth, Povey put the frighteners on him and he disappeared a bit sharpish."

Fox laughed. "How the hell did he persuade Proctor to collect that briefcase from the Agincourt Hotel then? I presume it was Povey who left the thing there."

"Yes, it was, sir, according to Julie. He told Proctor that there was a consignment of diamonds that he wanted placing. Proctor, like any other villain, was a greedy bastard and couldn't wait to get his hands on the gear. The rest we know. Then for good measure, seeing that Skelton was involved in 'handling' Linda Ward's gear, Povey took him out too."

"Sounds like a good result," said Fox.

"Very good, sir," said Gilroy, and leaning closer to Fox, added, "word is, sir, that the DAC's putting you in for a QGM."

"Tell him I've got one already," said Fox. "In fact, you can tell him that I'd rather have a new suit. That bastard Povey ruined a perfectly good Hackett that cost me a monkey only two months ago." Fox enjoyed playing up to his reputation for being the best-dressed detective at the Yard. "By the way, Jack, have you got the result of your promotion board yet?"

"Dipped it, sir," said Gilroy.

"Bad luck, Jack." Fox grinned. "Still, you'd've made a bloody awful chief inspector. And I'd've had to find another DI."

"That's the way it goes, sir," said Gilroy with a shrug. He knew that Fox had just paid him a compliment, but it would have taken a policeman to recognize it as such. "There are a few members of the Squad outside, sir. They'd like a word."

Fox groaned. "Better let them in, Jack," he said. "Oh, and thanks."

Gilroy nodded, embarrassed at Fox's rare display of gratitude. "Right, sir," he said.

Seconds after Gilroy's departure, a troop of Flying Squad officers entered the room. Each was carrying a briefcase. "Hallo, guv'nor," they chorused.

Fox glanced at the briefcases. "If they contain claims for expenses and overtime, they can wait," he growled.

Joe Bellenger put his briefcase on the end of the bed so that it was facing Fox. When he opened it, a short spring-loaded sign leaped into the vertical position upon which the single word BANG! was painted in large red letters.

"You bastards," said Fox, attempting to keep a straight face.

Once the raucous laughter had subsided, Detective Sergeant Crozier opened Fox's bedside locker and glanced at the door where Kate Ebdon stood guard. "All right, Kate?" he asked.

"All clear, skip," said the Australian detective.

As one, the Squad officers opened their brief-cases and, with a speed that would have done credit to a top-class shoplifter working in reverse, began to fill the locker with bottles of Scotch and packets of cigarettes.

"Hope you come back soon, guv," said Crozier. "The bloody place is in chaos already."

Fox ignored the implied compliment. "What about your enquiry in Cannes?" he asked, unable to forget the job even when confined to a hospital bed.

"Lasage came up trumps, guv'nor," said Crozier. "He found that Povey and Michelle White were both born in France, which is why we couldn't find any entries at St Catherine's House."

"And once Bert Glass heard that Povey was dead, sir," chipped in Kate Ebdon, "he admitted to posting the gear to Sailor Pogson that you found in the safe at City Road. He hadn't said anything before because Povey threatened him with GBH if he grassed."

"And just what d'you suppose is going on in here?" The stentorian voice of the sister cut through the conversation as she stood in the doorway, all starched and bristling. "Out, all of you."

Sheepishly, the members of the Squad, any one of whom would unhesitatingly have tackled an armed robber, made for the door.

"There's a Lady Jane Sims here to see you, Mr Fox," said the sister. "I've told her not to stay too long."

Jane Sims entered the room, her arms full of the largest bunch of flowers Fox had ever seen outside Covent Garden, and laid them on the end of the bed. She sat down and took Fox's right hand in her own. "I can't let you out of my sight for a moment, can I, Tommy Fox?" she said.

If you enjoyed *Rough Diamonds*, please share your thoughts on Amazon by leaving a review.

For more free and discounted eBooks every week, sign up to the *Endeavour Press* newsletter.

Follow us on Twitter and Instagram.

Printed in Great Britain
by Amazon

61870483R00123